Richard Anthony Proctor

The Expanse of Heaven

a series of essays on the wonders of the firmament

Richard Anthony Proctor

The Expanse of Heaven
a series of essays on the wonders of the firmament

ISBN/EAN: 9783337755270

Printed in Europe, USA, Canada, Australia, Japan

Cover: Foto ©Andreas Hilbeck / pixelio.de

More available books at **www.hansebooks.com**

EXPANSE OF HEAVEN:

A SERIES OF ESSAYS

ON THE

WONDERS OF THE FIRMAMENT.

BY

R. A. PROCTOR, B. A.,

AUTHOR OF "OTHER WORLDS THAN OURS," "THE MOON," "LIGHT SCIENCE FOR LEISURE HOURS," ETC.

"Let there be lights
High in th' expanse of heaven, to divide
The day from night."

NEW YORK:
D. APPLETON AND COMPANY,
1, 3, AND 5 BOND STREET.
1889.

CONTENTS.

EXPANSE of HEAVEN.

A DREAM THAT WAS NOT ALL A DREAM.

Behold even to the moon, and it shineth not; yea, the stars are not pure in His sight. How much less man, that is a worm? and the son of man, which is a worm?—Job xxv. 5, 6.

On a time I dreamed, and my dream was on this wise.

In a vast black space there appeared a glowing orb about three yards in diameter, as it seemed to me; but it was nearly a quarter of a mile away from me, and its real nature I could not perceive. It shone with a mighty light, whiter than the driven snow, and more intense than the light from the heart of the fiercest furnace.

Close by me I perceived a tiny globe, about an inch in diameter, travelling slowly along, and turning round and round as it travelled. Amidst the intense darkness which prevailed, this globe would have been wholly lost but for the glowing orb I have just spoken of, which lit up one-half of the surface of the small body. Looking closer, I perceived a yet smaller body, little more than a quarter of an inch in diameter, which seemed to be moving round the other at a distance of about $2\frac{1}{2}$ feet.

But as I looked, wondering what these small bodies might be, a power of keener vision was given to me, and I saw many animalcules, inconceivably minute, upon the surface of the layer of the two small globes. I could perceive that the greater part of the surface of this globe was covered with a film or moisture, and in this film were myriads of living creatures, moving about according to their several powers, some pursuing others, some pursued, but for the most part intent in seeking what they might devour. Over the dry part of this tiny globe, which I could have held (so it seemed in my dream) between my finger and thumb, were other creatures in countless myriads, though not in all parts equally numerous.

But what astonished me mightily was to perceive among the creatures moving over this little globe certain beings, not larger than the rest, nor remarkable in any respect save in this, that they appeared to act as though they possessed powers of reasoning. I could see that they constructed microscopic dwellings for themselves, and formed roads over their tiny domain, and made other constructions intended apparently for the convenience of their race. They even ventured, in minute floats, upon the film of moisture, which they crossed and recrossed in the most venture someway, considering that, film though it was, it was many times deeper than the largest of the floats in which these strange creatures crossed it. Indeed, sometimes when the film was agitated as by some one breathing on it, these floats upset, and many of the tiny creatures upon them were drowned. At some places I could perceive threads, infinitely finer than the threads of a spider's web, laid down under the film of moisture, and in many places such threads were extended over the dry part of this one-inch globe. The object of this arrangement I could not at first understand, but I learned presently that these creatures used the threads as a means of conveying messages to each other!

But I have no space to tell of all that I could perceive or that went on in this small globe. I must speak only of certain matters which struck me as chiefly interesting.

These little creatures, so small that the most powerful microscope yet made by man would altogether have failed to show them, were actually able to learn a great deal about objects outside their tiny abode. They could not only see the great glowing body which as I have said lay nearly a quarter of a mile from them, but they had found out how large it was, how far away from them, how bright, how hot, and even how heavy. This in creatures so utterly insignificant, as it seemed to me—so weak and small that with a touch of my little finger I could have destroyed many millions of them—appeared very wonderful. They were quite unable to leave their tiny world. It did not even give them a fixed stand-point, for it moved slowly onwards, as I have said, turning round and round, so that for half the time the shining globe was not even in sight. Yet these little beings had measured and weighed and tested it with results surprisingly accurate. They had found out, what I could not perceive from where I was placed, that this great globe, fully three yards in diameter, was in its way a sort of furnace, the flames on its surface being sometimes a foot high and sometimes even two feet. Its whole surface, they had found, was in a state of wonderful disturbance, being, on a small scale, like a sea of fire, and covered all over with intensely hot vapour extending to a height of nearly half an inch. But, even more wonderful to tell, these tiny creatures had found out what was burning (or at least glowing) in that large body. They had also learned the very rate at which the flames I have spoken of rose up above the surface of the glowing orb, or spread themselves over it.

This seemed to me so wonderful that I left the little globe to pursue its course, and went to the large bright body. It was not quite a quarter of a mile away, I found; but (precisely as these small creatures had somehow learned) about 320 yards from the small globe. When I got to a certain distance from it, I found the heat so great that I did not care to approach it more nearly. It was surrounded on all sides by glowing matter, not nearly so bright or so hot as its own substance, but still shining very resplendently. I found that the little beings on the small globe I had lately left were quite right in their general surmises about this large body. I could see the flames they had discovered, and could watch for myself many of the processes they had recognised by means of ingenious devices on a less than microscopic scale. The great glowing orb, though nine feet in diameter, was turning steadily round—a fact which my minute friends had known a long time before. Or rather I should say that the minute race of beings had known the fact for a long time, since the existence of these creatures was quite ephemeral, and even as my dream proceeded, though it appeared only to last a few days, many of these reasoning but 'to any thick sight invisible' creatures had been born, lived out their lives, and died.

Then I looked round on the dark space which surrounded me on all sides. I could perceive, but only as two points of light, the small globe on which were the little creatures so wonderful in understanding, and the smaller body which moved round it. But I could see also other small bodies. Not very far from me was one which was very brightly illuminated by the large glowing body. It was much smaller than the globe I had first seen, though larger than its companion. It was moving more quickly, and I could perceive that it was moving round the bright body at a distance of rather more than a hundred yards. Nearly twice as far away from the flaming central body I saw another globe, about one inch in diameter like the first, though from my present central position it looked larger and very much brighter. And at a distance, about half as great again as that of the small globe first seen, I saw a body rather more than half an inch in diameter, and of a somewhat ruddy colour. I paid a visit to this small body, which was travelling, I found, at a distance of about five hundred yards from the great glowing body. It was a pretty little object, with greenish markings between the red parts which gave this body its ruddy aspect.

I could now see that, yet farther away—in fact, more than half a mile from the bright central body—there were many very small objects, little more than grains of powder they seemed to me, travelling in a sort of ring around the glowing body I had left.

My dream was not yet over, however. For I presently perceived yet other bodies, travelling at greater distances. About a mile from the central body was a globe much larger than any I had yet seen, except of course the fire-globe three yards in diameter which seemed set as a sort of ruler over these small orbs. The body now seen was fully ten inches in diameter. It was beautifully coloured, being striped with red and yellow and purple and brown belts, which seemed to me to owe their regularity of arrangement to the rapid turning of this body. It will seem surprising, if anything in a dream can be surprising, that although this globe was ten inches in diameter while the globe first examined was but one inch in diameter, yet the larger globe was turning round much more quickly, making, in fact, five complete turns while the smaller made but two, for I tried both with a stop watch, and am therefore able to speak positively.

A singular circumstance about this large globe was that around it there were moving four little bodies, the largest being only about a third of an inch in diameter. These moved at distances of $2\frac{1}{4}$ feet, $4\frac{1}{2}$ feet, 7 feet, and $12\frac{1}{2}$ feet from the ten-inch globe on which they seemed to attend.   These little bodies, though no larger than peas, formed to my judgment a pretty little scheme, their motions in particular being singularly regular and very nicely adjusted.

But nearly twice as far away from that great glowing orb three feet in diameter, which I now began to regard as far the largest body I was likely to see, I found a most remarkable system.   There was a globe about $8\frac{1}{2}$ inches in diameter, and striped with belts much like the larger one I had just left, only it was of a more sombre tint on the whole.   Around this globe there was a set of flat rings not touching the globe anywhere, though in some unseen way they were so associated with it as to accompany it unceasingly.   These rings, regarded as a single system, had a span of upwards of twenty inches, and a breadth of nearly four inches.   But there were several of them, unequally bright, and on a closer survey I could perceive that they were made up of a multitude of tiny grains each pursuing its own career as if journeying around the globe which was within the ring.

Even this, however, was not all.   For this globe,

besides this curious little system of rings, had, like the globe before visited, a family of small bodies travelling round it at different distances. There were no less than eight of these tiny orbs. I noted that the sixth in order of distance outwards was nearly half an inch in diameter, and travelled at a distance of about $8\frac{1}{4}$ feet. The outermost of all, though not nearly so large—in fact, little more than a quarter of an inch in diameter—was distinguished by the wide span of its circular path, which lay at a distance of more than twenty-four feet from the centre of the ringed globe!

I was now about two miles from the great glowing mass, which looked very small because of its great distance. I could perceive, however, that farther away—some four miles from the glowing orb—there was another of the small globes, and though I did not visit it, my increased powers of vision enabled me to perceive that it was about four inches in diameter, and had four small bodies travelling round it. Yet farther away, some six miles from the central fire-globe, there was another orb of about the same size as the one just mentioned, and having only one small body attending upon it, or at least only one such body that I could perceive.

I now returned in my dream to the small body which I had first seen, and found the tiny reasoning creatures which I had watched before still continuing busily at work, collecting food, building houses, making roads, undertaking voyages, and—alas, poor little creatures!—quarrelling among themselves, and engaging in combats by which thousands of their number were destroyed. I found that many of the matters I had ascertained during my journeyings were quite as well known to the more studious of these beings as to myself. In this power of learning facts about objects so far away from them the tiny creatures seemed to me to be very wonderfully gifted. I was, however, rather surprised to find that some among them prided themselves as much on these powers as though in some way they had acquired them by their own exertions or goodness. To note the ways of some of these creatures —which to my vision seemed so insignificant and in fact contemptible, while they were manifestly very weak and short-lived—one would have supposed they had been mighty enough to construct not only their own little abodes, but the great nine-feet fire-globe which stood at the centre of the whole scheme of globes I had visited, as well as all these globes and the systems attending upon them. I was preparing to rebuke their folly, proposing in my dream to show them how wretchedly small and weak they were, and how little reason they had to pride themselves even on their certainly wonderful knowledge, since the more they learned the more clearly they ought to recognise their own insignificance: I was about, I say, to enter upon much wise discourse on this subject and kindred matters—not failing, in particular, to show them how very much stronger and greater I was than they— when to my annoyance and disgust I found all my dimensions rapidly becoming reduced, till I was no larger than they were; I found myself drawn down to the surface of the tiny globe on which they lived—in fact, I found myself one among them, and that all I had intended to say to them they might with equal truth say to me. And then I perceived that the small globe was the earth on which I lived, and the great fire-globe was the sun, while the other orbs I had visited were the planets and their satellites. And when I considered that I had learned nothing about them which I had not known before, I was so troubled that I awoke—and lo, it was a dream. Yet was the dream not without its lesson, and its lesson was this :—

' Speak to the earth, and it shall teach thee. . . . Who knoweth not that the hand of the Lord hath wrought this? In whose hand is the soul of every living thing, and the breath of all mankind. . . . Praise ye the Lord from the heavens. Praise Him in the heights. Praise ye Him, sun and moon; praise Him, all ye stars of light; praise Him, ye heavens of heavens.'

THE SUN.

I saw another sign in heaven, great and marvellous. . . . Great and marvellous are Thy works, Lord God Almighty.—REV. xv. 1, 3.

IN long past ages there were nations that worshipped the sun. He was their God; he seemed to them as a being of might, 'rejoicing as a giant to run his course,' and capable not only of influencing the fortunes of men and nations, but of hearkening and responding to their prayers. A vain thought truly, for the creature was worshipped and the Creator forgotten. And yet of all the forms of religion in which created things were worshipped sun-worship was the least contemptible. Indeed, if there is any object which men can properly take as an emblem of the power and goodness of Almighty God, it is the sun.

The sun is an emblem of the Almighty in being the source whence all that lives upon the earth derives support. Our very existence depends on the beneficent supply of light and heat poured out continually upon the earth by the great central orb of the planetary scheme. Let the sun forget to shine for a single day, and it would be with us even as though God had forgotten our existence, or had remembered us only to punish; myriads of creatures now living on the earth would perish, uncounted millions would suffer fearfully. But let the sun's rays cease to be poured out for four or five days, and every living creature on the earth would be destroyed. Or, on the other hand, even a worse (or at least more sudden and terrible) fate would befall us if an angel of wrath 'poured out his vial upon the sun, and power were given unto it to scorch men with fire.'

Yet again, the sun is an emblem of the Almighty in the manner in which he bestows benefits upon us and is forgotten. Day after day we enjoy the sun's light and heat; clouds may conceal him from our view, much as troubles may cause us to forget God; and the heat he pours out may seem sometimes insufficient or excessive, even as in our ignorance we are dissatisfied with the blessings bestowed by the Almighty. Yet these very clouds are among the good works we owe to the sun—they bring the rain which 'drops fatness upon the earth :' and without the changes of the season there would be neither the time of harvest nor the time of vintage. The cold of winter and the heat of summer, at which we often repine as excessive, are as necessary for our wants as the cool breeze and the genial warmth of spring or autumn.

We commonly forget, also, that the sun, besides sustaining us by his light-giving and heat-supplying powers, keeps us always near to him by that mighty force of attraction which his vast bulk enables him to exert. When we look at the sun as he rises (even as 'the glory of God coming from the way of the east') how seldom is the thought present in our minds that in that ruddy orb there exists the most tremendous power, swaying not only this vast globe on which we live, but orbs yet vaster than she is, and travelling on far wider courses; that the light and heat which seem to be gathering force as he rises, are in reality poured forth with fulness, even while as yet, owing to our position, we receive but little of them—nay, that during the dark hours of night they have been poured forth abundantly upon the earth; and that so rich is the sun in power and beneficence, through the might of his Creator and ours, that our earth is nourished and supported by the two thousand millionth part of the heat and light which he pours forth !

It will not be unprofitable to consider a little of what astronomy teaches about this stupendous orb, this emblem of the power and goodness of the Almighty—an emblem infinitely feeble, it must be conceded, even when the teachings of astronomy are considered, for we know that there are countless millions of such orbs, and of yet vaster orbs, within the reach even of the astronomer's telescope, but an emblem in this respect most apt, that our feeble imaginations are utterly unable to conceive its splendour, magnificence, and power.

This country on which we live is so minute, compared with the earth, that in a small globe or model of the earth it appears but as a scarcely distinguishable triangular speck. Yet we cannot conceive the dimensions of our own country, and far less, therefore, those of the whole earth. Nevertheless, let it be remembered that the swiftest steamships, ploughing the seas night and day without cessation, require twelve weeks to complete the journey to the opposite side of the earth. Now let anyone draw a straight row of one hundred and seven minute circles or round dots, all equal in size and touching each other, and let him try to conceive a great cubical or die-shaped heap of little globes, the heap having along each edge just such a row of globes as has been drawn; then the combined volume of all the globes forming that heap would exceed any one of the globes, in just the same degree that the sun's volume exceeds the earth's. It would, in fact, take more than twelve hundred thousand earths to make so large a globe as the sun.

But it is not by his size that the sun's might is to be measured. Many comets have been far larger than the sun, which nevertheless have had scarcely any power of attraction. The sun's might, however, is such as we might expect from his enormous bulk. The quantity of matter in the sun exceeds that in our earth no less than 315,000 times; and his attractive energy is proportionately enormous. If our earth, without being increased in bulk, were increased in density until she contained the same quantity of matter as the sun, the weight of every object on the earth's surface would be increased 315,000 times. A half-ounce weight, such as we use to weigh our letters, would press upon the earth as heavily as at present does a weight of four and a half tons. A man's body would be crushed down as by the weight of 315,000 men, or more than 20,000 tons. A body raised to a height of a single inch from the ground and then let fall would strike the ground with a velocity three times as great as that of the swiftest express train.

It is the might which the sun thus possesses by virtue of his enormous mass which enables him to control the motions of the family of planets circling continually around him. The movements of these bodies are so beautifully adjusted to their distances from the great body which rules them, that each describes a path very nearly circular. The nearer globes he draws more strongly towards him, but their swifter motions enable them to maintain their distance; the farther planets travel more slowly, but at their distances the sun's power is correspondingly reduced.

A cold and inert mass of matter, however, would be able to do all that the sun does by his mere mass, and yet be utterly unfit to be, like him, the ruler over a scheme of circling worlds. The glory of the sun is not in his strength alone. As Sir John Herschel has well said, 'Giant Size and Giant Strength are ugly qualities without beneficence. But the sun is the almoner of the Almighty, the delegated dispenser to us of light and warmth, as well as the centre of attraction; and as such the immediate source of all our comforts, and indeed of the very possibility of our existence on earth.'

If we would rightly measure the sun's activity as a

dispenser of God's gifts of light and heat, we must consider what our earth alone receives. On a glorious summer's day, when the air seems aglow with the sun's light and on fire with his heat, we are strongly impressed with the sense of the sun's intense activity. And yet in our temperate latitudes we seldom experience any approach to the burning heats of the tropics. But even in the full heat of a tropical noon, the solar energy actually expended over the whole region which any one spectator can discern is but a minute part of that which he is exercising every instant of time on the half of the earth turned towards him. It has been calculated that the heat received by the earth during twenty-four hours would be sufficient to raise an ocean 260 yards deep, covering the whole surface of the earth, from the temperature of freezing water to that of boiling water. And this, be it remembered, is less than the 2000 millionth part of the heat which the sun pours out into space during the same interval of time. Ceaselessly the wonderful stream of heat-waves is poured out on all sides. So energetic is it that the heat emitted in a single second would suffice to boil 195 millions of cubic miles of ice-cold water. Or, to take another illustration, which recent experience as to the value of our coal supplies will bring home to many of us with peculiar force—in order to produce by the burning of coals the supply of heat which we receive from the sun, there would have to be consumed on every square yard of the sun's surface no less than six tons of coal per hour; while, if a globe as large as our earth had to maintain such a supply of heat, it would be necessary that on every square yard of its surface more than three tons of coals should be consumed in every *second* of time.

We cannot wonder that the source of so vast a supply of heat should be the scene of tremendous processes of disturbance. The furnace whose fires maintain the life of the solar system is not merely aglow with intense light and heat, but is in a state of fierce turmoil. The most tremendous conflagrations ever witnessed upon our earth —great fires, by which whole cities have been destroyed —serve to suggest something of what is going on upon the sun, only that all the processes of such catastrophes must be supposed to be intensified a million-fold. As in great fires there is a constant roar and tumult produced by the rush of air currents which the fire itself has generated, so in every part of the sun, on every square yard of that enormous surface, the most hideous uproar must prevail as fierce cyclonic storms, bred by solar fires, rush with inconceivable velocity over the flaming surface. In the most tremendous storms known upon earth the wind does not travel a hundred miles per hour, and the winds which rage amid the flames of a conflagration are of slow motion compared with true hurricanes; but the cyclonic storms which stir the fiery breath of the solar flames career often with the inconceivable velocity of more than a hundred miles in every second of time. And the flames themselves are on a scale altogether inconceivable by us. A considerable proportion attain a height exceeding ten times the diameter of our earth; and some have been observed which have attained twice that height. But tremendous as are the motions taking place in the solar flames, even more wonderful are the effects of solar eruptions. By these tremendous throes matter is carried sometimes at the rate of four or five hundred miles per second [1] from the visible surface of the sun. This velocity not only exceeds many hundred-fold the swiftest motion known to us—the flight of a cannon-ball [2]—but even surpasses the velocity with which the swiftest of the celestial bodies travel on their courses. Our earth travels about $18\frac{1}{2}$ miles per second, Mercury more than half as fast again; and one or two comets have been known to travel with a velocity of more than three hundred miles per second as they made their perihelion swoop round the sun. [3] But no known celestial object has ever possessed

[1] Motions at this rate have not been actually observed; but matter has been seen to move upwards from the surface at such a rate that a simple calculation shows the rate of emission to have been certainly five hundred miles per second, and probably very much greater. For a remarkable instance, observed by Prof. C. A. Young, of America, see my treatise on 'The Sun' (2nd edition), chap. vi.

[2] Light and electricity travel very much more swiftly, but in the flight of either there is no transmission of matter.

[3] To attain this velocity they must approach very closely to the sun; and in point of fact, the great comet of 1680 (Newton's) passed so close to the sun that the nucleus, or centre of the head, was nearer than the summits of some of the largest solar prominences. The nucleus of the remarkable comet of 1843 passed yet closer.

a velocity approaching the tremendous rate at which glowing matter has been expelled from the sun's interior.

Such are some of the marvellous processes taking place in that orb which to the unaided vision of man seems calm as the depths of a summer sky, although

> Beyond expression bright
> Compared with aught on earth, metal or stone.

When we compare what the eye of man sees with what is actually going on in the sun, and consider further how small a way even the astronomer has advanced towards the interpretation of the wonderful orb which rules the solar system, we may well exclaim with the great apostle of the Gentiles, 'O the depth of the riches both of the wisdom and knowledge of God! How unsearchable are His judgments, and His ways past finding out!'

THE QUEEN OF NIGHT.

I.

And God made two great lights, great for their use
To man; the greater to have rule by day,
The less by night altern.—MILTON.

He appointeth the moon for seasons; the sun knoweth his going down.
                                          PSALM civ. 19.

I HAVE spoken of the reverence with which men in long
past ages contemplated the sun. Even before it was
known how much we owe to the sun, how he is the source
of nearly all the forms of force existing upon the earth;
and the delegated almoner of the Almighty's benevolence
to His creatures in this and other worlds, men recognised
in some sort the importance of the great luminary, and
many nations worshipped him as a god. But with this
worship there was commonly associated a subordinate
worship of the moon; and among some nations the moon
was esteemed the greater deity. It is not difficult to find
a reason for moon-worship. When we watch the moon
for any length of time—for an hour or two, even on a
single night—we find that she is not at rest among the
stars. She partakes, indeed, to a considerable degree in

that turning motion by which the whole starlit dome is carried from east to west around its polar axis. But she also has a motion of her own towards the east; so that if at any hour she be seen close to some conspicuous star, it will be found that after an hour or two she has shifted her position quite appreciably towards the left—that is, eastwards as we face the southern heavens. And if her position be noted on the following night, it will be seen that she has passed far to the east of the star. We can readily understand that these movements, although they escape the attention of many in our time, who know little even of those simple celestial motions which can be detected in a few hours,[1] were quite early noticed by men who lived much in the open air at night. The moon's motions must, for instance, have been detected in very early times by the Chaldæan shepherds who—

> Watched, from the centres of their sleeping flocks,
> Those radiant Mercuries, that seemed to move
> Carrying through æther in perpetual round
> Decrees and resolutions of the gods.

It was this motion of the moon, this apparent *power* iu

---

[1] The Astronomer Royal, remarking a few years ago on a work in which I endeavoured to show in a simple way how the star-vault varies in aspect from hour to hour, and from night to night, told me that he believed quite a considerable proportion of even well-educated persons were unfamiliar with the fact that the stars rise and set with the same sort of motion as the sun. It requires the actual light and heat of the sun, and the actual necessity of changing one's place if one would either remain in sunlight or in shade, as the case may be, to render well known the fact that the sun changes his place in the sky as the mid-day hours proceed.

her to shift her position, so as to view our earth, as it were, from new standpoints, which doubtless suggested to the ancients the idea of worshipping her as a deity. We see some trace of this fancy in the words of Job, when, making protestation of his integrity in the worship of God alone, he says, 'If I beheld the sun when it shined, or the moon walking in brightness, and my heart hath been secretly enticed, or my mouth hath kissed my hand'[1] (that is, if he had worshipped these heavenly bodies), 'this also were an iniquity to be punished by the Judge; for I should have denied the God that is above.'

Although the moon does not render such important services to the earth as the sun does, yet even viewed in this aspect, there is much in the moon's action which may help to explain the worship once paid to her.

The moon has been appointed for seasons; the Al-mighty spake—

> Let there be Lights
> High in th' expanse of Heaven, to divide
> The day from night; and let them be for signs
> For seasons, and for days, and circling years ;
> And let them be for lights, as I ordain
> Their office in the firmament of Heav'n.

---

[1] We had a curious illustration of this Eastern method of expressing reverence in the comments made upon the manner in which the Shah of Persia acknowledged the cheers of the Germans. An English writer described the action as scooping·with the hand as if to lift water, which was forthwith carried to the mouth; and, oddly enough, this writer mistook the motion as intended to imitate our military salute. It really symbolised the act of one who lifts the hem of another person's garment to his lips in token of respect.

Our month, although not according with the lunar month, nevertheless had its origin in the study of the lunar motions, as indeed the name of this interval of time sufficiently indicates. I need hardly remind the reader, again, of the part which the moon takes in fixing the dates of the Jewish movable festivals, while our own movable festivals in like manner depend on the moon's motions, the Paschal full moon determining Easter Day, and the other movable feasts following accordingly.

The benefits rendered by the moon as a light-giver at night need hardly be insisted upon. Whewell has well remarked, in his Bridgewater Treatise, that 'a person of ordinary feelings, who on a fine moonlight night' (moonlit is the more correct expression) 'sees our satellite pouring her mild radiance on field and town, path and moor, will probably not only be disposed to "bless the useful light," but also to believe that it was "ordained" for that purpose.' The great mathematician Laplace adopted an opposite view. Setting himself boldly, one may say defiantly, against the wholesome belief that there is method and design in the works of the Creator, he sneers at the belief of ' those partisans of final causes who have imagined that the moon was given to the earth to afford light during the night.' This ' cannot be so,' he remarked, ' for we are often deprived at the same time of the light of the sun and the moon,' and he proceeds to show how the moon might so have been placed as to be always ' full,' in other words, always opposite the sun, so

that the arrangement described by Milton as prevailing on
the first day of the moon's existence might have continued
for ever :—

> Less bright the moon,
> But opposite in levell'd west was set
> His mirror, with full face borrowing her light
> From him ; for other light she needed none
> In that aspect ; and still that distance keeps
> Till night, then in the east her turn she shines
> Revolv'd on Heav'n's great axle ; and her reign
> With thousand lesser lights dividual holds,
> With thousand thousand stars, that then appear'd
> Spangling the hemisphere. Then first adorn'd
> With her bright luminaries that set and rose,
> Glad evening and glad morn crown'd the fourth day.

In fact, Milton would seem to have entertained the belief
that this state of things not only characterised the first
day of the moon's creation, but continued until the Fall;
for in the tenth book, after describing how the sun was
set 'so to move, so shine

> As might affect the earth with cold and heat
> Scarce tolerable,'

he proceeds to indicate some change in the moon's motions—

> To the blank moon
> Her office they prescribed—

a new office, so differing from her former office as to form
fit part of

> Growing miseries, which Adam saw
> Already in part.

Laplace's device, however, involves the necessity of a

moon of different size and distance. He shows how a moon about four times as far off as our moon really is would revolve around the earth in the same time as the sun apparently does, and would thus present always a full aspect—if originally placed opposite the moon. It is a slight objection to this imagined state of things that, for Laplace's moon to appear as large as ours, it should have a diameter about four times as great, and be in fact as large, as our earth, while the motions assigned to it require that it should not be more massive than the present moon. Thus it would have to be made of material exceedingly light, about sixty times lighter than the present substance of the moon. This would be about seventeen times lighter than water, and more than four times lighter than cork. We know of no such substance, and therefore it seems idle to discuss further Laplace's daring notion. But this also may be remarked—that although such a moon as he described might for a very long period continue always exactly opposite the sun, yet in the course of time this moon would gradually fall away from that position; for the motions both of the earth and of this imagined moon could not possibly remain absolutely uniform. Thus at length a time would come when this moon, instead of being always 'full,' would be always 'new,' that is, always on the same side as the sun, and so give no light at all, even if she did not eclipse the sun.

On the whole, we may be content to accept the moon

as we find her, and to 'bless her useful light,' without
being particular to enquire whether another moon might
not have given us more light or under more convenient
conditions. Indeed, the astronomer would be content
with much less moonlight than we actually have, since the
moon's light is very unfavourable for the study of the
stars. Not only do the greater number of lucid stars (so
astronomers term those which can be seen with the naked
eye) disappear when the moon is bright, but the range of
the telescope is proportionately reduced. The astronomer
cannot hope to penetrate the star depths as effectually
during the moonlit hours as at other times. Delicate
objects like comets and star-cloudlets can scarcely be
studied at all when the moon is shining.[1] And the astronomer must certainly contemplate with any feeling but
admiration the arrangement proposed by Laplace. As it
is, there is a sufficient approach to the state of things
described in the article on 'Life within a Cluster of
Suns'[2] to make 'the want of night' no imaginary mis-
fortune to the astronomer.

[1] None but those who have tried the experiment can believe how seldom
the astronomer has a really dark clear night, with the atmosphere in good
condition for observing. I have myself had occasion to note this circumstance somewhat markedly; for I have desired to gauge the star depths
with a very fine reflecting telescope kindly placed at my disposal by Lord
Lindsay. But when I set aside those nights when twilight continues all the
night, those when the moon shines, cloudy or hazy nights, and nights
when the air is disturbed and unfit for telescopic work, I find the time
really available for this special work amounts only to a few hours in each
year.

[2] See p. 211, 'A Cluster of Suns.'

One remarkable feature of the moon's service as a light-bringer has been regarded as specially suited to subserve the wants of man. I refer to the phenomenon called the harvest moon. Without entering into explanations which would be out of place in these pages, I may simply state that in autumn the moon for several days, about the time of 'full,' rises night after night very nearly at the same time, so as in fact to remain above the horizon nearly all night. This is manifestly convenient to those engaged in harvesting operations, insomuch that, as Ferguson states, 'Farmers, better acquainted with the facts than astronomers till of late, gratefully ascribed the early rising of the full moon at that time of the year to the goodness of God, not doubting that He had ordered it so on purpose to give them an immediate supply of moon-light after sunset, for their greater conveniency in reaping the fruits of the earth.'

It is clear that the action of the moon in raising a great tidal wave is of important service to the inhabitants of the earth. It is probable, indeed, that the tides are absolutely necessary to preserve the ocean waters in a healthy condition by continual movement. But the tidal wave discharges special services exceedingly important to mankind. The building and launching of ships would be rendered a task of much greater difficulty if it were not for the alternate rise and fall of the sea. No one, again, who is familiar with life at the seaside, and particularly in cities placed near the mouths of great tidal rivers, can fail to recognise abundant evidence of the importance of the variation of the sea's level in many nautical and commercial processes.

But perhaps the greatest benefit conferred by the moon on mankind is one which few are aware of. It may truly be said that each year hundreds of lives that would otherwise be endangered are rendered safe by her means. It is known that when our seamen pass far beyond the sight of land, their safety depends on their observations of the celestial bodies. By such observations they are enabled to learn where they are, or, in technical words, their latitude and their longitude—that is, their distance north or south of the equator, and their distance east or west of some fixed station, such as Greenwich. Now their latitude is easily determined by observations of the sun or stars, whose altitude when due south depends solely on the latitude. But it is different with the longitude; for when we travel due east or west we do not find the apparent paths of the sun and stars changing at all. The only change which takes place is in the time at which the celestial bodies rise and set. It is of course noon when the sun is due south, wherever the observer may be (at least in our northern hemisphere). But it is not Greenwich noon, unless the observer is due north or south of Greenwich. If he is east of Greenwich it is past Greenwich noon when it is noon for the observer's station, and if he is west of Greenwich it is before Greenwich noon when the sun is due south. If he has a clock showing Greenwich time he can thus learn how far east or west he may be. Now the moon, properly observed, serves for the seamen the part of a clock which can never go wrong. The stars serve as the marks on the great dial-plate of the heavens, by which the position of the moon—the moving hand— can be determined with the utmost nicety. Calculations are then applied to show precisely where the moon would be seen among the stars if the observer were at the centre of the earth instead of at his actual station. And then a reference to the Nautical Almanac shows precisely what is the Greenwich time. Thence the observer learns how far east or west he is of Greenwich. And often, after many cloudy nights have passed, the observation of the moon has shown the sailor that owing to currents and misjudged rate of sailing, he has been far out in his reckoning; and he has been saved by the moon from a great danger. So that we may find a new meaning in the words of the inspired Psalmist—'They that go down to the sea in ships, that do business in great waters; these see the works of the Lord, and His wonders in the deep.'

II.

I HAVE hitherto considered the moon with reference chiefly to the services which she renders to our earth. I showed that, as a subordinate light-giver, as a measurer of time, as chief ruler of the tides, and, lastly, as a celestial index which shows the experienced seaman where he is on the wide expanse of ocean, the moon subserves most important purposes to the inhabitants of the earth.   I propose presently to consider the moon in another aspect; to enquire into her actual condition as a member of the solar system, and to describe briefly the interesting circumstances which have been ascertained by means of the telescopic scrutiny of her surface.   Before passing, however, from the former branch of my subject, I would make a few remarks on the convenience of the present arrangement as compared with that which the great mathematician and astronomer Laplace suggested as better suited for our requirements.

It will be remembered that Laplace showed how a moon might so circle around the earth as to be at all times exactly opposite the sun, and therefore always 'full,' rising also always when the sun set and setting when the sun rose.   I mentioned in my last paper certain difficulties attending this arrangement even when considered with reference to the particular result which it was designed to bring about.   I also touched on the inconvenience of some of the results which would have followed from it, and particularly on the loss we should sustain if we never had a perfectly dark night.   But it is even more important to notice how seriously all the other services rendered by the moon to ourselves would have been affected if the moon's motions had been those devised so ingeniously by Laplace.

Let it be remembered that to be always opposite the sun the moon must circle round the earth in the same time as the sun, or once a year. Thus the moon would no longer afford any subordinate time-measures. It is manifest that this would be a decided loss.

Again, the sun and moon at present join in controlling the tides, in such a way that when the moon is opposite the sun or on the same side as the sun, we have a tide resulting from the combined action of the sun and moon ; while when the moon is half-way between these positions, as at first and third quarters, we have a tide which is merely the excess of the lunar tide-wave over the solar tide-wave. If the wave produced under the former circumstances be represented by the number 7, then the wave under the latter circumstances will be represented by the number 3 ; for the solar and lunar tide-waves are as 2 to 5, and they always coalesce so as to produce a single but variable tide-wave. Now it is clear that this variation of the tide-wave adds importantly to the service which the tides render to man. It is extremely convenient to have occasional very high tides, while it would manifestly be inconvenient to have the range of the tidal wave always at its greatest value. Now, if Laplace's arrangement prevailed we should have the moon always co-operating with the sun, for they work together equally whether they be on the same or on opposite sides of the earth. Thus we should always have ‘ flood ’ tides, or rather we should know of no such differences as now distinguish flood-tides from neap-tides. This would be a second serious loss.

And lastly, as to the service which the moon renders to seamen by her motions among the stars, it is easily shown that she would at once lose a great part of her value in this respect if she circled round once a year instead of once a month. She would move then with less than a twelfth of her present rate of motion (for there are more than twelve lunar months in a year). Now this would correspond almost exactly to the case of a clock which had lost its minute hand, so that we had to determine the time from the position of the hour hand. We know that owing to the very slow motion of the hour hand we could never tell the time within several minutes by its means. We judge always by the minute hand. So with the moon. Her comparatively rapid motion enables the sailor to determine the time (not the time of day, but what may be called ' earth-time ') very closely; whereas if she moved with only one-twelfth part of her present motion, she would be practically useless as a time-indicator. Nor let the reader imagine that the difference of her value in this respect would be insignificant in its effects. Time in this case means position; an error of time means an error of position; and an error of position means danger. The danger is greater or less according as the error is likely to be greater or less. Now, unfortunately, a very small error of time corresponds to an error of distance quite sufficient to involve very great danger. Let us suppose, for instance, that a ship is in latitude sixty degrees—that is, somewhat farther northwards than the north of Scotland—and that she is making her way towards the American coast ; now suppose that observations of the moon have given the time very nearly right—say only half a minute wrong—and let us enquire how far wrong the estimated place of the ship would be. A degree in sixty north latitude contains half as many miles as at the equator, where, as we know, each degree contains sixty ' knots,' or nautical miles, or about sixty-nine common miles. Hence in latitude sixty north, each degree contains about thirty-four and a half miles. The earth turns through fifteen degrees each hour, and therefore through one degree in four minutes. So that an error of four minutes in the time would be equivalent to an error of thirty-four and a half miles in the determination of the ship's place. Half a minute would give an error, therefore, of about four and a half miles, quite enough to cast a ship upon some iron-bound shore when her captain judged that she was still at a safe distance.[1] It will be seen, therefore, how serious would be

---

[1] That erroneous notions may not be suggested as to the way in which our seamen actually provide against such dangers as are here indicated. I must remark that in point of fact there is no reliable method for determining a ship's place at sea with such accuracy that a captain could approach shore confidently (at night, for instance) within a few miles. All that he can expect from observation is such an approach to accuracy that until he is at a moderate distance from shore, no special look-out for land need be maintained. Of course the more accurate his means of determining true earth-time, the shorter will be the period during which (if he is worthy of

the mischief if all such errors as must inevitably arise in such cases were increased twelve-fold.

I cannot but think that the lesson we may derive from these considerations is a very instructive one. Let it be remembered that Laplace was a man of most remarkable powers. As a mathematical astronomer he comes next after Newton, of whom it has been justly said that he surpassed the whole human race in mental power. Laplace has not been judged to have spoken unadvisedly when, referring to Newton's work, he said that Newton was fortunate in being the earlier born, implying that he himself had the power to have discovered the great law of gravitation, had not Newton first accomplished the work. This, which would have been regarded justly as arrogance in another, has not been so imputed to Laplace even by those who question whether Laplace in Newton's place would

the trust reposed in him by crew, passengers, and employers) he will take no rest, and relax not one instant from watchfulness. To show what could be done if there were perfect means of determining the time, the following narrative may be cited :—When the 'Great Eastern' is carrying a telegraph cable across the Atlantic, her captain of course knows the true Greenwich time within a single second, for it is flashed to him from Valentia. He can therefore determine his true place with great accuracy. Now it chanced that on one occasion the captain of the 'Great Eastern,' while thus in telegraphical communication with Greenwich through Valentia, had occasion to search for a buoy which had been left floating (attached to a sunk cable) in a particular latitude and longitude. He made for the spot according to his calculated latitude and longitude, and (according to the account) after the final directions had been given to the effect that the ship should follow a certain course for a certain time, he went below to examine a chart. When the time came he was about to go on deck, hoping to have made his course so truly that the buoy would be in sight; but at that very instant the ship's side was struck by the buoy.

have done so much as Newton actually achieved. This is the highest praise which could be given to any astronomer short of saying that he was Newton's equal. Now see how the great mathematician failed when he employed his powers to show in what way the work of the Almighty might be improved. He showed how a certain advantage might have been obtained had a certain special arrangement been adopted. So far all was well. But he omitted to observe how much more would be lost than would be gained by the proposed alteration. His scheme was conceived in the spirit of the remark made by Alphonsus, king of Portugal, who, speaking of the system of the universe as understood in his day, said that if the Almighty had consulted him when the universe was about to be created, he could have given useful advice. Alphonsus was in one sense right, since his remark, ugly though it sounds, was really intended to imply no more than that, in his opinion, astronomers had not in his day discovered the true system of the universe. But had Laplace been consulted when the moon's position and path were designed (to use such words for want of better), and if his advice had been adopted, we should have had a moon which would have subserved but one out of four highly important services actually rendered to us by her. Well might Laplace have been answered by the Almighty, even as of old He answered Job out of the whirlwind, 'Who is this that darkeneth counsel by words without knowledge? Gird up now thy loins like a man ; for I will demand of thee, and answer thou me. Where wast thou when I laid the foundations of the earth ? declare, if thou hast understanding. Who hath laid the measures thereof, if thou knowest ? or who hath stretched the line upon it ? Whereupon are the foundations thereof fastened ? or who laid the corner stone thereof; when the morning stars sang together, and all the sons of God shouted for joy ? . . . Hast thou commanded the morning since thy days; and caused the dayspring to know his place. . . . Knowest thou the ordinances of heaven ? canst thou set the dominion thereof in the earth ? . . . Wilt thou also disannul my judgment ? wilt thou condemn me, that thou mayest be righteous ? '

I will draw this portion of my subject to a conclusion by calling attention to one feature of the moon, which, though it does not tend in any way to increase the comforts of the human race, has been of great importance so far as their acquisition of knowledge has been concerned. I refer to the near agreement in point of apparent size between the sun and the moon, two globes which differ so remarkably as to their real dimensions. The agreement is so close that as the sun and moon slightly vary in apparent size, according to their slightly varying distances, the moon looks sometimes slightly greater and sometimes slightly less than the sun. Now, it is easily seen that if this relation had not existed—and it is in a sense merely fortuitous, not existing in the case of any other planet which has a moon—we should know very much less than we actually know about our sun. If the moon had a disc much smaller than the sun's there would never be a total eclipse of the sun, and all those wonderful objects which make their appearance when the sun is totally eclipsed— the coloured prominences and the sierra, the glowing inner corona, and the radiated fainter glory which lies outside the corona—would have been altogether unknown to us. But we should scarcely have learned more if the moon had had a disc much larger than the sun's. For in that case when a total eclipse began, all the region round the sun, except that close to the part of the sun's face concealed *last*, would be hidden by the moon's much larger disc. At the middle of totality, the red prominences and sierra, as well as all the brighter part of the corona, would be altogether concealed from view. And, lastly, at the end of totality the same state of things would prevail as at the beginning, only now it would be close to the part of the sun just about to appear, that for a moment or two the red prominences would be visible. Manifestly it would be quite hopeless under such circumstances to attempt to obtain any satisfactory observations of the solar surroundings. We now see during totality the complete ring of prominences for two or three minutes, and. the whole of the corona is shown. Even as thus shown it has been sufficiently difficult to ascertain the nature of these objects. But with a moon much larger than ours we could have learned scarcely anything respecting them, and with a moon much smaller we should have known absolutely nothing of the solar appendages.

III.

With how sad steps, O moon, thou climb'st the sky,—
How silently and with how wan a face !—WORDSWORTH.

IN this, the third and concluding part of my essay on the Queen of Night, I propose to consider her not as a mere satellite or attendant on the earth, but as a planet or other world, possibly, though not probably, an inhabited world.

It may seem strange, perhaps, to some of my readers to find the moon spoken of as a planet. We are so accustomed to view the moon as a relatively small body circling around our earth, and directly subordinate to the require ments of her inhabitants, that it is only by an effort of the imagination that we can rise to the conception of her real position in the scheme of worlds circling around the sun. But in reality the moon is governed in her motions mainly by the sun; she circles around him rather than around the earth, though, viewed from our terrestrial standpoint, she appears to obey the earth's influence more directly than the sun's. If the moon could be watched from some distant point whence the whole solar system could be seen, her course around the sun would be seen to resemble that followed by a planet. This course may be described as nearly circular, and slightly eccentric, insomuch that while her mean distance is about ninety-one millions of miles, she is some 1,500,000 miles nearer to the sun in December and January than in June and July. This, let it be noticed, is precisely what we should say of the earth's path; and all that has to be added to the description of the moon's path is that, in a period of about four weeks, she passes alternately farther from the sun and nearer to him than her mean path by about 240,000 miles, a mere trifle, it will be seen, compared with the dimensions of her actual path round the sun. Nor is it true, as I have sometimes seen stated in books on astronomy, that the moon follows a spiral or twisted path, owing to her movement around the earth, combined with her movement round the sun. If a perfectly exact representation of the moon's path were made in very fine wire, on a tolerably large scale, it would require the nicest scrutiny to distinguish the wire curve from a perfect circle. Again, if we represented the earth's path by a wire circle a foot in diameter, and one-thirtieth [1] of an inch in thickness, the moon's path would be wholly included within the substance of that wire, passing alter-

[1] Rather less than a thirtieth, more exactly a thirty-third part. The reader should take an ordinary foot-rule, divided into inches and tenths of an inch; then one-third of one of these tenths will correspond to the greatest range of the moon within and without the earth's path, where this path is represented by a circle a foot in diameter. On the same scale the sun would be represented by a little globe rather less than two-thirds of the tenth of an inch in diameter, and about one-tenth of an inch from the centre of the circle.

nately close to its inner side and to its outer side, at points dividing the ring nearly into twenty-five equal parts.

We see, then, that so far as the moon's path is concerned, she may be regarded as a planet. Nor is she markedly inferior in bulk to some of the other planets forming the sun's inner family, consisting, as we know, of Mercury, Venus, the Earth and Moon, and Mars. She is certainly the smallest of this family, but compared with Mercury, she is not so small by far as Mercury is compared with the earth, and she is not much smaller compared with Mars than Mars is compared with the earth. This will be easily seen from the following numbers, which represent the volumes of the five planets which circle nearest to the sun, arranged in order of magnitude :—

The Earth	1000
Venus	855
Mars	168
Mercury	58
The Moon	20

And it must be remembered also that the absolute dimensions of the moon are by no means insignificant The moon's diameter is about 2,160 miles in length ; she has a surface of 14,600,000 miles, and a solid content of about 10,000 millions of cubic miles. If we consider her surface as the feature by which she is most readily brought into comparison with our earth, then it is to be noted that the earth's surface only exceeds the moon's about 13½ times, and the moon's surface is fully as large as Africa and Australia together, or nearly as large as North and South America without their islands.

In mass or quantity of matter the moon is somewhat more markedly inferior to the other four planets, as the following list of numbers, showing the relative mass of the five planets, sufficiently indicates:—

The Earth	1000
Venus	885
Mars	118
Mercury	65
The Moon	12

But still, it will be seen, the earth exceeds Mercury, in mass as in volume, to a greater degree than Mercury exceeds the moon; and Mars holds much the same relative position between the earth and the moon in this list as in the list of numbers representing the volume of the five planets. Moreover, the quantity of matter in the moon cannot be looked upon as absolutely insignificant, when we consider that the average density of the moon is more than three times as great as the density of water, and that she contains, as above mentioned, about 10,000 millions of cubic miles of matter. If the moon could be weighed against a quantity of water—say in some vast balance placed on the surface of the sun or of some other very large and massive orb—it would be found that about

34,500 cubic miles of water would be required to counter-balance the moon's weight.

"There is one circumstance, however, in which the moon shows a sort of dependence upon the earth, producing a very striking distinction between her and the other planets. She turns round on her axis in such a way as always to turn the same or nearly the same face towards the earth. As she turns uniformly, but does not travel at a quite uniform rate, and as she also turns on a slightly inclined axis, she sometimes shows a little more of her eastern and western sides, or again of her northern and southern sides, than at other times; but her average rate of turning is absolutely identical with her average period of motion round the earth, and accordingly she never sways more than a certain portion of her surface into view or out of view by these libratory or balancing motions.

Now this rate of rotation is exceedingly slow. For we know that the moon takes about a month in circling round the earth; and therefore she takes about a month in turning upon her axis. In other words, the moon's *day* lasts about four of our weeks; and if we suppose it divided as we divide our day, into twenty-four equal parts, then each of these parts lasts more than one of our days—in fact, a lunar hour lasts nearly 29½ of our hours. Day-time lasts on the average rather more than a fortnight of terrestrial time; and night lasts as long. Here, then, there is a very singular contrast between the state of matters on the moon and on our earth.

The contrast is rendered even more striking by the circumstance that the lunar year is shorter than our year. This will seem strange at first sight, because I have said that the moon travels round the sun on a path almost identical with the earth's, and of course in the same time. Now, we all know that our year is the time occupied by the earth in going once round the sun: and it might seem that the lunar year must necessarily be the period occupied by the moon in going once round the sun, this period being our common year. But a peculiarity which very slightly affects our own *year of seasons,*[1] making it in reality more than twenty minutes shorter than the *year of circling round the sun,* affects the moon's year in a much greater degree, insomuch that while the *lunar year of circling round the sun* lasts, like ours, 365 days, six hours, and nine minutes, the *lunar year of seasons* lasts only 346 days, fourteen hours, and thirty-four minutes.

It follows that there are not quite twelve lunar days in a lunar year. *Each of the four seasons lasts rather less than three days.*

But the seasons are also very slightly distinguished one from the other. Lunar winter differs from lunar summer no more than on our earth the 16th of March

---

[1] The peculiarity is in fact a swaying of the earth's axis like the slow reeling of a mighty top, each reel occupying about 25,866 years. The corresponding motion of the moon's axis is completed in about 18 years and 7 months.

differs from the 26th, or than the 27th of September differs from the 19th.

If the contrast between winter and summer is slight, however, the contrast between day and night is very remarkable. In order clearly to understand this, we must not only consider the great length of the lunar day, but the condition of the moon as respects those circumstances which on our own earth temper the mid-day heat and the cold of midnight. In the telescope the moon appears to be a perfectly waterless globe, her arid surface being covered with ring-shaped mountains, mountain-ranges, peaks, fissures, and rocks, except in certain regions, called seas, where the surface (really solid) is apparently quite smooth. It was formerly supposed that these smooth regions, which are rather darker than the rest of her surface, are seas; and, by a singular perversity, astronomers who have been but too ready to introduce new names among the constellations have continued to call these regions 'seas,' long after it has been demonstrated that they are land-surfaces. It is certain, then (at least as respects the side of the moon turned earthwards), that none of those beneficial effects which result on earth from the presence of extensive water-covered regions can be produced on the moon. No clouds can temper the heat of the lunar day, or at night prevent the too rapid escape of the heat which had been garnered up, so to speak, in the daytime; nor can any of those more subtle processes take place which result from the presence in our air of the unseen vapour of water.

Nor is this all. So far as we can judge, the moon has *no air*; at least no sign of air has ever been perceived by astronomers, even when they have applied the most delicate tests by means of the most powerful instruments. It is certain at any rate that whatever air there may be is very small in quantity compared with our air. Thus in the daytime the sun's heat is poured down with unmitigated effect upon the moon's surface, which during the long fortnightly day must be positively broiled by the solar rays; while at night, or rather so soon as night begins, the heat all passes away into space, and then for hour after hour of the long lunar night an intensity of cold must prevail far exceeding the bitterest cold of our Arctic and Antarctic regions.

It has been thought that on the farther side of the moon a different state of things may prevail, that oceans and an atmosphere may be there, and, possibly, living creatures not differing very greatly from those on our earth. I must confess that the evidence on which this opinion has been based does not appear to me convincing. And, apart from this, we see far enough round the other side to detect some signs of air, if not of oceans, if any existed there. If the whole surface of the moon be represented by the number 1000, the parts we see at one time or another amount in all to 589, while the parts never seen amount in all but to 411. Then there is this consideration, which to most minds will not seem without weight :—The part of the moon turned earthwards is, of course, the only part whence the earth can be seen. Now, it would certainly be a singular, and one may even say an unwise, arrangement (at any rate, the wisdom of the arrangement is not manifest to us) by which the inhabitants of the moon should be so confined to a certain lunar region as to be deprived of all opportunity of beholding the beautiful spectacle presented by our earth, as, with varying phases, she shows her huge disc (more than thirteen times larger than the moon's as seen by us), with its continents and seas, passing in orderly sequence into and out of view, with its aspect changing as the seasons progress, and with all the other charming phenomena which she must present to lunar inhabitants, if any such there are.

More reasonable appears the conclusion that either the moon is not now inhabited, or, if she is inhabited, that it is by classes of beings quite unlike any with which we are familiar.

THE EVENING STAR.

Now glows the firmament
With living sapphires; Hesperus, that leads
The starry host, rides brightest.—PARADISE LOST.

IN April there shines towards the west a star so far surpassing all others in the heavens in brightness, that it might well be believed to be the most important of all the orbs discernible by us. It is Hesperus, the star of the evening, the planet Venus; and, in reality, so far from being the largest of all the orbs we see, there are but two celestial bodies, besides the Moon, which are smaller than this beautiful planet. The planet Jupiter, which can now be seen at midnight, and is far inferior in brightness to Venus, is in reality a globe surpassing her more than thirteen hundred times in volume. And even Jupiter sinks into utter insignificance by comparison with the least of the fixed stars; while the splendid Sirius, which shines less brightly far than Jupiter, probably surpasses Venus in bulk more than a thousand millions of times.

Yet Venus is a globe of great magnitude when we compare her with all terrestrial measures of size. That star which seems like a very bright but tiny light in the sky, has, in reality, a surface which our swiftest modes of travelling would enable creatures like ourselves to survey only in a long period of time. Supposing that surface ocean-covered, then a vessel travelling as fast as our swiftest steamers would be more than two months in completely circumnavigating it. It gives a signal proof of the mistaken ideas we are apt to form, to look at that bright point of light now illumining our evening skies, and to consider that a steam vessel travelling around it, and ploughing the waves so swiftly that the sea-foam would dash in great white masses over its prow, would have to pursue its course unceasingly for seventy or eighty days in order to complete the circuit of that seemingly minute body.

It may be said without noticeable inaccuracy that Venus is a globe as large as our earth. Some telescopic measures have led astronomers to the conclusion that she is larger than our earth, while others (and these are commonly regarded as the best) appear to show that she is somewhat smaller than the earth. She has no moon, and is in that respect inferior to her sister planet Terra. But in many circumstances she so closely resembles the earth, that it is difficult to imagine that she is not, like the earth, an inhabited world. She is nearer to the sun, indeed, in the proportion of about 73 to 100, and consequently she receives more light and heat than the earth, in the proportion of about 100 times 100 to 73 times 73, or nearly 2 to 1. This seems at first sight to render her unfit to be the abode of living creatures; for even in our temperate latitudes the increase of the sun's light and heat in a twofold degree would undoubtedly destroy nearly all the forms of life now existing on the earth. But we are apt to forget that the forms of life we are accustomed to are not necessarily the only possible forms of life. It is almost impossible to say under what conditions life is possible or impossible. Men of science have lately been taught this in a very striking manner. For, judging by what they know of the state of things at the bottom of the deep sea, they concluded that there could be no living creatures there. They reasoned that the pressure exerted by the water would crush the life out of any known creature, which was unquestionably true. A piece of the hardest and densest wood, sunk to those depths, has the water literally forced into its very substance, and the tremendous mail of the crocodile, or the thick skin of the rhinoceros, would be unable to resist a tithe of the enormous pressure exerted by the water at the bottom of deep seas. Yet it is now known that creatures not only exist down there, but that, notwithstanding the great darkness which must prevail there, these creatures are provided with the means of seeing. So unlike are they to all other creatures, however, that they are unable to live out of their native depths, and when dragged up by the dredges, they burst asunder and are killed long before reaching the surface. This should teach us that although it may be proved that in some inaccessible world, like Venus, or

any of her fellow planets, the conditions which prevail
are not such as would be convenient to terrestrial creatures,
or are even such that no creatures known to us could endure
them even for a few minutes, life may nevertheless exist.
It is indeed tolerably certain that if there are living
creatures in Venus (as for my own part I little doubt), and if
among these creatures there are any which possess reasoning
powers such as ours (which is not so certain), it must appear
to such reasoning beings in Venus at least as difficult to
understand how our earth can be inhabited as we find it
to conceive what nature of creatures they may be which
exist in Venus.

The year of Venus is much shorter than ours, amount-
ing in fact only to 225 days, or rather less than $7\frac{1}{2}$ months.
So that if we suppose the year to be divided into four
seasons as with us, each of these seasons lasts rather
less than two of our months.   But with the tremendous
heating and illuminating power which the sun must
exert on Venus, the progress of vegetation must be much
more rapid than on our own earth, and therefore so long a
year is not required.   Yet it must not be imagined that
the short year of Venus of itself renders the condition of
the planet unlike that of any part of our earth.   There
are regions on our earth where the hottest and coldest
seasons are not separated as they are here in England by
six months, but by three.   This happens in the equatorial
regions, where the seasons we call spring and autumn are
the hottest part of the year, while the seasons we call

summer and winter are the coolest, or rather (since coolness, at least by day, is unknown in equatorial regions) are the least warm seasons of the year. And I have often thought, in connection with the subject of life in other worlds, that if the inhabitants of the earth were in some way prevented from travelling to other countries than those in which they were born, but were able to learn something of the climate of other regions, they would be apt to believe that life was quite impossible anywhere but in their own latitudes. For instance, if .we did not know that the torrid zone was inhabited, and could not visit that region, but knew nevertheless how tremendous the heat is there, how short the interval from greatest to least heat, and so on, how ready we should be to believe that neither animal nor vegetable life can exist there. And in like manner as to the Arctic regions. Supposing we knew only that there are parts of the earth where the sun is sometimes unseen for several successive weeks, and sometimes remains without setting for as long a period, while even in the heart of summer a cold more intense than our bitterest winters prevails, how startling would be the thought (familiar though it now seems to us) that there are not only living creatures in the Arctic regions, but that a race of men exists and thrives there, even preferring their strange abode to the temperate regions which seem to us so much more pleasant!

It is remarkable, indeed, that while our lips are ready to speak of the goodness of God to all His creatures, and of His infinite wisdom and power, we very often treat the question of life in other worlds as though the Almighty's power and wisdom were limited, and as though He would cause other worlds to be inhabited not by creatures suited to the conditions prevailing in those worlds, but by creatures such as we are familiar with, although such creatures would certainly be most miserable, if they could exist at all, in any world but ours. May it not justly be said in answer to such reasoning, ' Oh that God would speak, and .open His lips, and that He would show the secrets of wisdom, that they are double to that which is ! Canst thou by searching find out God ? canst thou find out the Almighty unto perfection ? It is as high as heaven ; what canst thou do? Deeper than hell ; what canst thou know? The measure thereof is longer than the earth, and broader than the sea.'

There is another circumstance in the condition of Venus which, according to our ideas, seems inconsistent with the well-being of her inhabitants, but may nevertheless be recognised by reasoning beings on Venus as affording excellent illustrations of the beneficence of the Almighty. I refer to the slope of her axis to the path in which she travels. It is known, of course, to my readers that it is the slope or tilt of the earth's axis which occasions the changing seasons of our earth, and they doubtless remember the striking descriptive passage in Milton's ' Paradise Lost '—

> Some say, He bid His angels turn askance
> The poles of Earth twice ten degrees and more
> From the Sun's axle; they with labour push'd
> Oblique the centric globe.   Some say, the Sun
> Was bid turn reins from th' equinoctial road,
> Like distant breadth to Taurus with the seven
> Atlantic Sisters, and the Spartan Twins,
> Up to the Tropic Crab; thence down amain
> By Leo, and the Virgin, and the Scales,
> As deep as Capricorn, to bring in change
> Of seasons to each clime; else had the spring
> Perpetual smiled on earth with vernant flow'rs,
> Equal in days and nights.

But in Venus, if the observations of certain telescopists can be relied on, the poles are ' turned askance ' two score degrees and more; and thus all the seasons are exaggerated : or rather, there results a state of things differing in all respects from our terrestrial seasons. This would not be the proper place to discuss the effects actually resulting in different parts of Venus (and, besides, I have already given a full account of those effects in my ' Orbs Around Us '); but one single case corresponding to that of our own country on the earth will serve to show how very strangely the seasons progress in Venus. We know that here in London the sun at noon in spring and autumn rises about $38\frac{1}{2}$ degrees above the horizon (the point overhead is 90 degrees from the horizon). But in summer he rises higher, ' twice ten degrees and more,' or in fact to a height of about 62 degrees, at noon; while in winter he is as much lower at noon, and so attains only a height of about 15 degrees. Everyone knows, too, how much longer the day is in summer than in winter. Hence we have the pinching cold and scorching heat of our extreme winter and summer. But in Venus, at a place in the same latitude as London on earth, a much more remarkable change must take place. For there, as here in London, the sun at noon in spring or autumn must be about 38½ degrees above the horizon; but at noon in midsummer he is almost exactly overhead (in point of fact *more* than 90 degrees from the southern horizon— that is, he is rather on the northern side of the point overhead). At noon in midwinter he is not seen at all; for the slope of Venus's axis amounts to more than 50 degrees, and therefore the winter noonday sun is depressed more than 50 degrees below the place of the spring or autumn noonday sun, which, as we have seen, is but 38½ degrees above the horizon. In winter, then, in a place situated on Venus as London is on the earth, there is no day. And it is easily seen that there is no night in summer. In fact, such a place presents the same peculiarity in this respect which is observed within our Arctic and Antarctic regions. But it also resembles places within our torrid zones, in having the noonday sun overhead in summer. When it is added that the change from the extremely hot summer (with a sun twice as large as our own overhead at noon, and still high above the horizon at nominal midnight) to the bitter cold of winter (with the sun far below the horizon at nominal noon) takes place in less than four of our months, it will be seen that if there

is a London on Venus the Londoners there must be of
singularly strong constitutions. It is thought a trying
change for the ordinary Londoner to visit the hotter
regions of the tropical zone; and it is an even more
trying change for him to penetrate within the Arctic
regions. But to have a summer more than twice as hot
as our hottest torrid weather, a cold as extreme as that of
our Arctic winters, succeeding each other at intervals of
four months, would certainly kill in a year or two not
merely the ordinary Londoner, but the hardiest specimen
of the hardiest races of mankind. But assuredly 'Touching the Almighty we cannot find Him out; He is excellent
in power and in judgment, and in plenteousness of justice;
He will not afflict.'

THE RUDDY PLANET.

The snows that glittered on the disc of Mars
Have melted, and the planet's fiery orb
Rolls in the crimson summer of its year.—HOLMES.

DURING May there shines in the south a ruddy orb which can scarcely be mistaken for a fixed star. It is the planet Mars pursuing his course (now retrograde) through the constellation of the Virgin. In this constellation there is but one star which is comparable in brilliancy with the planet Mars—the star Spica Azimech, which marks the ear of corn carried in the maiden's hand; and the eye recognises at once a marked difference between the sparkling light of the star and the steady glow of the ruddy planet. It may in passing be noticed that a fine opportunity is afforded the young astronomer of observing the chief distinction between a planet and a fixed star. It is quite commonly imagined that only long and patient watching can reveal the movements which are characteristic of the planets (and whence, indeed, they derive their name, since the word planet signifies ' a wanderer ').

But even in a few hours Mars perceptibly changes his place among the fixed stars; and if he be watched night after night during a favourable opportunity—

let us say from the end of May until the end of June —he will be seen to traverse a very considerable portion of one of the great loops in which he circuits the zodiac. I can imagine few more instructive or suggestive exercises than thus to track a planet which, like Mars, or Jupiter, or Saturn, is conspicuous from time to time in our night skies as distinguished from the twilight skies on which the planet Venus pursues her course. The task is not at all a difficult one. All that is necessary is to prick down on a sheet of white paper the stars of the constellation which the planet is traversing. The ordinary almanacs tell us which constellation this chances to be, and any good star-atlas will give the conspicuous stars.

Then each night the young astronomer should notice where the planet is situated among these stars, and should jot down its place accordingly in his star-sheet. When a few days have passed he will begin to recognise the nature of the track which the planet is pursuing, and he will have pursued himself a portion of the track by which the earliest astronomers were gradually led to the knowledge of the true arrangement of that wonderful scheme of orbs over which the sun bears sway. Nay, if the planet he has selected has been Mars—now the best placed by far for the purpose, and always remarkable when so placed for the rapidity of his motions—the young astronomer will have been repeating, in a rough way, the observations which led Kepler to the knowledge of those laws on which Newton based the whole system of modern astronomy.

It appears to me that the study of the heavens is not less instructive in this aspect than in the wonderful facts which it has revealed. I find, indeed, a special charm in the contemplation of the great problems of astronomy as they presented themselves to men before the time had come when the great secret of the universe was to be revealed. There is much in the thoughts suggested by such contemplation to afford encouragement on the one hand, and to teach modesty on the other. If we feel gratification, and some degree of pride in the intellectual powers given to man, when we consider the marvellous way in which the truth in these matters has been attained, we must nevertheless perceive how prone man is to error, when we recall how for century after century a false system of astronomy was complacently taught at all the great seats of learning.

There is another excellent reason for studying the actual motions of the celestial bodies when favourable opportunity occurs. This reason is that set forth by Milton, when he makes the archangel say to Adam :—

> To ask or search I blame thee not; for Heaven
> Is as the book of God before thee set,
> Wherein to read His wondrous works, and learn
> His seasons, hours or days or months or years.

And no other subject of observation is pleasanter or more

instructive than the movement of the planets, as they
pursue

> Their wand'ring course,—now high, now low, then hid,
> Progressive, retrograde, or standing still.

Let us pass, however, to the consideration of the
planet Mars as exhibited to us by the teachings of
astronomy.

We note, then, first, that Mars is strikingly contrasted
to the two planets hitherto considered—Venus and Jupiter
—unlike though these two planets are to each other.
'One star differeth from another star in glory.' We may,
indeed, almost say that in the whole heavens there are
not two orbs which resemble each other. In considering Venus we were struck by the great amount of light
and heat which she receives from the sun. With Mars
all this is reversed. For whereas Venus is the planet
which travels next to the earth on the inside, or towards
the sun, Mars travels next to the earth on the outside, or
away from the sun. Accordingly he receives much less
light and heat than the earth ; his actual supply (considering mile per mile of surface) varies from one-half to
one-third of the earth's supply, this great variation being
due to the eccentric nature of the path on which he
travels. Thus, while Venus receives twice as much light
and heat as the earth, Mars never receives more than half
as much as the earth, or one-fourth of the supply afforded
to Venus. Mars also differs remarkably from Venus and
our earth in size, and it is in this respect that he affords

the most remarkable contrast to the planet Jupiter. For we have seen that Jupiter is very much larger than the earth, exceeding her more than twelve hundred times in volume, and more than three hundred times in mass or quantity of matter. Now Mars is very much smaller than the earth, being, indeed, much nearer to the moon both in point of size and in point of mass. In size he is about one-sixth part of the earth ; in mass he is about one-ninth part. He is, in fact, the smallest of all the planets except Mercury (and of course the members of the ring of small bodies travelling between Jupiter and Mars). Moreover, he is contrasted to Jupiter in the fact that he has no moon, whereas Jupiter, as we have seen, is surrounded by a noble family of moons. What renders the contrast between these planets more remarkable is that they are next neighbours in the solar system, so far as the primary planets are concerned. According to the astronomy of Newton's day, and until the present century, there were in order the planets Mercury, Venus, the Earth, Mars, Jupiter, and Saturn ; and thus, next to the two giants Jupiter and Saturn, but nearest of all to the greater giant Jupiter, there came the least of all the planets except Mercury.

But although Mars is a small and seemingly insignificant member of the solar family, he is in reality by no means the least interesting of the planets. He is, indeed, the one about which we know most. Venus comes nearer to us, but when she is nearest we cannot see her, since she then lies directly towards the sun. Jupiter, again, looks larger than Mars, and we seem at first sight to perceive more in the belted globe of the giant planet than in the small red disc of Mars. But all the processes at work in Jupiter are seen under the diminishing effect of a distance of some 360 millions of miles, whereas Mars, when favourably placed, is but some 50 millions of miles from us, on the average, and sometimes when he approaches at his very nearest, he is less than 40 millions of miles from us.

Under the telescope Mars presents appearances somewhat like those which we may imagine that our earth presents as seen from Venus or Mercury. There are reddish tracts which we may regard as the continents of the planet, and there are greenish regions which may very well be oceans. Assuming this to be the case, we can note at once a marked difference between the arrangement of land and water in Mars and in our own earth. Our oceans exceed the continents nearly three times in extent. On Mars land and water are about equally divided. Again, the arrangement of land and water on our earth is such that in reality the continents may be looked upon as great islands. The two Americas form one great island. Europe, Asia, and Africa another; Australia a third; and then there are a multitude of smaller islands. In Mars a very different arrangement prevails. The relation is not absolutely reversed—that is to say, the oceans in Mars cannot be regarded as great lakes; but an intermediate

arrangement prevails, land and water being so intermixed
that the great continents are connected with each other,
as well as the great oceans. There are of course some
islands and some lakes, but the chief divisions of land and
water are connected as described.[1]

The next feature of Mars which has to be noticed is
the presence of two white patches around the poles of the
planet. These have long been regarded, and very reasonably, as the Arctic and Antarctic snows and ice fields of
Mars. It occurred to Sir W. Herschel to study their appearance in order to see whether, as the Martial year progressed, they changed in size, waxing larger in winter and
waning again in summer. For Mars has seasons as our
earth has, his polar axis being sloped to the level of the
path in which he travels, much as the earth's axis is
sloped to the level of her path. The slope is rather greater,
and therefore the seasonal changes must be somewhat more
marked, but the difference is not very great. It follows
that during the progress of the Martial year, which lasts
687 days, there must be spring and summer and autumn
and winter in one hemisphere of Mars while in the other
there are the seasons autumn, winter, spring, and summer.
Now Herschel found, as he expected, that with the progress of these seasons the polar snows of Mars wax and

---

[1] A coloured chart of Mars on the Stereographic projection is given in
'Other Worlds,' and a chart on Mercator's Projection in 'Orbs Around Us.'
From these charts globes of the planet have been formed by Mr. Browning,
the optician, and by Captain Busk (in the latter case Messrs. Malby have
made the globes).

wane much as happens with the snow and ice in our own Arctic and Antarctic regions.

But even more like what takes place on our earth is the apparent formation of great masses of cloud, hiding from view the Martial lands and seas, sometimes for many successive hours. Indeed, it would seem that in the winter season of Mars the sky is commonly overcast, for the features of the winter half of the planet are not nearly so well seen as those of the half where summer is in progress. And then again it would seem as though at early morning and again in the evening fogs and mist prevail in Mars, for the parts of the planet which have lately come into sunlight, as well as those which are about to pass away to the night half of the globe, always show a whitish light which altogether conceals the features of land and water.

Perhaps, however, the most remarkable circumstance of all in connection with the ruddy planet is the fact that astronomers have been able to prove that there *is* water on Mars. The mere appearance of greenish tracts on the planet may suggest the idea that water exists there; but yet we could not be at all sure that this is the case. Again, the white polar caps of Mars are very well explained by the supposition that they are snow-covered regions; yet this supposition might be altogether erroneous. And it might seem as though nothing short of a visit to Mars could place the existence of water on the planet's surface altogether beyond dispute. But by means of the wonderful powers of the new instrument of research called the spectroscope, it has been proved beyond all possibility of question that there is water on Mars. The way in which this has been done is in reality sufficiently simple, though it would not be easy to explain it fully in these columns. This much, however, may be said in the way of explanation. When the sun's light is examined with a spectroscope, the white sunlight is changed into a rainbow-tinted streak crossed by a multitude of dark lines. When the sun is low down, so that his light traverses the lower parts of the air, certain new dark lines and bands are seen in the rainbow-tinted streak called the solar spectrum; and it has been proved that some of these new lines are solely due to the vapour of water in our atmosphere. Now, the light of Mars is reflected sunlight; and therefore when examined with the spectroscope, it gives the rainbow-tinted streak and the dark lines which form the solar spectrum. But *also* it gives the dark bands known to belong to the vapour of water; and these bands are seen when Mars is high above our horizon, so that the bands cannot be due to the vapour of water in *our* atmosphere. Hence it follows that there is the vapour of water in the atmosphere of Mars. This vapour can only be raised (in sufficient quantities) from the surface of seas and oceans; hence we can infer safely that the greenish tracts are oceanic. And it is clear that, having moisture in the Martial air, we should expect cloud, rain, and snow—

precisely in accordance with the planet's telescopic appearance.

We appear, then, to have many remarkable indications of resemblance between Mars and our own earth. And it might appear a natural conclusion to this chapter to assert that Mars is, in fact, a miniature of our own earth, and in all probability inhabited by such creatures as we are familiar with. In another chapter, in which the subject will be completed, it will be seen whether this conclusion is to be accepted, or whether Mars, like Venus, affords evidence of the wonderful diversity of conditions which exists throughout the universe of God.

LIFE IN THE RUDDY PLANET.

He looketh to the ends of the earth, and seeth under the whole heaven;
to make the weight for the winds, and He weigheth the waters by measure.
—Job xxviii. 24, 25.

WHEN I was considering the planet Venus, and noting
those circumstances in her condition which differ in the
most marked manner from the corresponding circumstances in the case of the earth, I took occasion to point
out that the Almighty has doubtless so provided for
creatures living in Venus that the conditions which seem
to us unfavourable are in perfect accordance with the
requirements of the inhabitants of that planet. I might
follow the same course in the case of Mars; but it appears
to me that it will be well to take another view of the
matter. I shall therefore invite the special attention of
my readers to the unfitness of Mars to be the abode of
such creatures, animal and vegetable, as exist upon our
earth. In other words, I shall endeavour to show how
admirably adapted the earth is to the wants of her
inhabitants; for, in reality, this is the lesson to be
learned from the unfitness of her nearest neighbours,
Mars and Venus, to be the residence of terrestrial
races. The reader will not forget, however, that all

which I shall thus urge must be interpreted in the way thus indicated; he must carefully bear in mind that the very circumstances of the condition of Mars, which I am to insist upon as unfavourable for terrestrial beings, are in all probability those which reasoning beings on Mars, if such exist, have the greatest reason for regarding as proofs of the beneficence of the Almighty towards the creatures inhabiting that planet.

I pass over for the moment the small supply of light and heat received by Mars, because the actual effect of the solar rays must depend partly on the nature and extent of the Martial atmosphere, which are not certainly known. I wish at present to deal only with known facts respecting Mars, so as to have nothing uncertain in this portion of my reasoning.

I take first, then, the length of the Martial year. Mars requires very nearly 687 days to complete the circuit of his path round the sun. In other words, his year exceeds ours by 322 days. If we imagine this year of Mars divided like ours into twelve months, each of these months would contain 57 or 58 days. Now, it is an interesting and significant circumstance that the constitution of the greater number of our vegetables, plants, &c., is specially adjusted to the length of our year. If our year were suddenly lengthened, even by but a single month, the vegetable world would be altogether disordered; 'the functions of plants,' as Whewell has said, 'would be entirely deranged, and the whole vegetable

kingdom involved in instant decay and rapid extinction.'
It would be easy, though it would occupy a considerable
amount of space, to show this by a multitude of instances.
But I shall content myself with touching on an interesting circumstance in the natural history of plants, to
which Linnæus was the first to call special attention. I
refer to the fact that plants have each a special season for
their various functions. Thus, 'if we consider the time
of putting on leaves, the honeysuckle protrudes them in
the month of January; the gooseberry, currant, and elder
in the end of February or beginning of March; the
willow, elm, and lime-tree in April; the oak and ash,
which are always the latest among trees, in the beginning,
or towards the middle, of May. In the same manner the
flowering has its regular time: the mezereon and snowdrop push forth their flowers in February; the primrose
in the month of March ; the cowslip in April; the great
mass of plants in May and June ; many in July, August,
and September; some not till the month of October, as
the meadow saffron ; and some not till the approach and
arrival of winter, as the laurustinus and arbutus.' A
complete series of such instances would form what has
been poetically termed a ' Calendar of Flora.'

The different plants require the same portion of time
for the competition of their several changes, although
each has its special time of year for throwing out leaves,
flowering, budding, and so on. It is clear, then, that any
considerable change in the length of the year would be

fatal to vegetable life. The first year of the new kind would be perhaps merely a year of confusion. As Whewell well remarks, ' What would become of the calendar of Flora if the year were lengthened or shortened by six months?' But the second year, or the third at latest, would bring about the destruction of nearly all the orders of plants now existing on our earth.

Whatever, then, may be the state of Mars as respects animal life, it is quite certain that all forms of vegetable life in Mars are unlike those existing on our earth. We may take it for granted that there is not a single plant now living in Mars which would thrive or even exist if it could be removed to our own earth.

The day in Mars differs so little in length from our own day, that it would be difficult to show that either animal or vegetable life in Mars would differ much on this account alone from such life on our earth. The Martial day exceeds our own by a little more than half an hour. Thus what has been called the Dial of Flora, or Flower-clock, in which the opening and closing of flowers mark the several hours, would be put very little out of order if our day changed to the Martial day. Probably nearly all flowers would adapt themselves readily enough to the change; though it is to be noticed that Whewell,[1] after a careful consideration of the evidence,

---

[1] All that I quote from Whewell in the present paper has been taken from his ' Bridgewater Treatise on Astronomy,' not from his book on the ' Plurality of Worlds.'

arrives at the conclusion that ' the power of accommodation which vegetables possess in this respect is far from being such as either to leave the existence of the periodical constitution doubtful, or to entitle us to suppose that the day might be considerably lengthened or shortened without injury to the vegetable kingdom.'

But we come next to a feature of very great importance in the economy of Mars, the attraction of gravity at his surface. The reader is aware that the attraction of gravity at the earth's surface depends on the quantity of matter in the earth, and also on the size of the earth. If the earth contained as much matter as at present, but had a diameter only half as great as at present, gravity would be four times as great as it is now; in other words, everything on the earth would weigh four times as much. But if the earth were of the same size as at present, but contained more or less matter, the attraction of gravity would be correspondingly increased or diminished. Now, in the case of Mars we find a very much smaller quantity of matter, as I mentioned in my last; and if we only considered this difference, we should infer that gravity was only one-ninth as great at the surface of Mars as at the earth's surface. But the diameter of Mars is less than the earth's in the proportion of about 11 to 20; and this tends to increase gravity in the proportion of 20 times 20 to 11 times 11—that is, as 400 to 121, or about 10 to 3. . Now, if we first decrease our terrestrial gravity to one-ninth its value, and then increase the result as 10 to 3, we get finally a decrease in the proportion of 10 to 27. This shows that a body which would weigh 27 pounds on the earth would, if removed to Mars, weigh only 10 pounds; using the word 'weigh' to mean the actual pressure downwards, for of course in the ordinary way of measuring weights by a balance there would be no difference.

Now, this difference in the downward pressure of all objects on Mars, as compared with terrestrial objects of equal mass, would produce results of a very mischievous nature if it were suddenly to be extended to our earth. In the first place, the mere change in the weight of all objects, including the bodies and limbs of animals, would lead to a variety of unpleasant results. Whewell remarks that in such a case 'we should discover the want of the usual force of gravity by the instability of all about us. Things would not lie where we placed them, but would slide away with the slightest push. We should have a difficulty in standing or walking, something like what we have on shipboard when the deck is inclined; and we should stagger helplessly through an atmosphere thinner than that which oppresses the respiration of the traveller on the tops of the highest mountains.' And he very well notes that all this shows the real importance of those dark and unknown central portions of the earth which we are apt to regard as 'deposits of useless lumber without effect or purpose. We feel their influence on every step we take and on every breath we draw; and the powers we

possess, and the comforts we enjoy, would be unprofitable
to us if they had not been prepared with reference to those
as well as to the near and visible portions of the earth's
mass.'

Another instance of the importance of the actual
value of the force of gravity is found in the correspon-
dence between the force with which the sap of plants is
impelled upwards, and the downward action of gravity
restraining this upflow. It may, perhaps, be thought at
first by many readers that the upward force producing the
flow of sap is but slight, since this flow is so gentle a
process; but it will suffice to mention the experiments of
Hales to show that this is not the case. He found, for
instance, 'that a vine in what is called the *bleeding
season* can push up its sap in a glass tube to a height
of twenty-one feet above the stump of an amputated
branch.' It is clear that any considerable change in the
force of gravity would be most injurious to plant life.
An increase of gravity would cause the activity of the
vegetable circulation to be greatly reduced ; an increase of
gravity would unduly hasten the rising of the sap, 'and
probably hurry and overload the leaves and other organs,
so as to interfere with their due operation.'

Another illustration, and a very beautiful one, is
pointed out by Whewell in the positions of flowers. ' Some
flowers grow with the hollow of their cup upwards ; others
"hang the pensive head" and turn the opening downwards.' It is obvious that an increase of gravity would

force the upright plants to hang their heads, while a decrease to the value of gravity which actually exists in Mars would cause the drooping heads to stand erect. But it has been shown by Linnæus that on the position of the heads of flowers, combined with the greater or less length of the pistil and stamens, depends the fertility of the plant. So that, as Whewell remarks, ' the whole mass of the earth, from pole to pole, and from circumference to centre, is employed in keeping a snowdrop in the position most suited to the promotion of its vegetable health.'

But the most important effect of all is that which would be produced on the atmosphere. If gravity were reduced to precisely the value it has in Mars, our air would immediately be released from more than half the coercive force now drawing it downwards to the earth. It would still be drawn downwards, but so much less that the density of the air at the sea-level would be reduced in the same degree as gravity—that is, in the proportion of 10 to 27. The mercurial barometer would, in fact, stand at about 11 inches instead of 30. This corresponds to the effect which takes place in an elevation of about five miles. Now, there are no creatures but certain races of birds which exist on our earth at this enormous elevation, and probably very few races of terrestrial animals could survive the change to so rare an atmosphere.

Now we are indeed here touching upon a somewhat doubtful feature of the condition of Mars, whereas I have set myself as a law in the present essay the avoidance of all doubtful points. We do not know whether there is more or less air around Mars than around our earth; but nevertheless we can be quite certain that in one way or another a state of things must exist which would be very unfavourable to the creatures living on our earth. If on the one hand; the quantity of air is so much greater in Mars that the actual density of the air at the sea-level is the same as with us, then this air, when moving in winds and storms, must be much more effective in overthrowing objects like our terrestrial animals and vegetables, simply because they are so much less strongly kept in their place, in consequence of the feeble gravity of Mars. Besides, if the air is no denser on Mars than with us, there must prevail an intense cold, in consequence of the greater distance of Mars from the sun; and if we have a denser air, the Martial hurricanes become still more destructive. On the other hand, if the Martial air is rarer than ours, the cold is still more intense, and thus the condition of Mars is seen to be on this account altogether unfit for such creatures as exist upon our earth.

We see, then, that for many distinct reasons Mars cannot be the abode of living creatures resembling those with which we are familiar. And we learn to recognise the loving care with which the requirements of terrestrial creatures have been adapted to the circumstances under which they subsist, when we note that even in Mars, the planet which, perhaps, on the whole most nearly resembles our earth, all forms of terrestrial life would quickly perish.

THE PRINCE OF PLANETS.

ON any evening during the month of April there can be seen, towards the south, a star far brighter than any other in the heavens, except (for a part of the time) the evening star towards the west. The star in the south is the mighty Jupiter, the leader of all the planets, exceeding all the rest together as well in volume as in mass, and so far surpassing our earth in these respects that he may fairly be regarded as a body serving an altogether different purpose in the scheme of creation. I propose to give a brief account of this wonderful globe, pointing out in particular the circumstances which distinguish him from this earth on which we live.

But first let us consider the wonderful contrast between the aspect of this planet as seen by the unaided eye and his real condition as revealed to us by the telescope. Regarding him as he shines on a dark and clear night, we seem to see a bright but *small* object. Compared with the moon, for instance, Jupiter seems little more than a point of light. Then, watching him from hour to hour, we observe that he appears to be *at rest* among the stars, though sharing with them in the motion by which all the orbs of heaven are apparently carried from east to west in consequence of the earth's rotation upon her axis. To the untutored mind Jupiter presents no single feature teaching his real nature and his importance in the creation.

And now, in turn, let us consider what astronomy tells us respecting him.

That small but brilliant orb is a globe so large that, compared with it, our earth is no larger than a pea compared with an orange. Twelve hundred and thirty orbs as large as our earth would be required to form such a globe as Jupiter's. In mass he does not exceed our earth so greatly; but still it would require the mass of three hundred earths to make up Jupiter's. That star which seems to us a point compared with our moon, is attended on by four orbs, the least of which is as large as our moon, while the others are larger than the moon, one being as large as the planet Mercury.

But even more wonderful is the thought of the enormous rate of motion with which that vast orb is being carried along with its attendant family through space. In each second Jupiter's giant bulk moves eight miles, a rate exceeding about five hundred times the velocity of the swiftest express train. I have said that his attendant family is carried along with him. But besides this motion which they share with him, these orbs (which no eye perceives without telescopic aid, so completely are they lost in the glorious light of their ruling planet) are themselves travelling around Jupiter with motions of enormous rapidity. Nay, the nearest moon travels even faster on its course round Jupiter than Jupiter travels on his course round the sun. It moves no less than eleven miles per second; so that at one part of its course, when its motion conspires with Jupiter's, it is advancing nineteen miles per second, while at the opposite part of its course it is moving backwards at the rate of three miles per second. The other moons have corresponding varieties of motions; and yet these enormous and complex movements are not merely rendered undiscernible by vastness of distance, but the orbs which take part in them are actually invisible until the giant eye of the telescope reveals them to us.

When we know that Jupiter is an orb so mighty, and the centre of a scheme so remarkable, the thought is naturally suggested that he must be the abode of living creatures. It is almost impossible for us to conceive any other purpose for which so noble a planet can have been framed. And let the unbeliever sneer as he will, the thoughtful mind will recognise in such a consideration a valid argument. It is true that men have repeatedly erred when they have attempted to reason from their limited conceptions of the purposes of the Almighty; and it would be incorrect to argue that Jupiter is an inhabited world because the earth is inhabited, and therefore the planets are apparently intended to be inhabited. But if it could be shown that the only purpose which Jupiter could possibly subserve was that of supplying an abode for living creatures, this would form a very strong argument to most persons, and an irresistible argument to many, in favour of the opinion that Jupiter actually is inhabited.

And yet when we consider the circumstances under which this giant planet exists, we can scarcely suppose that there are living creatures on its surface. There is, in the first place, its enormous distance from the sun, whereby the light and heat received at Jupiter is reduced to less than the twenty-fifth part of that which we receive. It is no doubt true that the actual climate of the planet may depend much on the nature of the Jovian atmosphere; for we see that at the summits of high mountains on the earth, even in tropical regions, a cold so intense prevails that snow perpetually clothes the mountain peaks. But an atmosphere can after all only as it were garner up the heat that it receives; it cannot increase the quantity received. And so far as we know, the only way in which any atmosphere such as we could live in could thus store up the heat received, is by the action of the vapour of water. But it may be doubted whether the sun's direct heat on Jupiter could be capable of causing the water on Jupiter to evaporate to any considerable extent. It is the sun's heat which loads our air with the vapour of water, and then this vapour (especially at night) prevents the heat from escaping so rapidly as it otherwise would. But the feeble sun of the Jovian sky could hardly raise any water vapour into his atmosphere.

Let us, however, enquire what the telescope tells us about the atmosphere of Jupiter. It is clear that we might expect to find the signs of a great stillness in that atmosphere, if the sun's action alone effected it. For we know that all the disturbances of our own air are due to the sun's heat; wind and cloud, storm and rain, are alike generated by his action. So that where his direct action is so much less as it must needs be in the case of Jupiter, we might expect an unchanging aspect to be presented. But the reality is very different. Examined by a powerful telescope, Jupiter shows all the signs of the most tremendous atmospheric disturbances. There are great bands of clouds all around him, so arranged as to imply the existence of very strong winds resembling our trade winds. But these cloud zones change sometimes so rapidly in shape as to show that either some of the clouds have rapidly discharged their contents in rain and new clouds have been very rapidly formed, or else that great cloud-masses have been carried along with enormous rapidity by winds of hurricane force. In some cases it has been difficult to determine which of these events has taken place, but in others it has been manifest that tremendous storms must have occurred. In passing, indeed, I may remark that it matters very little so far as the main argument is concerned whether we take one view or the other; since it is clear that the formation and dissipation of cloud-masses over enormous regions (regions in many cases exceeding the whole surface of our earth in extent) must indicate forces of great activity in Jupiter, quite as satisfactorily as the existence of violent hurricanes. Nevertheless, the mind is more prone to recognise the activity of those forces which occasion actual movement than that of the silent but most energetic forces which produce or dissipate great cloud-masses. Now, there have been cases where it has been manifest that the most tremendous hurricanes must have agitated the atmosphere of Jupiter. For it has been possible to watch the gradual motion of cloud-masses on Jupiter, and thence to determine the rate of the wind which carried them, as certainly as one can tell the rate at which a terrestrial cloud is moving by noting the rate of motion of its shadow. And these gradual motions of cloud-masses on Jupiter, when interpreted by what we know of the real dimensions of Jupiter, have been found to indicate the existence of winds blowing at the rate of nearly 200 miles per hour.

The most remarkable circumstance about these Jovian hurricanes remains to be mentioned, however. Our terrestrial storms rage sometimes for five or six days in succession, but this is very unusual. Ordinarily the fiercest storm blows itself out in less than three days. Now, Jovian hurricanes have been known to last for six or seven weeks. When this circumstance is considered in connection with the rate at which these storms blow, it is impossible to resist the impression that Jupiter is little suited to be the abode of living creatures.

Sir John Herschel states, in his treatise on Meteorology, that a wind-storm blowing at the rate of 90 miles per second is capable of overturning all but the most strongly built houses and of uprooting the stoutest forest-trees. And every mile per second added to the velocity of such a storm increases its destructive power in a marked degree. Fortunately such storms occur but seldom, are limited in their range, and last but a short time. What, then, would happen if a storm raged for a couple of months, over a region exceeding the whole surface of the earth in extent, the velocity of the wind being more than twice as great as that of the most tremendous and destructive hurricanes known on our earth ? No living creatures known to us could survive such a storm; the strongest buildings men have erected would be destroyed by it in a few minutes; every region over which it raged would be desolated. Yet such storms are not infrequent in Jupiter.

But, after all, the main inference derivable from these hurricanes does not relate to their effects, but to their cause. Such hurricanes would doubtless make Jupiter an unsuitable abode for men ; yet it is not wholly inconceivable that creatures more strongly framed and capable of building more solid edifices might live comfortably enough even where such tornadoes occurred from time to time. But when we enquire how these storms can be produced, we are led to an opinion which is strongly opposed to the idea that Jupiter can be inhabited. It is incredible that the feeble sun of Jupiter occasions these storms. Wind can only be generated by heat; and great winds are occasioned by great contrasts of temperature. Where are we to look for such heat and such contrasts in Jupiter? Since we cannot ascribe these effects to the sun, we are forced, I think, to regard them as due to some cause inherent in the planet itself. It would seem as though an intense heat must prevail in Jupiter's substance, and that to this heat not only the Jovian hurricanes but the Jovian cloud-bands themselves must be ascribed. To speak plainly, it would seem as though Jupiter were so tremendously hot that the waters on his surface continually throw up vast masses of water-vapour—nay, when we remember the enormous quantity of water which must be present in his cloud-bands, it would seem almost certain that the whole of those waters which would otherwise form oceans on his surface, are converted into steam, which in the upper parts of his atmosphere condenses into the form of visible water-vapour, or cloud.

If such is actually the condition of Jupiter, life can scarcely exist on his surface. It is, indeed, always possible, as I have said in speaking of Venus, that life may exist under conditions which to our feeble conceptions appear altogether intolerable. But there is a great difference between such conditions as we considered in the case of Venus and the state of a globe such as Jupiter seems to be. The relations of heat and cold of Venus differ only in degree from the relations with which we are familiar on earth; but a globe actually hot enough to turn enormous masses of water into steam could only be inhabited by creatures incapable of being injured by fire, and it is difficult for us to imagine that there can be such creatures.

It would indeed seem as though the actual globe of Jupiter were red-hot; since from time to time, when the great white cloud-belt which surrounds his torrid regions has been dispersed, a strange fiery hue has been observed over this zone, which strongly suggests the idea of a glowing central globe. And when the light of Jupiter has been measured it has been found to exceed that which would be given by a globe of equal size simply reflecting the sun's light.

It would seem, then, that this noble planet, surpassing all the other planets together, as well in bulk as in mass, is not an inhabited world. We seem forced to the conclusion that his bulk is useless, his mass and might powerless for good. We cannot imagine that he was constructed to afford light in the earth, beautiful though he may be as a star in our skies; it is an idle thought, I conceive, that his noble system was intended merely to afford a subject of study to terrestrial astronomers, profound though the problems are which the movements of his moons afford; the solar system does not require for its safety the perturbations which the mass of Jupiter occasions in the motions of the planets. Yet I propose to endeavour, in my next chapter, to show that even to our feeble conceptions there is enough in what we know of the Prince of Planets to show that he may fulfil purposes such as we can understand. For the present I leave the questions which I have raised to the consideration of my readers, reminding them, however, that even if it could be demonstrated that Jupiter serves no purpose conceivable by us, it would be unreasonable to conclude that he had been made for no useful purpose. For 'behold God exalteth by His power: who teacheth like Him? who hath enjoined Him His way? or who can say, Thou hast wrought imperfectness? Remember that thou magnify His work, which men behold. Every man may see it; man may behold it afar off. Behold God is great, and we know Him not.'

JUPITER'S FAMILY OF MOONS.

WE have seen that Jupiter, although the chief planet of the solar system, is probably not the abode of any living creatures, and is certainly unfitted to be the abode of such creatures as we are familiar with. Yet his enormous bulk and mass, the noble sweep of his orbit, the importance, beauty, and symmetry of the system over which he bears sway, all suggest the idea that he was not created in vain. Nor can we readily conceive any purpose he can fulfil save that of supplying or helping to supply the wants of living creatures. In fact, it is in this way that we view all the celestial bodies. We are not contented when studying the sun, for example, with the mere consideration of the wonderful processes taking place upon his surface and around him; but we enquire how these processes are related to his power of supplying our wants, and the wants of all that live upon the earth, by means of the light and heat which he emits. We study our moon in the same spirit; we see that whether she be herself inhabited or not, she was not created in vain—she rules our tides, she gives us an important though intermitting supply of light by night, she serves as a measure of time, she helps to guide the seaman over the trackless waves of ocean, and she subserves our wants in a variety of other ways. And it is the same method of viewing the celestial bodies which has led nearly all men to believe in the existence of multitudes of other worlds than ours.

Now, when we apply these considerations to Jupiter and his system, we find in his moon-family an increase to the difficulty which has already engaged our attention. For what are those four orbs intended? If Jupiter is not inhabited, they serve none of the requirements which our own moon fulfils. If Jupiter is inhabited, the moons still seem to be of little use. For we can see that Jupiter has a very dense and vapour-laden atmosphere, and it is altogether improbable that any of the moons can be seen from his real surface, supposing he has a surface, which is very far from being a certainty. But even if we suppose that his moons can be seen, they can supply very little light during the planet's night. A different opinion has long been entertained, owing to the details of the matter being left unconsidered. Sir David Brewster, for instance, in his pleasant little work called ' More Worlds than One,' has dwelt upon the moons of Jupiter as obviously fulfilling the important purpose of compensating the planet for the small amount of light received from the sun; and he speaks of the wonderful beauty of the scene presented by Jupiter's moons when all visible at once. But if we consider the actual circumstances under which these moons are placed, we shall find that they cannot be even so effective as our own single moon in supplying light to their primary planet, while we know well that the light of ten such moons as ours would be but a poor compensation for the loss of twenty-four parts (out of twenty-five) of the sun's light and heat. These moons lie at such distances from Jupiter, that while the nearest looks considerably larger than our moon,[1] all the others look far less. The farthest, indeed, must show a disc little more than a quarter of our moon's in diameter, and about a fourteenth of the moon's disc in apparent size. But of course all these moons together cover a considerably larger part of the sky (when they are all seen at once) than ever is covered by our moon. It might seem, then, that they must give much more light. But then it must be remembered that they are themselves only illuminated by the same small sun which shines in the Jovian skies. Supposing them to be constituted like our own moon, the apparent brightness of their discs must be about a twenty-fifth part only of that of hers. When due account is taken of this circumstance, it is found that the full-moon brightness of

---

[1] At least when nearly overhead; but owing to the enormous size of Jupiter, there is a great difference in the apparent size of his nearest moon when high above the horizon and when low down. When overhead this moon is at its nearest, and shows a disc exceeding our moon's by more than a fifth part in diameter, and nearly half as large again in apparent size. But when near the horizon this moon is very little larger than our own.

the four moons of Jupiter amounts only in all to a sixteenth part of the brightness of our full moon.   And even
this is not all.   The four moons never can be all full
together, though they can be all above the horizon at
the same time.   The innermost, which of course looks the
largest, is always eclipsed by the vast shadow of Jupiter,
when directly opposite the sun; so that this moon is never
seen full.   The same applies to the second moon, which is,
however, eclipsed on a much shorter part of its course.

It appears, then, that the moons of Jupiter are utterly
unfit to compensate for the defect of sunlight.

But before we dismiss the Jovian family as useless
moons, after already dismissing Jupiter as a useless world
(speaking always of his adaptation to the wants of creatures
living upon him), let us enquire whether we may not, by
reversing the functions of planet and planet-family, obtain
an explanation of both.   Why should not the moons of
Jupiter be inhabited, instead of Jupiter himself, and
Jupiter be appointed to compensate them (not they him)
for the smallness of the direct supply of solar light and
heat?

Here we must not be staggered by the great superiority
of Jupiter in bulk and mass.   We must remember

> That great .
> Or bright infers not excellence : the earth,
> Though, in comparison of Heaven, so small,
> Nor glist'ring, may of solid good contain
> More plenty than the sun that barren shines,

Whose virtue in itself works no effect,
But in the fruitful earth ; there first received,
His beams, unactive else, their vigour find.

Jupiter's relation to his family of four moons does indeed resemble in a somewhat marked manner the relation of our sun to the four worlds—Mercury, Venus, the Earth, and Mars—which travel nearest to the central luminary, and are most peculiarly to be regarded as the sun's family. Jupiter surpasses each of his moons in bulk and mass in a degree corresponding to that in which the sun surpasses the four small planets just named (not equally, but the disproportion is of the same order). The third of his moons is the largest, just as this earth, the third of the sun's inner family of four planets, is the largest of that family. The other three moons are about equal together in mass to the largest, just as Mercury, Venus, and Mars are about equal together, in mass, to the earth, and the distances at which the moons travel are proportioned to each other somewhat like those observed in the case of the four small planets.

We know that the distances of Mercury, Venus, and the Earth, and Mars from the sun are fairly represented by the numbers 4, 7, 10, and 16; those of Jupiter's family of moons are fairly represented by the numbers 4, $6\frac{1}{2}$, 10, and 18, which, under the circumstances, indicates a sufficiently close resemblance. In particular I would invite the reader to notice how complete is the contrast between the positions which the moons of Jupiter bear as compared with that occupied by our own moon. The largest of Jupiter's moons has a mass less than the 110,000th part of Jupiter's; our moon, on the contrary, is about equal to the eightieth part of the earth. As respects mass, our moon is in fact rather to be regarded as the fifth and smallest member of the inner family of planets, than as occupying a totally inferior position as a body of another order. The earth exceeds Mercury very much more, as well in mass as in volume, than Mercury exceeds the moon. Jupiter's moons, on the other hand, belong as distinctly to an inferior order, when compared with him or his fellow giants among the planets, as our earth when compared with the sun.

Now, our difficulties begin to diminish when we regard the moons of Jupiter as the abode of life, and Jupiter as the ruler of the system, subordinate. of course to the sun. For we must remember that every one of Jupiter's moons is in reality a planet travelling round the sun. Each one of them has its year, its day, and probably its seasons. For anything, indeed, that is known, the inhabitants of each may regard their little world as the centre of the universe; since to a creature placed on one of those moons all the circumstances would be presented which caused the ancients to regard our earth as the fixed centre of created things. Jupiter must appear to them as a gigantic moon; and he really is capable of compensating them to a noteworthy extent for the small amount of light supplied to them by the sun. Certainly this is the case with the nearest moon, since Jupiter must show a disc exceeding our moon's more than fourteen hundred times in apparent surface, and supplying more than fifteen hundred times as much light as our full moon. Even in the case of the outermost moon the apparent surface of Jupiter's disc must exceed that of our moon about sixty-five times, and supply about eight times as much light. It may be noticed that we have not reduced fourteen hundred or sixty-five to their twenty-fifth part, as might appear to be the proper course on account of the diminution of the sun's light in this degree at Jupiter's distance. The reason will be found in what was stated in the last paper respecting the brightness of Jupiter. He is almost three times as bright as a body equally large, and placed where he is, but having a surface of no greater reflective power than the moon's.

This leads us to the consideration that possibly a portion of the light of Jupiter may be inherent—in other words, that he may be glowing with the intensity of his own heat. Certainly the excess of his light is not sufficient to prove this, for as a matter of fact he only gives out as much light as he would reflect if his whole surface were covered with such clouds as ours.[1] Still, as his light is seen in the telescope to be not uniformly white, but to owe its whiteness as a whole to a mixture of many distinct colours, while some of his belts present an actual

---

[1] Everyone who has seen the moon by day, when there are small summer clouds in the sky under full illumination, must have noticed how much inferior the moon's brightness is to that of such clouds.

red colour, as though there were red-hot matter glowing underneath his vaporous envelope, the idea is strongly suggested that he may glow with some small degree of inherent light, and may be capable of supplying a considerable quantity of heat to the orbs which circle around him.

This is not so fanciful as perhaps many readers may at first suppose. If we imagine Jupiter to give out as much heat as though he were a globe as hot as iron when it is beginning to show red with increase of heat, he must warm at least his nearer satellites in an efficient manner. The quantity of heat he would supply to his nearest satellite would be that which a circular sheet of iron, one foot in diameter, and maintained at a dull red heat, would give out to objects two yards from it. This would be by no means a contemptible addition to the supply derived directly from the sun. And it is to be remembered that this heat and any accompanying light would be given out not only, like the reflected sunlight, when Jupiter is full, but whenever he is above the horizon. Thus may it be said of these moons, that

> By tincture or reflection they augment
> Their small peculiar, though for human sight
> Too far remote.

Apart, however, from such considerations as these, it will be manifest that whatever differences may be presented in the moons of Jupiter as compared with our earth, the only known abode of life, are differences of degree only and not of kind. They are not by any means of such a nature as to preclude the conception that life exists on these worlds.

If this be indeed the case, how wonderful must be the scene presented to the inhabitants of these moons by the great planet round which they circle! He must, in fact, replace with them the great object of our own wondering contemplation, the sun. For to them the sun is a minute body, showing a disc scarcely equal to one twenty-fifth of the sun's disc as we see him; but the glorious disc of Jupiter, varying at the several moons from an area 1,600 times as great as their sun, to an area 35,000 times his, and marked by the wonderfully beautiful colours of which our telescopes afford a faint idea, must be an amazing object of contemplation. The changes also which take place in his aspect as he turns round on his axis, and also as real changes take place in his cloud envelope, must be singularly impressive and suggestive. We may well believe that if there are reasoning creatures on the worlds which circle around Jupiter, they have as good reason as we ourselves to say, ' The heavens declare the glory of God, the firmament showeth His handiwork.'

THE RING-GIRDLED PLANET.

I HAVE often thought that among the most instructive of those lessons which the celestial orbs teach us is the avoidance of rash judgments as to the ways and works of the Creator. We are so often mistaken when we judge by appearances. Some star or planet appears to our judgment inferior to the rest, either in size or brightness, or beauty of colour, and we should be apt to judge that it was among the least important of God's works; and lo, when we see it rightly, it is a miracle of beauty and symmetry, marvellous in its dimensions and in the complexity of its structure, and manifestly a scene where forces the most stupendous are daily and hourly in action.

Certainly there is no known orb which presents so strikingly the contrast I have referred to as the planet Saturn. To the naked eye this body is a dull-looking star, far inferior to Jupiter and Venus in apparent size— nay, even surpassed in lustre by Mars and Mercury, the least of the primary planets. Slowly he drags his course onward from station to station, his slow advance alternating with yet slower retrogression. He was chosen by the alchemists as the representative of the heavy and lustreless metal lead, deleterious in its influence on the body, and of little intrinsic value. The astrologers selected him as the planet working the most mischievous effects on the fortunes of the human race. He was held to be not only a mean but an evil planet, aptly named after the old time-god, whose cruelty was matched by his dullness and stupidity.

How different is all this to the reality! We turn on Saturn a powerful telescope on some calm clear night, when the air is well suited for observation, and we see the most beautiful picture conceivable—a glorious orb, the surface resplendent with the most beautiful colours, blue at the poles, yellow elsewhere, crossed by a creamy white central belt, and flecked with spots which under favourable circumstances show brown, and purple, and ruddy tints. The most wonderful part of the picture, however, is the amazing ring-system, not a mere ring as it is so often shown, but a complex system of rings, each curiously variegated in colour, while the innermost (richly purple under favourable observing conditions) is unique among celestial objects in being transparent, so that the orb of the planet can be seen through this ' crape veil ring,' as astronomers have called it.

The return of Saturn to our midnight skies presents a favourable opportunity for an enquiry into what has been learned respecting this beautiful planet, the most complex in construction of all the members of the solar system, inferior only to Jupiter in dimensions and mass,

while surpassing even that prince of planets in the extent
and importance of the scheme over which it bears sway.
I shall proceed in this enquiry on the plan which I have
heretofore adopted in these pages—not restricting my
remarks to the mere physical wonders of the object dealt
with, but endeavouring to present my subject in such a
way as to indicate something of the purposes which Saturn
may be supposed to fulfil in the scheme of creation.　I
shall be unable indeed to proceed so far in this direction
as I should wish, or as some readers may expect.　For
indeed I hold that many writers who, with an excellent
purpose in view, have attempted to show forth the
Creator's praise by indicating the plans He had in view
when this or that arrangement in the universe was designed, have erred, mistaking their conviction that 'God
worketh all things according to law,' for the power of
ascertaining what that law may be.　Yet it seems a useful
and judicious exercise of the reason to endeavour to
ascertain, where possible, the special purpose which
various created things subserve in the economy of the
universe.

Let us first picture to ourselves the wonderful dimensions of the ringed planet.　He has a somewhat flattened
globe, whose mean diameter is about 9 times that of
the earth, so that his surface exceeds hers about 81
times, while his volume exceeds hers more than 700
times.　But his mass does not exceed the earth's mass to
so enormous a degree.　For, regarding him as a whole,

his mean density is less than that of any known planet, being less than a seventh of the earth's, so that he exceeds her in mass only about 90 times instead of 700 times. But even this is still a very great disproportion; and, in fact, if all the planets except Jupiter were formed into a single mass, this mass would be little more than a third of Saturn's.

The globe of Saturn seems to be enwrapped within a dense cloud-laden atmosphere, resembling in many respects that which surrounds the planet Jupiter. In fact, for anything which is certainly known, Saturn may have no solid globe at all; for nothing fixed has ever been recognised in Saturn. We see an orb so enwrapped in cloud that all we can perceive, even when the outermost cloud layers pass away from any part of the disc, is an inner cloud envelope, which, for anything we know to the contrary, may not be the innermost. Indeed, one is perplexed, in enquiring into Saturn's deep and apparently dense atmosphere, by the difficulty of understanding how that atmosphere can possibly endure the enormous attraction to which we know it to be subjected. *There* is the attracting mass of Saturn drawing that atmosphere always down towards the planet's surface (if it has a surface) with such force that if much deeper than ours the atmosphere would actually be compressed into the liquid or solid form.

But there is another singular circumstance closely related to the one just mentioned. We might expect that the enormous globe of Saturn, containing ninety times as much matter as the earth, would be greatly compressed by the attraction of its own parts on each other. For when we say that his mass exceeds the earth's ninety-fold, we in fact imply that his attractive energy, his might as a ruler of matter, exceeds the earth's in that degree. And what draws the earth's globe together, and compresses its inner parts to their present degree of density, is the attractive energy of its mass; so that we might expect the inner parts of Saturn to be compressed in proportion to his much greater mass, and his density consequently much greater. But, as I have said, his density is less than a seventh of the earth's.

How is it, then, that on the one hand Saturn's atmosphere is so deep and yet so mobile as we perceive it to be, while his mean density is less than that of water? This is a question of great importance in connection with the question of Saturn's habitability. For when all the circumstances are carefully considered, no way of removing the difficulty is recognised, except the supposition that the density of Saturn remains small and his atmosphere remains mobile by reason of an intense heat pervading the whole of Saturn's mass. We know of no power except heat which could prevent the enormous mass of Saturn from producing the effects due to its gravitating energy. We see in the sun's globe an illustration of the power which heat possesses in this respect. The sun's mass exceeds the earth's not ninety times, but *three hundred and fifteen thousand times,* and yet his mean density is less than one-fourth of hers. But his fiery heat enables us to understand this circumstance. It vaporises the materials which we regard as the most stable, and expands the vapours thus produced. It swells the whole bulk of the sun, reducing his mean density not only below the density due to his enormous mass, but even below that due to a mass such as our earth's.

Saturn, however, does not, like the sun, show manifest signs of being pervaded by an intense heat. He does not glow with inherent light; and if he emits (as the supposition we are dealing with requires) an intense heat, the distance at which we are placed from him prevents us from becoming sensible of the fact. It is clear, of course, that he is not nearly so hot as the sun; and obviously we should not expect this, since his mass is but the 3,500th part of the sun's, while his density is more than half as great as the sun's. It would suffice to account for Saturn's actual density, if he is so hot only that although his real globe is glowing with the intensity of his heat, his atmosphere is non-luminous and loaded, moreover, with opaque clouds thrown up from the heated mass within. In this case he would appear much brighter than he would if his visible surface were like our white sandstone, for the clouds in his atmosphere would reflect much more light than any kind of earth known to us, shining, in fact, with a whiteness nearly equal to that of driven snow. And probably a certain quantity of the light from his glowing interior would pass to us between the clouds of his deep atmosphere.

This corresponds closely with the facts observed in the case of Saturn as of his brother giant Jupiter. Both these planets shine much more brightly than they would do if their surfaces consisted of any known kind of earth. This has not only been shown by careful measurement of the light received from these planets, but by yet more satisfactory evidence obtained by photographing them. Lying so much farther from the sun than our moon does, much less light falls upon each square mile of their surface, and if they were opaque, and of the same reflective power as the moon, Jupiter would require about twenty-five times the period which is required to photograph the full moon, and Saturn about ninety times. But Dr. De La Rue, the eminent English photographer, finds that the photographic power of the moon exceeds Jupiter's only about as 3 to 2, and exceeds Saturn's only as about 15 to 1. This, indeed, would imply that a considerable part of each planet's light is inherent, a result which agrees with the estimates of their brightness obtained by Professor Bond of America. But we may be content to accept the lower estimate of Zöllner, the German astronomer, who found that Jupiter shines as if he were a globe of white cloud, and Saturn as though nearly of the same reflective capacity. This is sufficient to show that these two planets are quite unlike the earth. Combining with the reasoning based on Saturn's low mean density, the cloud-encompassed condition of his atmosphere, and his relative brightness, suggestive of some degree of inherent luminosity, we seem justified in arriving at the conclusion that, like Jupiter the Prince of Planets, Ring-girdled Saturn is not a fit abode for living creatures.

But if, in Jupiter's case, we could turn from the primary planet to a scheme of dependent orbs, and regard *these* as the habitable worlds and their primary as a subsidiary sun, much more is this the case with Saturn. For, in truth, the scheme over which Saturn bears sway is a miniature, and no contemptible miniature, of the solar system itself. Within an extreme span of upwards of four millions of miles (two millions on either side of Saturn's globe) there circle eight worlds, the least of which is probably at least a thousand miles in diameter, while the largest, appropriately called Titan, is certainly larger than Mercury, and probably as large as Mars. Then within the path of the innermost of these bodies— these *moons*, as astronomers term them—there is the wonderful ring-system of Saturn. The span of this system of rings amounts to about 176,000 miles—that is, its outermost edge lies about 88,000 miles (more than eleven times the earth's diameter) from Saturn's centre. The complete system has a breadth of about 37,600 miles; but the innermost part, to a breadth of nearly 9,000 miles, is dark. Through this dark ring, where it crosses the planet, the outline of Saturn's disc can be clearly perceived. In fact, this wonderful dark ring is transparent. The bright parts of the system form two rings, separated from each other by a dark, but not perfectly black, circular division, about 1,700 miles broad; but it is supposed that each of these two rings is subdivided into a great number of rings, and a circular mark, as though the outermost were divided into two connective rings of nearly equal width, has been seen by several observers.

Such is the wonderful system over which Saturn bears sway, his mighty mass guiding his eight satellites on their paths around him precisely as the sun's mass guides his eight planet-dependants on their course. It has been shown, too, that the ring-system consists of multitudes of small satellites, guided also by the attraction of Saturn, even as the thousands of bodies in the ring of asteroids are guided by the attraction of the sun.

It seems to me that, apart from the reasoning already adduced, we have to choose between two views of the Saturnian system. Either the scheme of satellites and the system of rings are intended to subserve some useful purpose with respect to Saturn, or Saturn subserves some useful purpose with respect to these systems. Now, the satellites can supply very little light to Saturn. All together (if they *could* be all full together) they would supply but a sixteenth part of the light which we receive from our moon when she is full. How so insignificant a supply of reflected light can make up to Saturnians for the fact that the direct supply of solar heat is but one-ninetieth of that which we receive, I leave the believers in

Saturn's habitability to explain. But the ring-system, which also has been spoken of as supplementing the deficiency of solar light, does just the reverse. It deprives the Saturnians for long periods together, in some regions for several successive years, of the light they would otherwise receive. And this it does in the winter of those places. At this time, also, it reflects no light to them during the night. In summer the rings do not cut off any of the sun's light, and they shine at night with a considerable degree of brightness, marred only by the circumstance that at midnight the great shadow of the planet falls on nearly the whole of the visible part of the ring. But no supply of reflected light during the summer nights can compensate for the deprivation of the whole of the sun's direct light *in winter* for several of *our* years together.

We seem compelled, then, to adopt the view that Saturn subserves useful purposes to the worlds which circle round him. To these he certainly supplies much reflected light, and possibly a considerable proportion of inherent light. He probably warms them in a much greater degree. And it seems no unworthy thought respecting him that even as he sways them by his attractive energy, so he nourishes them as a subordinate sun by the heat with which his great mass is instinct. If our sun, so far surpassing all his dependent worlds in mass, yet acts as their servant in such respects, we may reasonably believe that Saturn and Jupiter act a similar part towards the orbs which circle round them.

NEWTON AND THE LAW OF THE UNIVERSE.

WHILE the study of astronomy affords many wonderful subjects for meditation in the celestial glories which it reveals to us, it also gives food for profitable reflection in the lessons which it affords us respecting the mental powers given to man by his Creator.

It is, for instance, a strange and suggestive circumstance, that man insignificant in his dimensions and in all his physical powers, when viewed in comparison even with the earth on which he lives, and compelled to remain always upon that orb, which is utterly insignificant · compared with the solar system, should yet dare to raise his thoughts beyond the earth and beyond the solar system, to contemplate boldly those amazing depths amidst which the stellar glories are strewn.

That he should undertake to measure the scale on which the universe is built, to rate the stars as with swift yet stately motion they career through space, to test and analyse their very substance, to form a judgment as to processes taking place upon and around them, though not one star in all the heavens can be magnified into more than the merest point—all this affords noble conceptions of the qualities which the Almighty has implanted in the soul of man.   Nor can I express assent here with the conceptions of Milton (otherwise so nobly free in his ideas of the duties of men), where he describes Raphael as dissuading Adam from enquiry into the profounder problems of nature, when our first parent, by his countenance, seemed

> Ent'ring on studious thoughts abstruse . . .

'This to attain,' says Raphael,

> 'Imports not, if thou reckon right: the rest
> From man or angel the Great Architect
> Did wisely to conceal, and not divulge
> His secrets to be scanned by them who ought
> Rather admire; or, if they list to try
> Conjecture, he his fabric of the Heavens
> Hath left to their disputes, perhaps to move
> His laughter at their quaint opinions wide
> Hereafter; when they come to model Heaven
> And calculate the stars . . .
> Solicit not thy thoughts with matters hid;
> Leave them to God above; him serve, and fear!
> Of other creatures, as him pleases best,
> Wherever placed, let him dispose; joy thou
> In what he gives to thee, this Paradise
> And thy fair Eve.   Heaven is for thee too high
> To know what passes there.   Be lowly wise;
> Think only what concerns thee, and thy being;
> Dream not of other worlds, what creatures there
> Live, in what state, condition, or degree,
> Contented that thus far hath been revealed
> Not of Earth only, but of highest Heaven.'

Far nobler, as it seems to me, is the thought of our Poet-laureate :—

> Let knowledge grow from more to more,
> But more of rev'rence in us dwell,
> That mind and soul according well
> May make one music as before.

> But vaster. We are fools and slight,
> We mock Thee when we do not fear.
> Ah, teach Thy foolish ones to bear,
> Teach Thy vain worlds to bear Thy light.

Certainly man ' then seems likest God ' when he exercises the noblest of the powers which God has given him.   God sees; and, in his infinitely feebler way, man sees : but we express the attributes of the Almighty more fully when we say God sees and knows, that is, God sees and understands ; and, in like manner, we indicate a nobler quality in man—a more distinguishing attribute—when we note his power of understanding what he sees.

Slowly, it is true, does the power of the mind give to man the mastery over the more hidden ways of nature. One after another tries and fails, though gradually accumulating the knowledge by which, in the end, the secret will be learned.   At length the master-mind arrives which is to utilise the garnered knowledge of ages.   On a sudden the scattered portions of the chain of evidence are linked together, and the chain is complete.   A great work has then been achieved—a work which the Almighty had as fully intended that the human race should accomplish as any of those material successes by which men have obtained mastery over nature and the forces of nature.   I would not join with those who have spoken of the scientific apotheosis of man.   Indeed, I conceive that science teaches no lesson more plainly than the feebleness of man, and the narrow range of the mental powers of individual men—even the most eminent in science. But the scientific successes of mankind stand far higher than any others which they achieve, except those only in which they master themselves. We may not be satisfied in studying nature until we have passed 'from nature up to nature's God;' but scientific research is a good guide, if rightly followed, for a great part of the journey.

Few instances afford a more remarkable illustration of the true nature of scientific research in this respect—not merely in the wonders which it reveals, but in its own wonderful nature—than the enquiry by which the great Sir Isaac Newton was led to the discovery of the law of gravitation.

For many long years astronomers had been engaged by observation, calculations, and reasoning based on these processes, in the endeavour to ascertain the laws according to which the planets move. After a long struggle to retain the earth in her apparent position as the chief body and true centre of the universe, they had been led by the masterly investigations of Copernicus to the theory that the sun is the ruling orb of the solar system. Then the ingenuity of Kepler, following on the laborious and skilful observations of Tycho Brahé, had revealed certain laws of planetary motion. It was shown by him that the planets revolve in ellipses (very nearly circular) around the sun, placed, not in the centre, but at one of the points called the *foci* of the ellipse. He had ascertained also that each planet, in travelling around this common *focus,* so moves that if a long elastic cord were supposed to connect this planet with the sun, this cord would sweep over equal surfaces in equal times; a singular discovery reflecting great credit on Kepler's ingenuity and patience, since it is not such a law as would occur until after many others had been tried and rejected; and there was no reason known to Kepler why so peculiar a law should be followed. In fact, we know that he was engaged no less than nineteen years in testing various laws before he succeeded in discovering the true one. Then a third law, the most remarkable of all, was discovered by Kepler.

The other two laws related to each planet severally. But now he discovered a law connecting the various planets together, a law exceedingly simple, though like many other simple matters it can be made to sound exceedingly recondite by the use of a few long words. I dare say many among my readers would start away in disgust from this essay, if I assured them solely that the planets so move that their periods are in the sesquiplicate ratio of their mean distances. But the third law of Kepler may be more pleasantly indicated. It is this:—If we take the number of days in which a planet revolves round the sun, and multiply that number into itself once, and if we then take the number expressing the distance of the planet from the sun in miles, and multiply that number into itself twice over, we shall find that the two numbers we thus obtain bear always a constant proportion to each other. There is no difficulty in verifying the law as thus

stated; but the process is long, so I will give the law in
another form much more readily verified. Take the year
for the unit of time, this being the earth's period of revolution, so that in fact we call the earth's period 1. Call
her distance from the sun 1 also. Then the following
simple law holds: any planet's period multiplied twice
by itself is represented by the same number as the same
planet's distance multiplied once by itself. Thus a table
of the planets' elements gives us for Jupiter's period nearly
11·9 years, and for his distance 5·2 times the earth's.
Now, if we multiply 11·9 by itself once, we get the
number 141·61; and if we multiply 5·2 by itself, we get
27·04, which multiplied again by 5·2, gives 140·608.
This number we see is very nearly equal to the other; and
it would have been exactly equal, if we had taken the
exact number: for Jupiter's orbit is rather less than 11·9
years, and his distance rather more than 5·2 times
the earth's. The same would be observed if we tried any
other planet. Here, then, was a law by which in some
mysterious way the planets seemed to be associated
together, moving with a harmony corresponding in some
sort to that which the Pythagoreans of old had believed in.

It was thus that Kepler viewed this last discovery of
his. His fervent disposition was roused to earnest enthu-
siasm when he had found this law of harmony in the
universe. He felt instinctively that he was approaching a
yet grander discovery, or that at least he had shown the path

by which a greater truth was to be reached, and the law of the universe recognised. He might have spoken of himself, had he known what was to come, as the Moses of the astronomy of the future, who saw the promised land afar off, but entered not therein. But he chose rather to use the words of the ancient mystics : ' I will rejoice !' he exclaimed ; 'I will triumph in my sacred fury; for I have found the golden vases of the Egyptians !'[1]

But it was not till Newton came that the true meaning of these laws was ascertained, and very wonderful is the history of the process by which he solved the noble problem which Nature had presented to mankind for investigation. Everyone has heard the story of the apple, whose fall is said to have suggested to Newton the great discovery for which his name will be deservedly celebrated for all time. The story may be true in a sense, though not in the sense usually given to it. Newton certainly did not ask why the apple fell, since it was well understood in his day, and had been known for many centuries, that bodies fall to the earth by virtue of her attractive influence. But it is quite possible that Newton, who had long been engaged in profound meditation on the laws of planetary motion, should have suddenly seen revealed to him the possibility that a far wider law of attraction exists. His mind was full of the thoughts sug-

---

[1] Referring to the belief of the Pythagoreans that certain sacred secrets were preserved in golden vases shown to Pythagoras by Egyptian priests.

gested by the mysterious energies which appear to sway the motions of the planets; and here, suddenly, his attention was called to the mysterious energy by which the earth draws bodies to her surface. What if one and the same form of force is exerted in all such cases ? What if the sun draws the planets towards him, as the earth draws unsupported bodies towards her ? What if the law exemplified in the fall of the apple is a universal law, indicating a property of matter itself, not limited to this or that kind of matter, but common to all matter and exerted on all matter, operating as certainly on every particle of the thin air we breathe as on the heaviest metals ?

Newton at once saw that it was to the moon we should look for an answer to these questions. And, by the way, I might add to the advantages we derive from having a moon the fact that but for her we should assuredly not be now acquainted with the law of the universe. The moon supplied Newton with an intermediate stepping-stone enabling him to pass over the wide gap separating terrestrial gravity from the sun's action as ruler of the planetary system. The earth has an orb circling round her as the planets of the sun;[1] and the orb thus obeying her attrac-

[1] This is not inconsistent with what I formerly said as to the moon circling in reality around the sun. The fact is, that if we consider the moon's motion solely with reference to the earth, taking no account of their common motion around the sun, then the moon may be regarded as circling round the earth. It is only as viewed from some standpoint far away from the solar system that the moon must be regarded as an orb circling round the sun. Both views are just.

tion was shown by Newton to be subject to a degree of
force corresponding precisely to the force which the earth
exerts on bodies which fall to her surface, on the supposition that the force diminishes with distance from the
earth's centre, according to a certain easily explained law.
At twice the distance the law is reduced to one-fourth, at
thrice the distance to one-ninth part, and so on. Now,
the importance of this fact resides in the circumstance
that, granting this to be the law of diminution in the
sun's attracting force also, then—*all Kepler's laws are
explained.* The planets *ought* to travel in paths such as
they actually follow; they *ought* to move at rates varying
as their rates of motion actually vary; and, lastly, the
third law, which Kepler called the harmony of the system,
is, like the others, a *necessary consequence* of the law
according to which the solar action diminishes with
distance.

Only one kind of evidence was required to make the
demonstration of the law complete. The general motions
of the moon, the planets, and the planets' families had
been fully accounted for. But if the law of gravitation is
true, then these different bodies must disturb each other.
The planet Jupiter must disturb our earth, for example,
as she circuits round the sun, and must disturb the moon
as she circuits round the earth. Of all such instances of
disturbance the most marked and the one we could
recognise best should be the disturbance of the moon by
the sun. Instead of following the course round the earth

which she would have if the earth were the sole centre of her motion, the moon would be now swayed on one side and now on another side of her course, now hastened and now checked, by the sun's disturbing influence.

It was in dealing with these disturbances that Newton showed with what wonderful mental powers he had been endowed. He tracked the moon through all her movements, and measured the sun's action on her in all positions; he showed where she would be hastened, where retarded, where drawn away from the earth, where drawn closer, where her path would be more tilted, where less, where its eccentricity would be increased, where diminished. All the peculiarities of motion thus calculated from the law of gravitation were found to accord in the most convincing manner with those peculiarities actually observed in the moon's motions which had long perplexed astronomers. The demonstration of the law of gravitation was so complete, as it thus first came from Newton's hands, that within a very short time men of science were thoroughly convinced, and the law of gravitation has not been seriously questioned from that day to this.

Such is a brief history of the greatest scientific discovery ever made by man—the recognition, in fact, of the law of the universe—a law affecting every particle of matter, operating at all distances, ruling the tiniest sand-grains, and swaying the mightiest orbs—the universal law of gravitation.

THE DISCOVERY OF TWO GIANT PLANETS.

THE history of astronomy presents two remarkable instances of the discovery of planets. In the present day the discovery of objects which by courtesy are called planets is not an uncommon event. Not a year passes without the recognition of two or three and sometimes ten or twelve of those bodies termed asteroids, which travel between the orbits of Mars and Jupiter. These bodies, so far as their motions are concerned, resemble the planets. But they are very minute compared with even the smallest of that family of minor planets to which our earth belongs. Our moon and the satellites or secondary planets which attend on Jupiter, Saturn, and Uranus are gigantic bodies compared with the largest of the asteroids, or, as they are sometimes called, the planetoids. And then the zone of asteroids is so crowded that no very great interest or importance can be attached to the detection of new members of this family. Already their number is approaching the middle of the second hundred, and ' the cry is " Still they come." '

Luther, the German astronomer, has discovered nineteen, and until lately stood easily first among asteroid-hunters ; but Peters, of America, has been gaining steadily during the last two or three years, and a few weeks ago discovered his nineteenth asteroid, so that now Luther and Peters are level. Several other astronomers have discovered more than a dozen of these bodies; and our own countryman Mr. Hind, notwithstanding numerous other astronomical engagements occupying the greater part of his time, has discovered ten asteroids. It will be understood, then, that when a new asteroid is detected, astronomers hear of the discovery with equanimity.

The two instances with which I propose now to deal are of another kind, however, and each in its special way attracted deservedly a great amount of attention, while one of them has been characterised by Sir John Herschel as the greatest discovery since Newton's day. I refer to the detection of the two giant planets Uranus and Neptune, one discovered accidentally, the other by a process of reasoning so profound and difficult that few can even understand its force.

Although Uranus was discovered by accident, it will not be thought that on that account small credit should be given to Sir W. Herschel, the astronomer to whose redoubtable telescope this planet fell as a spoil. The accident was one which could not have happened but to an enthusiast in astronomical researches. He had penetrated into the star depths again and again with telescopes of his own construction, engaged in the attempt to solve problems of the utmost difficulty, when one night this new orb swept into his ken.

6

Even then he must have failed to know it for what it was, or rather he would have mistaken it for what it was not—a fixed star—but for the great power of the instrument he was employing; for so far off is Uranus, that notwithstanding its dimensions, which are so great that seventy-four such globes as our earth could be formed from it,[1] it appears in ordinary telescopes without any well-defined disc. Herschel himself could only see that the new orb differed somewhat in appearance from a fixed star, until, applying higher powers, he recognised the fact that he had discovered either a comet or a planet. Then he watched for the signs of motion which every comet or planet exhibits. He found in a short time that the stranger was in motion, and thus all doubt was dispelled so far as the question whether it was a star or not was concerned.

I do not describe the process of observation by which the true nature of Uranus was discovered, the planet's orbit determined, the size and mass of the stranger estimated,[2] and eventually a family of satellites found to be travelling around it. My present purpose is to consider only the discovery of this planet and its fellow giant Neptune. But one singular feature in the history of sub-

---

[1] This remark refers to the volume of the planet; in mass it only exceeds the earth $12\frac{1}{2}$ times.

[2] A full account of these circumstances, and of recent discoveries respecting Uranus, will be found in an essay called 'News from Herschel's Planets,' in the second series of my 'Light Science for Leisure Hours.'

sequent research must be mentioned, not only as bearing on the subject of the discovery of Uranus, but because it is also connected with the discovery of Neptune, as will presently appear.

So soon as astronomers had recognised the nature of the path of Uranus, so as to be able to predict the motions of the planet, they could also trace back its course, so as to find where it had been at any given time before its discovery. Now, when this had been done, it was found that Uranus had in reality been often observed before—no less than nineteen times in fact.

It had been observed by the eminent astronomers Flamsteed, Bradley, Mayer, and Lemonnier. Flamsteed had seen it five times, each time recording its place as that of a star of the fifth magnitude. But Lemonnier had actually seen the planet no less than twelve times. Unfortunately, Lemonnier was not an orderly man; 'his astronomical papers,' says one who has recently written on the subject, ' are said to have been a very picture of chaos;' and M. Bouvard narrates that he had ' seen one of Lemonnier's observations of this very star written on a paper bag which had contained hair powder.' So narrowly had the planet escaped recognition until its discovery should come to reward the most laborious of all astronomers—the great Sir W. Herschel.

Time passed on, and the slow-moving Uranus began to be regarded as a regular member of that family of bodies which astronomers watch over with special care.

The motions of the planet were carefully calculated and as carefully watched; the elements of the planet were assigned; and all seemed settled as respected its position in the planetary scheme. So complete was the mastery which astronomers had gained, since the discovery of the law of gravitation, over the movements of the planets, that long before Uranus had completed the circuit of its orbit, all the characteristic features of that orbit, as its inclination, eccentricity, and the period (eighty-four years), in which Uranus traverses it, had been satisfactorily determined.

This was a great triumph for the theory of gravitation; but a far greater triumph was at hand.

It was found that Uranus did not strictly follow the path assigned to it. Not only as time progressed was the discrepancy more clearly recognised, but it was found absolutely impossible to reconcile the observations made by Flamsteed and Bradley, before the discovery of Uranus, with the elements which nevertheless astronomers felt they could confidently assign to the planet. The disturbing influence of Jupiter and Saturn, the only planets which could affect Uranus appreciably, had of course been duly taken into account; and the masses of these planets had been far too satisfactorily ascertained to leave any doubt as to the effects which they could severally produce on Uranus. Yet the planet's motions still differed from those which theory assigned.

The idea was quickly broached that there must be an

orb travelling outside Uranus, and disturbing the planet by its attractions. Bouvard was the first, I believe, to suggest this natural explanation, which astronomers readily accepted as sufficient. The idea was certainly strange, and startling because of its novelty. Here was a planet which has been known only for half a century, and because it was now a little on one side and now a little on the other side of its estimated position, astronomers inferred that another planet as yet unseen was disturbing their new friend.

But was it impossible to discover the unseen planet by carefully taking into account all the discrepancies in the movements of Uranus? Probably the daring nature of this conception can only be appreciated by mathematicians, who know the enormous difficulty and complexity of the problem involved. To others it might seem, perhaps, that the displacement of Uranus would point directly enough to the place of the disturbing planet, just as, let us say, the strain on the angler's line would indicate very clearly the place of the unseen fish which produced that strain. But in reality this is a very incorrect way of viewing the matter.

It is one of the most difficult problems that can be imagined to determine the motions of a planet when all the circumstances which can affect that motion are known. For instance, long after the theory of gravitation had been established, the most skilful mathematicians failed one after another in explaining a certain marked peculiarity in the movements of Jupiter and Saturn, although in reality, as Laplace afterwards proved, that peculiarity was a necessary consequence of relations already known to exist between these two planets. Now, only conceive how enormously difficult the converse problem must be when the direct problem is so difficult. If when we take two known planets of given mass, distance, and so on, we find it extremely difficult to determine in what way each planet will affect the other, how exceedingly difficult—might we not even imagine, how utterly impossible—it must be to infer from the peculiarities of motion of one planet the distance, mass, and position of a planet hitherto unknown! This was the problem which lay before astronomers, and all save two shrank from the attempt to solve it. Of these two one was a young man who was preparing to take his degree at Cambridge—John Couch Adams, destined to be soon regarded as the greatest mathematical astronomer England has had since Newton's day. The other was the Frenchman Leverrier, Adams's senior in years, possessed of far more complete information of the facts of the case, and of far more abundant leisure to deal with the problem.

Young Adams first completed his work. He estimated the place of the as yet unseen planet, and announced it to the Astronomer Royal for England. Challis also, the head of the Cambridge observatory, received the news. Between these two observatory chiefs it might be thought that the new planet, if it lay anywhere near the indicated place, would be quickly discovered. But Professor Airy seemed to imagine that a mare's nest had been discovered. He put some questions intended to be posing, which the young Johnian was not eager to answer. Challis was more zealous in the cause of science. He did all he could be expected to do, especially when we remember that he quickly learned that the Astronomer Royal had small faith in the superior mathematical power of his young contemporary. It may perhaps surprise some readers to learn that Challis actually saw the planet. He saw it twice, and each time marked its place. The planet was *in the net.* Nothing, it should seem, could lose England the credit of the greatest astronomical feat since Newton's day. But, to quote an old proverb, the cards never forgive. The Astronomer Royal had challenged ill fortune for England, and ill fortune came. It was in September 1845 that Adams had communicated to Challis the place of the disturbing planet, and in October that in the pleasing confidence of youth he had forwarded the information to the Astronomer Royal.

In June 1846, or fully *eight months* after Adams's first intelligence, Leverrier 'assigned,' to use Challis's words, 'very nearly the same longitude for the probable position of the planet as Mr. Adams had arrived at.' But even then the information Leverrier gave was not so complete as that which Adams had given, for Adams stated the form and position of the orbit, the mass, and the mean distance of the hypothetical planet, whereas Leverrier 'gave no results,' says Challis, ' respecting the planet's mass and the form of its orbit.' Shortly after the Astronomer Royal began to think that possibly Adams might after all be right. But it was now too late. For the Berlin astronomers, six weeks after Challis had secured two observations of the planet, detected it from Leverrier's announced place. It is only necessary, to make the story complete, to mention that as soon as Challis, Sir John Herschel, and others announced what Adams had really effected, Arago and other French astronomers abused our great young Englishman as an interloper, as though it were incredible that the country of Newton should have produced the equal of Leverrier.

I must not dwell further, however, on the circumstances of this discovery, preferring to deal with the pleasanter considerations suggested by its nature. It seems to me in some respects even more striking than Newton's discovery of the law of gravitation. Newton explained the laws according to which known objects move ; Adams and Leverrier showed where a hitherto unknown object would be found when telescopes were turned to that part of the heavens. Newton recognised laws hitherto unknown. Adams and Leverrier by abstract reasoning inferred the existence of a world which men as yet had never seen.

But there is one consideration which is even more suggestive. The acutest reasoners among men have been able to detect a planet by means of the disturbances produced by its attraction acting on the planet which travels nearest to it.   But if the mental powers of man were increased he could analyse disturbances much more minute in their effects.   We can conceive so great an increase of power that, from the motions of one planet only, the nature of the whole solar system might be inferred.   But to the infinite wisdom of the Almighty a power of inference such as this is as the weakness of the infant's mind compared with the powers of a Newton.   To Him the least grain indicates the whole scheme of the universe, its present condition, past history, and future fate.   Not an atom in the remotest orb can move a hair's breadth without producing in every other atom throughout the universe an effect—infinitely minute to our perceptions—but as manifest to the Almighty as the noon-day sun to us.   Man reaches the limit of his powers in reasoning from one planet to the next; to the Almighty every atom in infinite space is eloquent of the universe itself.

THE LOST COMET.

And I looked, and behold, a great cloud came out of the north, and a
fire enfolding itself, and a brightness was about it, and out of the midst
thereof as the colour of amber, out of the midst of the fire.—EZEKIEL i. 4.

THESE words describe, not inaptly, what was seen on the
evening of November 27, 1872, in Italy and other countries
where the atmosphere was clear. Here in England there
was a display of shooting-stars, some forty or fifty thousand
of these bodies falling between the hours of five and
eleven. But wonderful as was this display, in Italy a yet
more unusual spectacle was witnessed, for at the height of
the display the smaller meteors were so numerous that the
appearance presented was that of a cloud of light around
the gemmed feet of Andromeda in the northern skies;
'a great cloud came out of the north, and a fire enfolding
itself, and a brightness was about it.' Moreover, since the
larger meteors shine for the most part with a yellowish
light, it may be said that 'out of the midst of the cloud
came a brightness as the colour of amber, out of the midst
of the fire.'

Soon after it was announced that the meteors forming
this wonderful display were travelling on the track of a

lost comet, known to astronomers as Biela's. A score of years had passed since this famous, though small, comet had been seen. In 1866, and again in the autumn of last year, astronomers had searched for it with special care, because, according to their calculations, it should have been favourably placed for observation. But not a trace of it had been detected. Then the expectation arose that as the earth was to pass, during the last week in November, through the track or wake of the comet, a meteoric display might be seen, even as had happened year after year when on November 13–14, 1866, 1867, 1868, &c., the earth passed through the track of Tempel's Comet. This anticipation was actually fulfilled, and it was readily shown that all the circumstances of the star-shower agreed with the theory that the falling stars were travelling in the path of the missing comet.

But a singular event followed. A German astronomer conceived the idea that as the comet's meteor-train had come as a star-shower ' from out of the north,' the meteors might be looked for as a cloud passing away towards the south. He telegraphed to an English astronomer occupying a station where the southern skies can be observed, and urged him to examine the part of the heavens directly opposite to the feet of Andromeda, whence the meteor shower had seemed to rain upon our northern regions. It was done: and lo! close to the very spot pointed out there was a faint celestial cloud, resembling in all respects a small comet. It was watched, and seen to be travelling in a course corresponding with that which the lost comet would have followed if travelling on that part of its path. In fact, the English astronomer announced definitely that he had found the comet which had been so long missing.

But it was not so. He had indeed found a nebulous cloud of light travelling in the track of the lost comet; but when enquiry came to be made by comet-calculating astronomers, it was seen that the cloud which had been seen in the south was far behind Biela's comet—millions of miles, if we count by distance, and nearly a quarter of a year, if we count by time.

Biela's comet is therefore still missing, though it cannot be said that we have seen nothing of it. Those meteoric visitants had undoubtedly once belonged to it; that cloud of light travelling southwards was unquestionably a portion of it, not a fragment recently detached (for such a fragment would not quickly be left so far behind), but a portion, which, many centuries ago, must have formed part of the long lost comet.

But how strange are the thoughts suggested by these circumstances! The history of Biela's comet had long been remarkable in cometic annals. In 1832 the comet had terrified the nations, because astronomers had announced that it would cross the earth's path.[1] In 1846

---

[1] The account of the terror then excited is very remarkable. The anxiety experienced in France led a Parisian Professor to beg the Academy of Sciences to refute the assertion that the comet would encounter the earth.

It divided into two separate comets, which travelled side by side with a gradually increasing distance between them, and with a singular interchange of light, now one onw the other being the brighter. In 1852 the comet returned yet again to our neighbourhood (the period in which it circles around the sun being about six years and eight months); and at that time the two companion comets could still be discerned, though the distance between them had enormously increased. Whether it returned in 1858-9 is not known, as its arrival on that occasion would have carried it to parts of the sky too close to the sun for telescopic scrutiny. In 1866, however, it should have been seen. Astronomers had become very familiar with the calculation of its motions, their predictions according better and better at each return with the actual motions of the comet; and the path assigned to it was so placed that the comet should have been well seen. But

'Popular terrors,' he wrote (I quote from Dr. Dick's 'Sidereal Heavens'), 'are productive of serious consequences. Several members of the Academy may still remember the accidents and disorders which followed a similar threat, imprudently communicated to the Academy by M. de Lalande, in May 1773. Persons of weak minds died of fright, and women miscarried. There were not wanting people who knew too well the art of turning to their advantage the alarm inspired by the approaching comet, and *places in Paradise were sold at a very high rate.* The announcement of the comet in 1832 may produce similar effects, unless the authority of the Academy apply a prompt remedy; and this salutary intervention is at this moment implored by many benevolent persons.' Recently an announcement of a similar kind, relating to the arrival of a comet on August 12, 1872, was received (so far as I have been able to learn) with exemplary equanimity. Certainly no 'places in Paradise' were disposed of on this occasion.

though carefully sought for with large and powerful telescopes, it was not then found; nor again was it seen on its return last autumn.

Let us follow the comet in imagination as it passed away from our neighbourhood in the year 1852, and try to conceive the dangers and vicissitudes to which it has been exposed, and to some one or other of which it may perchance have fallen a victim.

Biela's comet always arrived from out the north, and passed away from our neighbourhood southwards. Its course did not carry it very much nearer to the sun than our earth is; and, after passing southwards, until it was about eighty millions of miles from him, it gradually receded again, still passing farther and farther south of the general level in which the planets travel. For aught that is known, however, it may have been in this part of its course that the comet experienced the disturbances which so dissipated its substance as to render it undiscernible by terrestrial astronomers. We have reason to believe that meteoric systems are more and more densely strewn the nearer the sun is approached, that they cross and interlace in wonderfully complex fashion close by him; and it may have been in its passage through such labyrinthine meteor-systems that the comet lost its head in the most literal sense of the words. Such was the opinion of our great astronomer, the younger Herschel, who, writing in 1866, when the comet was first missed, said, 'Peradventure it has plunged into and got bewildered among the rings of meteorolites.' All that we know of the structure of a comet's head teaches us to believe that, minute and scattered as are the meteors comprising such rings, they are quite sufficiently compact to effect the destruction of a comet impinging full upon one of their clustering aggregations.

But let us suppose that the comet escaped this danger —and, in any case, we know that what has here been spoken of as destruction is not absolute annihilation, but only the destruction of the cometic form : it passed on, let us imagine, unscathed by the meteors which crowd round the sun's neighbourhood, and, gradually increasing its distance, it bore away towards those cold regions of interplanetary space which lie beyond the orbits of the earth and Mars. Obeying the mighty reining power of the sun's attraction, the comet travelled on its oval path, sweeping far to the south of the orbit of Mars, and presently, as its distance still increased, it began to return towards the general level in which the planets travel. What strange news would that comet have to tell, if it could describe all the scenes through which it passed in this portion of its path !

Meteor-streams unknown to terrestrial astronomers travel in countless thousands in those spaces. Isolated bodies, like those aerolitic masses which fall from time to time upon the earth, are moving hither and thither on their paths round the sun. And yet more wonderful must be the scene presented by the solar system itself, and the

star depths surrounding it. We are so in the habit of
regarding the visible half-sphere of the heavens as a star
canopy, at night, over the seemingly level earth, that it is
difficult to conceive the complete starlit sphere within
which each of the members of the sun's family really
travels. And how wonderful must be the aspect of our
sun seen from the interplanetary spaces without the intervention of that atmosphere of ours which veils his glories!
The coloured prominences, and the deeply-hued sierra,
would be clearly visible from such a standpoint, while
around all would be seen the glorious corona with its complicated structure branching outwards into space, and,
perhaps, mingling with the softer lustre of that immense
disc of scattered matter which astronomers call the
zodiacal light.

As our comet travelled towards the level in which the
planets move, it was exposed to a new form of danger.
Between the paths of Mars and Jupiter lies the zone of
small planets. It is probable that there are myriads of
these bodies of all orders of magnitude from the largest—
Vesta, Juno, and the others first discovered—to bodies
perhaps as minute as the least of the meteors. Astronomers have already discovered 130 of these small planets,
and continue yearly to discover more, while it is probable
that the smaller members of the family will for ever
remain undetected. Now, these bodies present a form of
danger to cometic wanderers which the large planets do
not occasion. They do not travel in the same general

level as the large planets, but at considerable inclinations thereto; and thus they range widely above and below that level. The width of the zone is also considerable. In fact, the zone does not form a flat ring like the ring of Saturn, but a system shaped like an anchor ring.[1] Through this zone, or at least its outskirts, the path of Biela's comet carries it; and it is not altogether impossible that it was while passing through this critical part of its orbit, that it suffered the injuries which have prevented it from returning in recognisable form to the scrutiny of our terrestrial astronomers.

But if it only escaped that danger, it was thenceforward safe until it again returned to the earth's path. It had to pass, indeed, the orbit of giant Jupiter, who is the great disturber of comets, insomuch that a fanciful mind might recognise no inapt description of this planet's qualities in the title ' cloud-compeller,' given by Homer to Zeus, the Jupiter of the Greek mythology. But there is no danger to Biela's comet in this part of its career, since his course carries him far to the north of Jupiter's orbit. Travelling still farther outwards to the point of its path farthest from the sun, the comet then returns, rounding the zone of small planets at a safe distance, passing far north of the course of Mars, and thence, with con-

---

[1] This is the technical name for such rings. Possibly to most of my readers a wedding-ring will seem to present an apter illustration. A wedding-ring would, in fact, be called by a mathematician an 'anchor-ring;' a term not unsuitable, perhaps, in other respects.

tinually increasing rapidity, descending towards the path
of the earth as a ' cloud coming out of the north.'

Since the comet was last seen it has thrice traversed
the enormous orbit here described, passing from a least
distance of about eighty millions of miles to its greatest
distance amounting nearly to six hundred millions of
miles. Whether it has been destroyed as a comet, or
whether it has only been so far dissipated as to be invisible
in our most powerful telescopes, we do not know. But in
either case it has pursued the same general course, for the
minutest fragment of its substance would obey as implicitly
the law of gravity as the once complete comet, or even
as the staider members of the solar family—-the planets.
Such have been the motions of this singular object, such
the vicissitudes to which it has been exposed. There is
much that is mysterious in these events, much that, to our
feeble conception, appears like a waste of energy. But
we must remember that though we are ignorant of the
purposes which the comet has fulfilled in its journeyings,
and of the effects which have resulted from its dissipation,
yet all that has happened to it during its career as a
member of the solar family was designed by Him who
' foresees the end from the beginning.' ' Great and marvellous are Thy works, Lord God Almighty!'

VISITANTS FROM THE STAR DEPTHS.

THERE are some astronomical facts which do not seem at a first view more surprising than others, but which yet, when studied thoughtfully, disclose the most startling thoughts for our consideration.. Among these I know none more remarkable than the fact that certain bodies reach our solar system from the stellar depths. The fact is easily stated; and at first we might be disposed to say that it is not particularly surprising. If the spaces round our solar system are tenanted by stars, why should they not be tenanted by comets, or by flights of meteors? and such bodies existing in the star depths, why should they not from time to time be drawn from out those depths by the sun's attractive energy, or be encountered by the solar system as it speeds onwards through space?

But so soon as we begin to enquire into this now undoubted fact, we find ourselves brought face to face with mysteries of the most perplexing nature, and we find that thoughts are suggested which impress upon us most startlingly the wonderful nature of the universe, not in extent only, but in duration, and in the vitality that pervades its every portion.

A comet is seen in the far distant depths of space as a faint and scarcely discernible speck. It draws nearer and nearer with continually increasing velocity, growing continually larger and brighter. Faster and faster it rushes on until it makes its nearest approach to our sun, and then, sweeping around him, it begins its long return voyage into infinite space. As it recedes it grows fainter and fainter, until at length it passes beyond the range of the most powerful telescopes made by man, and is seen no more. It has been seen for the first and last time by the generation of men to whom it has displayed its glories. It has been seen for the first and last time by the race of man itself. Nay more, according to the calculations made by astronomers, the comet has made its first and last visit to the solar system. Of all comets this cannot, indeed, be affirmed; but there are some whose motions will bear no other interpretation.

And now, what meaning are we to attach to a visit such as this? Whether we trace back the comet's past history so far as the imagination or the reason can disclose it to us, or whether we follow its future fate, we are alike appalled by the stupendous time-intervals which are revealed to us.

Whence came the comet? Trace back its path, and we find no place from which it *could* have started on its course until we consider the stars in the region of the heavens whence the comet appeared to travel. It would be idle to select any star in particular in that region as probably marking the spot whence the comet started. But suppose we take the brightest, some leading orb, lying at a distance not absolutely unmeasurable by man, like the distances of all the millions on millions of stars, except some ten or twelve; suppose even that the course of that comet as it approached was such that it might have come from the star Alpha Centauri, which, so far as is known, is the nearest of all in the heavens; then, at a moderate computation, the journey from the neighbourhood of that star has not occupied less than eight million years.[1]

[1] The calculation is not altogether simple. Nevertheless, I briefly sketch a process of calculation which, though not exact, yet suffices to show the *order* of time-intervals in question in this matter. I assume the mass of Alpha Centauri to be four times the sun's—which corresponds with the observed brightness of the star, our only means of guessing at its volume and mass. I take its distance as exceeding the sun's 210,000 times; and I divide this distance into two parts, one 70,000 times the sun's distance, and the other therefore 140,000 times the sun's distance. The smaller distance being taken nearest to the sun, it follows from the law according to which attraction diminishes with distance, that a particle placed at the point separating the two unequal distances is equally attracted by the sun on one side and the star on the other. Then I have only to calculate how long it would take in passing from the star to that point under the star's influence alone, and from that point to the sun under the sun's influence alone, to have a rough approximation to the time occupied in the entire journey—an approximation certainly not far from the truth, since in the mid-spaces the attractions of the two orbs have counterpoising influences, and it the sun helps the particle in retreating from the star, the star retards the particle as it draws onwards towards the sun. Now, it is easy to find how long a particle would take in falling to the sun from a distance 70,000 times greater than the earth's. For by Kepler's third law, described in the last paper, we have only to multiply 35,000 into itself twice, and to take the square root of the result, to get the period of a body moving in any orbit whose mean distance is 35,000 times the earth's; and we get in this way

Here is a consideration so stupendous that we may well pause before accepting it. Let us see whether there is any way of escape from it. It appears to me that we only come upon greater wonders in endeavouring to avoid this one. Suppose we assume that astronomers have been mistaken in those cases where they have imagined that comets come from the star depths. The observations required to be made are, it is true, somewhat delicate, and a very slight error of observation applied to a comet which really travels in a closed orbit around the sun—a very large and eccentric orbit—in a period of two or three thousand years, might lead to the mistake of supposing that the comet came from interstellar space after a journey millions of years in duration. The behaviour of the comet, while in our neighbourhood—that is, while it continued visible—would be almost exactly the same on either supposition. But we gain very little by supposing that the comet travels in a long oval. For of all the perplexing questions which the astronomer can deal with there is

6,550,000 years, half of which is the period occupied in falling 70,000 miles. Here at once we have more than $3\frac{1}{4}$ millions. And for the body falling to the star from a distance of 140,000 times the distance separating the sun from us, we have an equally simple process, so soon as we have noted that owing to the greater mass of the star, a body would only occupy half a year in completing an orbit as large as our earth's. We multiply 70,000 then twice into itself, getting 343,000,000,000,000, and taking (very roughly) the square root of this we get 18,600,000, one-half of which gives the number of half-years in the fall to Alpha Centauri, so that we get 4,650,000 years. Adding this to the other period, we get close on eight millions of years for the total period occupied by a body in travelling from Alpha Centauri to the sun.

none more perplexing than the question how comets come to travel in closed paths around the sun. That when once introduced into such paths they should continue to traverse them is easily explained; but how they enter on those paths is a mystery of mysteries, unless we assume, as nearly all astronomers do assume, that comets arriving from the interstellar spaces have been so disturbed by the attracting influence of some planet as to be forced to travel on a closed path.

We know that Jupiter and Saturn, or the less but still giant planets, Uranus and Neptune, have power enough so to disturb the motion of an arriving comet, passing near enough to one of these massive orbs; and we know of no other force which could possibly have led to such a result: so that this interpretation may be regarded as the only explanation which is sanctioned by scientific evidence. But then it has simply brought back our difficulty. If comets arriving from the interplanetary spaces have been thus captured, we still have their journey through those spaces to perplex and bewilder us by the stupendous time-intervals which they require.

We may be stopped indeed at the threshold of the enquiry by the suggestion that so many thousands of years ago the comets were launched upon the paths which they are now pursuing, and at such distances from the sun as to come into view at their respective times. But I may be permitted, I trust, to reject altogether such a solution as this, not assuredly because I question the Creator's power so to arrange matters if it had pleased Him, but because it is rendered manifest by the most certain scientific evidence that this has not been the Creator's pleasure, that, on the contrary, He has chosen to work all things by law. It is indeed only because this is so that science has any power to ascertain the meaning of processes going on around us. It is by the recognition of law in the universe that we are led from 'nature up to nature's God,' and they err who would stay the researches which lead to the discovery of the laws of the universe, by the simple explanation that 'God so willed.' That He did so is certain; but science is not therefore to be checked in its enquiries, as though there were fear of her discovering too much. The time has not yet come, nor is it likely to come, when science need take her shoes from off her feet, because of her too near approach to the great First Cause, and because in *that* sense the ground on which she stands is holy ground. She stands on holy ground now, and has always so stood, because she deals with the ways and works of the Creator. But she approaches no nearer to the First Cause in enquiring into the birth of the solar system than in watching the growth of an ephemeron.

And in truth the subject we are upon touches very closely on the question of the origin of our solar system If we deal with comets and meteor-systems as visitants from stellar space, we are at once brought into the presence of time-intervals so vast as to lead us to epochs when our solar system was in its infancy. The eight millions of years I spoke of just now form but the unit of time-measurement—that long interval simply 'counts *one*' in the working of the mighty machine. I took the shortest comet-journey, and I took but one journey; but according to all reasonable probability not one such journey, but thousands, must have elapsed since the time when—by whatever process—any given comet was first formed. We trace back a comet to the star region it came from, as if with the expectation of finding there its birth-place; but from *our* sun that comet starts on a journey which will carry it to another star region, and there it will arrive millions of years hence to arouse speculation in the inhabitants of other worlds. Why should we regard the last known journey of a comet as the first it has ever undertaken? It is as though the ephemeron should regard the only day of its short life as the first day which had dawned upon the universe.

But there is a way of viewing this subject which leads us at once either to the conclusion just indicated or to another equally wonderful conclusion based on the soundest principles of probability. Either a comet which reaches us from the interstellar spaces has made but one journey, or it has made many, flitting from star to star in journeys lasting millions of years. If we take the last view we begin to perceive by what stupendous time-intervals we must measure the duration of the universe. But if we take the other, what opinion must we form of the immense number of cometic voyages through space, when our sun, one amongst millions of millions of suns, is visited by so many comets, that Kepler (before the telescope had shown the real wealth of comet-matter) said that the comets of the solar system must be as the fish of the sea for multitude ? Every comet reaching our system indicates the existence of comets reaching or voyaging towards other systems than ours. We must picture the interstellar spaces, which seem wholly unoccupied, as in reality tenanted by millions of comets for each one of the millions on millions of suns. This opinion, indeed, is forced upon us whatsoever view we take as to the past history of individual comets. A wonderful wealth of matter is thus displayed to us. The whole universe is presented as a scene of amazingly complex activity; and to the wonder caused by its infinite extent and by the vastness of the orbs which people it, there are added the thoughts suggested by the amazing voyages which the messengers, as it were, from one scheme to another are continually making, and by the enormous duration of each single voyage.

But we have still to consider whence comets come. We may trace them through voyage after voyage, but that does not bring us to their starting-place. We have still to enquire how these strange objects came into existence. The enquiry may not indeed be successful, since it carries us back to epochs so remote that we may well shrink from endeavouring to ascertain what then was taking place. Nevertheless, modern science teaches us this lesson above all others, that there is nothing old as there is nothing new in the universe—that is, that no process or state is completely passed, and that no process or state now appears for the first time. We will then, in another chapter, make a survey of the domain of science, ' bringing forth things old and new ' for comparison with what is known about comets, in order that, if it be possible, we may form some idea of the origin of these mysterious objects. It may be that we shall find evidence not altogether indistinct or unsatisfactory to show that in our time and, as it were, under our very eyes comets are being brought into existence. Need it be said that if this is so, it is to our sun that we shall have to look for the processes by which comets are being generated, and the materials from which they are being formed ?

WHENCE COME THE COMETS?

WHAT I propose to say in this chapter will probably surprise many readers of these pages. It may seem to them that the ideas I am about to suggest are too wild and fanciful for acceptance. Yet before our enquiry begins let us recall to mind the wonderful and mysterious facts which have been learned respecting comets, and remember that the real explanation of those facts cannot but be surprising. Here are these amazing objects often exceeding the sun himself many times in size, spreading their huge tails over distances measured by millions of miles, undergoing the most wonderful changes of shape and dimensions, actuated apparently by forces quite different in their nature from the force of gravity and far more potent in their action, travelling from the interstellar spaces after voyages of incalculable duration, and lastly—most wonderful of all perhaps—returning into those far-distant spaces after subserving no useful purpose, so far as can be perceived, in the economy of our solar system. What can these objects be but wonderful? What theory can explain them but one that is as wonderful in its nature as the objects it is to account for? We are in the presence of stupendous facts, and we must not therefore be surprised if bold and startling ideas are suggested in explanation of those facts.

Two circumstances have recently aided speculation in this difficult and perplexing subject. One is the recognition, by means of the spectroscope, of the gaseity of the head and coma (or hair) of comets. The other is the discovery of an association between comets and meteor-systems. On the first fact I shall say little, because it rather promises future explanation than in itself affords sufficient evidence on which to base any opinion respecting comets. Doubtless when some splendid comet—like that with the aigrette-plume in 1858, known as Donati's, and the wonderful object which in the summer of 1861 shone for a few days above the horizon during the morning hours—shall have been subjected to careful spectroscopic analysis, we shall begin to know something respecting the actual structure and condition of cometic appendages. But for the present the most effective piece of knowledge in our possession is that which indicates a connection between meteors and comets.

Briefly stated, the fact—now perfectly demonstrated—is this : The only meteor-systems whose paths have been recognised are found to travel in the track or orbit of known comets. We cannot tell quite certainly what may be the nature of the connection thus indicated; but it would seem to be tolerably obvious that the meteors or falling stars which are seen for a few brief moments as

they are fired during their rush through our upper air are
bodies scattered on the track of comets by some process of
dispersion the nature of which may one day be ascertained.
And this view seems to be confirmed by Sir John Herschel's observations of the comet of 1862, which not only
showed the very kind of appearances we should expect on
this theory, but is otherwise remarkable as being the only
bright comet yet unquestionably associated with one of
our recognised meteor-systems—it is the parent comet,
in fact, of the famous August meteors, called also the
' Perseids,' and sometimes the ' Tears of St. Lawrence.'

Now, Sir John Herschel, *before* it had been demonstrated that the comet is thus connected with the August
meteors, recorded the following observations which he had
made upon it :—' The phenomena exhibited by its nucleus
and head were peculiarly interesting and instructive, it
being only on very rare occasions that a comet can be
closely inspected in the very crisis of its fate, so that we
can witness the actual effect of the sun's rays upon it.   In
this case the pouring forth of the cometic matter from the
singularly bright and highly condensed nucleus took
place in a single compact stream, which, after attaining a
short distance, equal to rather less than a diameter of the
nucleus itself, was so suddenly broken up and dispersed
as to give on the first inspection the impression of a
double nucleus.   The direction of the jet varied considerably from day to day, but always declined more or less
from the exact direction from the sun.'   It appears clear

that there was here a process of raising up, as it were, of cometic matter from the head or nucleus, under the sun's influence, and that then this matter was swept away as if by a repulsive influence exerted upon it by the sun, the rate of this repulsion being such that the direction of the stream of repelled matter regarded as a whole did not lie exactly from the sun, any more than the stream of smoke from the funnel of a moving steamer lies as a whole in the direction in which the wind is blowing.

But the special point for our consideration is that meteors follow and are obviously connected with comets. Now, we cannot examine meteors very well, because they never fall to the ground. The spectroscope has been applied to them as they have shot across the sky, but the attempt is like trying to shoot a bird with a single bullet, and the resulting observations are scarcely to be relied on. There is a way, however, of ascertaining the probable nature of meteors; because they obviously belong to the same class as those masses of matter called aerolites which sometimes fall upon the earth from out of the interplanetary spaces. These masses can be analysed, chemically, microscopically, and otherwise, and so we can learn something not merely of their present structure, but of their past history.

Now, the result of such enquiry is very curious. Sorby of Sheffield, the eminent mineralogist and microscopist, found, nine or ten years ago, that meteoric masses have been exposed to processes somewhat resembling those to which matter is subjected in the great furnaces of Sheffield. Here is his account of the matter :—Originally the material of aerolites was 'in a state of fusion; and the most remote condition of which we have any positive evidence was that of small, detached, melted globules, the formation of which cannot be explained in a satisfactory manner, except by supposing that their constituents were originally in a state of vapour *as they'* (that is, the same constituent elements) '*now exist in the atmosphere of the sun*; and on the temperature becoming lower condensed into these ultimate cosmical particles. These afterwards collected into larger masses, which have been variously changed by subsequent action, and broken up by repeated mutual impact, and often again collected together and solidified.' This would clearly suggest that these meteoric masses were originally expelled either from the sun or from one of his fellow suns the stars, *or else* that we must look back to some long past epoch in the history of the universe when a true chaos prevailed, regarding meteorites as the fragments left from the time of chaos. Let us see what the chemical analysis of meteorites may suggest as the more probable of these views.

The chemical evidence is singularly decisive. Professor Graham, the late Master of the Mint, and one of the greatest chemists of our day, examined the iron of an aerolite called the Lenarto Meteor from the place where it fell. He tested it with special reference to the quantity of hydrogen contained in it; for hydrogen and other gases can be occluded, as it is called, or as it were closed in, within the substance of iron. Now, observe what he says about the iron of this meteor:—' It has been found difficult to impregnate malleable iron with more than an equal volume of hydrogen under the pressure of our atmosphere. Now, the meteoric iron (this Lenarto iron is remarkably pure and malleable) gave up about three times that amount without being fully exhausted. The inference is that the meteorite *had been extruded from a dense atmosphere of hydrogen gas*, for which we must look beyond the light cometary matter floating about within the limits of our solar system.' . . . . ' Hydrogen has been recognised by the spectrum analysis of the light of the fixed stars by Messrs. Huggins and Miller. The same gas constitutes, according to the wide researches of Father Secchi, the principal element of a numerous class of stars, of which Alpha Lyræ (the leading brilliant of the Lyre) is the type. The iron of Lenarto has no doubt come from such an atmosphere, in which hydrogen greatly prevailed. *This meteorite may be looked upon as holding imprisoned within it, and bearing to us, the hydrogen of the stars.*'

We are led then to the startling conclusion that comets (for what applies to the meteoric trains must needs apply to the comets whence those trains proceed) have been expelled either from our sun or from one or other of the stars. We may dismiss the sun from consideration, so far as most of our cometic visitors are concerned, simply because any matter he flung forth would either travel for ever away from him to visit other systems, or if not expelled with sufficient force for that, would return after a journey of greater or less length to the globe of the sun whence it had been projected. The fact is that most of the comets expelled from our sun would visit other solar systems, while our solar system would be visited by stray comets, now from one star, now from another.

I might pause at this stage to enquire into the singularly interesting evidence which our sun himself affords as to the projectile power which he possesses. I might describe processes of solar eruption, actually witnessed and watched by astronomers, in which a velocity of ejection amply competent to carry matter for ever away from the sun was undoubtedly produced by solar volcanic forces. But such an enquiry would require an essay to itself, and I hope some day to be able to take up that special subject. In this place, let it suffice to say that the sun certainly possesses power to eject material from his interior, apart from that strange repulsive power—far more powerful than his attractive energy—which he exerts on the substance of comets' tails. And what is true of the sun may be regarded as true of each star, since we know that every star is a sun, and that many, if not most, stars are far mightier suns than ours.

But now a very curious consideration presents itself. Supposing that the large comets which visit our system were originally expelled from some one or other of the suns which people space, it must have been an amazingly long time ago that any such comet first came into existence. I showed in my last essay that eight million years would be the shortest time in which any comet could traverse the space separating our system from the nearest star. And then it must be regarded as altogether unlikely that a comet has made only one interstellar journey before visiting us. Far more probably every comet has made many journeys, flitting, as I have said, from star to star in journeys, each lasting millions of years; and we may say that certainly *some* comets have done so. Now, the stars are not unchangeable. Our own sun is undergoing continual changes, and probably will die out, and, as a sun, cease to exist, before many millions of years have passed, perhaps before many thousands have passed. It is also believed by astronomers that not many millions of years ago our sun was in a condition quite unlike that in which he at present exists. So that when some at least of the large comets which have visited our system began their being, our sun in all probability was not the sun he now is. He was probably larger and more nebulous, but less massive; he was younger and more active, but less powerful; the scheme over which he now rules was as yet unformed; the whole planetary system was quite unlike the scheme we now recognise.

But if this was the case with our sun and his system, doubtless it was the case also with most of the suns we call stars. We must assume, then, that either the large comets we have seen came some of them at least from suns in a condition quite unlike that of our sun as he now is, or else that the suns which in the far-off ages expelled those comets have long since ceased to be suns. Thus we either look back to a distant time when the sidereal universe was full of younger suns ruling over systems still incomplete, or else the eye of reason reveals to us countless invisible orbs, which once were suns, still peopling the realms of space, but no longer affording light and heat and life to the schemes which circle round them. Or we may adopt the inference, which perhaps some will consider more probable than either, that *both* views are just; in which case we must assume that even now, at this very time, there exist all orders of suns within the sidereal universe—suns still growing; suns ruling over schemes already formed around them; and, lastly, dead and used-up suns, waiting, as it were, for some future change, by which they will be restored to activity and usefulness.

But may we not reasonably apply these considerations to the minor system, of which the planets are the members? If within the star depths we recognise, at least with the eye of reason, these various states of being, may it not be that within the planetary scheme like varieties exist? We are too apt to consider that a dull uniformity pervades those regions which we have not explored; and though the study of our own domain has revealed an inexhaustible variety of nature, condition, and structure, we are unwilling to extend the lesson to the spaces around us.

We look on the stars as suns like our own, on the planets as orbs like our earth, on their satellites as moons like ours; and we regard the ring of Saturn with wonder, because we know of nothing wherewith to compare it. But may we not believe that the wonderful variety we recognise among terrestrial phenomena characterises the planetary scheme, and in a yet greater degree the amazing system of which our sun is but an unimportant member?

THE COMET FAMILIES OF THE GIANT PLANETS.

I HAVE already spoken in a previous article[1] of the comet called Biela's—and sometimes the Double Comet, or the Lost Comet, because it had first divided into two, and eventually vanished altogether away. I have now to consider the class of comets to which Biela's belonged— the comets of short period. In this class may be included all those which have been watched at two or three returns to our neighbourhood, so that Halley's comet, with its period of about seventy years, is included in the class, while, on the other hand, the periods of such comets range down to the short interval of three and one-third years, recognised in the case of Encke's comet. I do not propose, however, to enter into the history of any of these bodies. My special object is to discuss the relations they present in connection with the meteor-systems respecting which I have spoken in my last article.

It will be remembered that we were led to the conclusion that the great comets, as well as the great

---

[1] See p. 124, 'The Lost Comet.'

meteoric masses which from time to time fall upon the earth, were originally expelled from the stars. Now it might seem at a first view reasonable to conclude that the small comets also, and the meteor-systems which follow in their track, had a similar origin. For in great volcanic explosions on our own earth large masses of rock and other matter are accompanied by flights of smaller missiles, while sometimes the expulsion of large masses ceases for a while, and showers of scoriæ and cinders are alone expelled. If we assume that the eruptions taking place in suns are like terrestrial eruptions in this particular respect, so that now large masses, and now flights of small masses are ejected, we should find the smaller comets and their meteor-trains as readily explained as the large comets and the great aerolites which probably follow in their track.

But there are certain difficulties in the way of this explanation.

The comets of short period follow orbits which on the one hand do not pass near to the sun, while on the other, being closed curves, they necessarily differ altogether in shape from the paths pursued by bodies arriving from interstellar space. These comets, then, cannot possibly have been expelled from the sun, for matter expelled from the sun would either pass away from him or return to him, moving very nearly in a straight course. If we assume that these comets were expelled from stars, we have to explain how it is that their paths are now so differently shaped from those they would have had on first reaching our system after their journey through the interstellar depths.

The ordinary explanation of this circumstance is, that one or other of the giant planets—Jupiter, Saturn, Uranus, and Neptune—has disturbed one of these comets as it arrived after its interstellar journey, and has compelled it to take up the orbit in which it at present travels. If a comet were travelling towards the sun on such a course as to pass very close to Jupiter, it would be for a time chiefly under the influence of Jupiter's attraction, and its path might be so changed, and its velocity so reduced, that thereafter it would travel on a closed curve around the sun. And so with the other planets just named. Now, there is a circumstance in the movements of the comets of short period which accords well with this explanation. If a comet were at any time so near to the planet Jupiter, let us say, as to be treated in the way described, the future path of the comet would necessarily pass through the spot where the disturbance took place; and although in the course of many years the comet's path might be considerably changed, yet a part of the path would always pass somewhat near to the orbit of Jupiter. And in point of fact this peculiarity is recognised in a more or less marked degree with all the comets of short period. Their paths so cling, as it were, about the paths of the giant planets, that I long since gave to those thus related to Jupiter the title of 'Jupiter's comet family,' while Saturn, Uranus, and Neptune each have their dependent comets, those of Neptune forming a peculiarly symmetrical family.

But there is one consideration which renders it difficult to suppose that all these comets were thus gathered in from the interstellar spaces by the attracting energy of the giant planets. For any planet—even the mighty Jupiter—to capture a comet, the comet must pass very near to the planet. For a short time the comet must be more strongly controlled by the planet than by the sun; and this requires that a comet should pass nearer to the planet than its own satellites. Now, if we try to picture the circumstances under which a comet would arrive from outer space, we readily see that the chances are many millions to one against this happening. The span of Jupiter's orbit amounts to about nine hundred millions of miles, and an arriving comet would be unlikely to approach the sun on the level of Jupiter's path; it might arrive from above or below, and at any degree of slope. The orbit of Saturn is twice as wide as that of Jupiter; that of Uranus is twice as wide, and that of Neptune thrice as wide as the orbit of Saturn. Compared with these enormous distances, the distances within which a comet must approach these planets, in order to be brought into subjection and compelled to travel in a closed orbit round the sun, are altogether minute.

Either, then, we must assume that in the case of every captured comet there has been a most wonderful coincidence, or else that many millions of comets have arrived for each one that has been captured. And as it is certain that for every known comet of short period there must be hundreds or thousands unknown, we see that the latter supposition involves very remarkable ideas as to the wealth of cometic matter in the universe. Then we have the same enormous time-intervals to consider in the case of these small comets as in the case of the large comets already discussed, with the additional time required to reduce the smaller orbits to their present shape.

It is worth enquiring, therefore, whether there is no simple explanation—not, indeed, that we can hope to find any interpretation which is not of a surprising and even startling nature, but that perhaps one may be found which would give a more satisfactory and systematic account of the comets of short period.

Since these comets are associated in so peculiar a manner with the giant planets of the solar system, may it not be that they bear a relation to these planets somewhat resembling that which the large comets bear to the suns which people space? As the large comets would seem to have been expelled from these suns, may not the small comets have been expelled from the giant planets? We need not necessarily assume that these giant planets are still in the active and sunlike state necessary, we may suppose, for the expulsion of comets. Even this assumption is not altogether without evidence in its favour; and, indeed, I have long since been led, by evidence of another kind, to the conclusion that Jupiter and Saturn are secondary suns to the schemes of secondary planets which circle around them. But it may be on the whole safer to assume that the birth of the comet families of the giant planets took place in far distant eras, when these orbs were not merely as now instinct with an intense heat, but also aglow with light, so as to present, when viewed from other systems, the aspect which the small companions of unequal double stars present to our telescopists. Astronomers have long since seen reason for believing that all the planets, including our own earth, were once luminous with intensity of heat, and the giant planets, when in that condition, were probably comparable as light-givers to many of the minor suns of our galaxy. There seems nothing unreasonable, therefore, in the supposition that as the leading suns have expelled the large comets now followed by trains of meteorites, so these minor suns —Jupiter, Saturn, Uranus, and Neptune—ejected the small comets followed by flights of relatively minute meteors.

Now, it happens that there is one piece of evidence which seems strikingly to favour the theory here advanced. It is clear that captured comets would be as likely to be sent round the sun on their new orbit in one direction as another—advancing or retrograde—that is, in the same direction that the planets travel in, or in the opposite direction. *But* comets expelled from a planet would partake in the motion of the planet, and this motion, though it would be combined with the motion of ejection, would probably leave a balance of advancing motion. Supposing a person in a rapidly advancing open carriage were to throw stones in all directions around him, is it not clear that more of these would travel forwards than backwards, simply because the forward motion of the carriage would always be added to the motion imparted to the stone? If the open carriage belonged to a railway train moving at express speed, *all* the stones would move forward, even those which were flung directly backward, *as respected the train.*[1] Applying the principle here illustrated to the case of the comet families, we see that if they were ejected from the planets with which they are respectively associated, we might expect to find the greater number travelling the same way round the sun as the planets. Moreover, we see that this peculiarity would be more marked the greater the velocity of the parent comet, and that probably the comets depending on Jupiter, the most swiftly travelling of the giant planets, would *all* travel forwards. Now, this is precisely the state of the case. Far the greater number of the comets of short period travel advancingly, or like the planets; and while some few of those dependent on the outer planets, Neptune and Uranus, travel in a retrograde manner, *none* of those dependent on Jupiter so travel.

Yet another piece of evidence. For the same reason

---

[1] The experiment here indicated is not one that any reader should attempt to carry out in a practical manner.

that ejected comets would for the most part travel forwards, there would be a tendency among their orbits to lie near the level of the planetary orbits. At any rate, we might expect to find such a tendency among those depending on Jupiter. The case is precisely like that just considered, and can be illustrated in the same way. If stones were flung in all directions from a very swiftly moving train,[1] they would not only all move forwards, but there would be a tendency to horizontal motion, simply because every stone would partake in the horizontal motion of the train.

Even a stone thrown vertically upwards *from the train* would move slantwise with respect to the earth. Now, here again the facts of the case favour the strange theory I am dealing with. The comets which come from interstellar space show every variety of inclination to the general level of the planetary motions. Those depending on the outer planets are, for the most part, not very greatly inclined to that level. Those attending on Jupiter do not include one case of *great* inclination, and are for the most part very little inclined.

There is not much evidence, it may be admitted, in favour of the theory we are considering. Still the balance of evidence favours this theory rather than the theory that the comets of short period have been in the main

---

[1] I suppose, at least, that a stone cannot be flung with the speed of an express train ; but I have no certain knowledge as to the greatest velocity which an expert thrower can impart to a stone flung in the usual way.

drawn from the interstellar spaces. And so far as can be judged no other theory than these two can be imagined.

Now, whether we regard the giant planets as still engaged in the work of comet ejection or suppose that they have long since ceased to possess the powers necessary for that work, we have alike a curious subject of contemplation. In one case we see that a strange variety exists within the planetary system, where our earth and her fellow minor planets are fit abodes for life, while the giant planets are in a state of intense activity. In the other we see that a strange difference exists between the present condition of the outer planets and their condition in long past ages. I do not know which thought is the more suggestive; but I may note in passing that both thoughts may be admitted at the same time, and that in fact it is altogether more probable that both are just than that one must be rejected in favour of the other. Truly, when we view our solar system in the light of such considerations as these, we begin to see how much more wonderful the planetary scheme is than it has been represented in the text books of astronomy. We no longer are a uniform system, inert and lifeless, so far at least as life is measured by change, but a scheme full of variety, instinct with energy and vitality, changed in all parts from the condition it once had, changing in all parts towards new conditions—a living, growing, developing system, a fit world of life to be ruled over by the mighty, ever active sun. As we contemplate these wonders, we seem to find a new meaning in the words of the Psalmist, ' The heavens declare the glory of God; and the firmament sheweth His handywork. There is neither speech nor language, but their voices are heard among them.'

THE EARTH'S JOURNEY THROUGH SHOWERS.

THERE are some facts in astronomy the real significance of which scarcely strikes us as they are ordinarily presented. We note with more or less interest, perhaps with wonder, a series of statements in which great distances and large masses are referred to with an imposing array of figures, but we fail to recognise adequately what the statements mean. This is particularly the case with some of the more recent discoveries made by astronomers. They are so pregnant with meaning, so stupendous, not only in their direct significance, but in the inferences which flow from them, that time is required even to view them aright, and much more time to realise their full significance.

Perhaps there is no department of astronomy to which these remarks are more strikingly applicable than to meteoric astronomy. I have already touched on some of the remarkable inferences, as to cosmical relations, which may be deduced from recent discoveries respecting meteors and meteor-systems. I propose now to touch on the subject in its terrestrial aspect: to show what is actually taking place as our earth urges her way on her wide orbit round the sun, saluted on all sides by meteors—

Pelted with star dust, stoned with meteor balls—

though not always exposed to meteor showers of equal heaviness.

It is perhaps sufficiently startling to be told at the outset that nearly all shooting stars—nine hundred and ninety-nine out of every thousand, certainly—are missiles which rush towards the earth with a velocity far exceeding that of the swiftest cannon-ball. They are not missiles which miss their mark. They do not, as was once thought, merely graze our atmosphere. They come straight towards the earth, and many among them must make straight towards living creatures on the earth. And though they are for the most part small, they are by no means so small as to be unable to destroy life. Their swift motions make up for their smallness, and the actual momentum of some of the tiniest of these bodies is equivalent to the momentum of a cannon-ball.

We might afford to make little of the danger (for danger there would be but for a circumstance presently to be mentioned) were the number of these bodies small. If ten or twenty saluted the earth during the twenty-four hours, the chance that even in the course of a century any living creature would be struck would be small. For the earth is large, and living creatures occupy but a small portion of its surface. But, I think, many among my readers have no adequate conception of the enormous number of meteors which each year fall upon the earth. A million a year would bring some degree of danger. But the actual number is far greater. It has been estimated by Professor Simon Newcombe, of America, on grounds which are perfectly reliable, that including telescopic meteors (that is, meteors so small as only to be visible when they happen to pass across the field of view of a telescope) no less than 146,000 millions of meteoric bodies fall each year upon the earth. If one in a thousand struck a human being the inhabitants of the earth would be decimated in a single year.

How then is it, it may be asked, that we never hear of even an accident from ordinary meteors, though accidents from aerolites have not been altogether unknown? Here is this great vessel, the earth, sailing through space, and saluted every twenty-four hours by 400 millions of missiles, each flying towards her with many times the velocity of the swiftest cannon-ball. This goes on by day and by night, when living creatures are far from shelter as well as when they are protected in their various abodes; and yet the inhabitants of earth are perfectly safe from all danger. It is not merely that they have been so far fortunate as to escape hitherto, but that they really are as safe as though the earth were protected by those three-feet armour plates which will one day, we are told, defend our floating batteries.

The real protection of the earth is the air which surrounds her. Soft as the air is, the resistance it opposes to swift motion is very great. The swifter the motion the more effective is the resistance. In the case of the meteoric missiles falling on the earth the resistance is so great, owing to their enormous velocity, that they are consumed and presently vaporised in their rush through the upper parts of the air. For the most part they appear to penetrate the air to a depth of about twenty miles below the height at which they are first rendered visible by the intensity of their heat. For they mostly appear when still at a height of seventy miles and vanish when at a height of about fifty miles. But the actual course they pursue through the air is nearly always much longer, because they do not descend vertically but aslant. It is easily intelligible that the extreme rarity of the air at these heights is compensated by the vastness of the distance through which the meteor travels in a very short time. For most of the meteors are travelling through the air, when they·begin their passage through it, at the rate of twenty or thirty miles per second, and though their velocity is much reduced in the course of their. flight, yet, as everyone knows who has seen shooting stars, they execute their long flight through the upper air-strata in which they are destroyed at a very high velocity, being seldom visible more than a few seconds. Thus the air forms a perfect protection to our earth. The words of Milton respecting the air, although used by him in another sense, yet by a happy accident apply with singular fitness to the services actually rendered by the air according to recent astronomical discoveries respecting meteors :—

> God made
> The firmament, expanse of liquid, pure,
> Transparent, elemental air, diffused
> In circuit to the uttermost convex
> Of this great round ; partition firm and sure
> . . . . lest fierce extremes
> Contiguous might distemper the whole frame.

Nevertheless, although none of the meteors reach the surface of the earth in their original solid form, their substance must in the long run sink down through the air until it settles on the earth. For though they are vaporised through intensity of heat, yet they can remain in the vaporous state but a few seconds, presently changing into the form of mere dust by a process of condensation, precisely resembling that which changes the invisible vapour of water in our air into the form of visible clouds of water globules. This meteoric dust being extremely fine must sink very slowly, but in the long run every particle of it reaches the earth.

Evidence has been obtained on this point—though even without such evidence no doubt could well be entertained on the subject. Dr. Reichenbach collected dust from the top of a high mountain, which had never been touched by spade or pick-axe ; and in analysis he found this dust to consist of almost identically the same elements as those of which meteoric stones are composed—nickel, cobalt, iron, and phosphorus. Dr. Phipson also, in his interesting work on 'Meteors, Aerolites, and Shooting Stars,' remarks that 'when a glass covered with pure glycerine is exposed to a strong wind, late in November, it receives a number of *black angular particles*, which can be dissolved in strong hydrochloric acid, and produce yellow chloride of *iron* upon the glass plate.'

It is a strange thought that the breath we draw contains matter which has circled in the meteoric form around the sun, visiting in its course the space where Mars and Jupiter, Saturn, Uranus, and Neptune [1] pursue their paths.

And here the question suggests itself whether the supply of meteoric dust is necessary to the well-being of the inhabitants of earth. That it is not on the whole injurious is manifest, for the supply has continued for ages, and will continue for many ages to come. It is not at all unlikely that it is to some degree necessary for our well-being, though the doses of meteoric matter which we receive are altogether infinitesimal. But the supply is variable, since sometimes there are showers of meteors, while at others there are but a few scattered meteors for several days in succession. May it not be that meteors in excess are bad for the inhabitants of earth? or else (for we have no satisfactory evidence

---

[1] This applies of course only to certain meteors. Some meteors do not travel beyond the path of Jupiter; and probably only a small proportion pass beyond the orbit of Neptune.

either way) that a great deficiency in the supply might lead to mischief?

It has been suggested that some of the pestilences which history records were produced by meteoric influences. It seems tolerably clear that the worst plagues were due to the great plague-generator, Uncleanliness. But some of the plagues were so sudden in their origin, lasted so short a time, and had such singular features, as to suggest the idea of extra-terrestrial influences. Amongst these may be mentioned the sweating sickness of the fifteenth and sixteenth centuries, which was not only characterised by the peculiarities in question, but, by its recurrence thrice in forty-six years, has suggested the action of a recurrent cause like the return of meteoric clusters circling around the sun.

Note, for instance, Bacon's description of this sickness in his Life of Henry the Seventh :—

' About this time,' he says, speaking of the year 1485, ' in autumn, towards the end of September, there began & reigned in the city, and other parts of the kingdom, a disease then new : which, by the accidents and manner thereof, they called the sweating sickness. The disease had a swift course, both in the sick body, and in the time and period of the lasting thereof; for they that were taken with it, upon four and twenty hours escaping, were thought almost assured. And as to the time of the malice & reign of the disease ere it ceased, it began about the one and twentieth of September, & cleared up before the end of October, insomuch as it was no hindrance to the king's coronation which was the last of October ; nor, which was more, to the holding of Parliament, which began but seven days after. It was a pestilent fever, but, as it seemeth, not seated in the veins or humours, for that there followed no carbuncle, no purple or livid spots, or the like, the mass of the body being not tainted; only a malign vapour flew to the heart and seized the vital spirits ; which stirred nature to strive to send it forth by an extreme sweat. And it appeared by experience that this disease was rather a surprise of nature than obstinate to remedies, if it were in time looked into. For if the patient were kept in an equal temper, both for clothes, fire, & drink, moderately warm, with temperate cordials, whereby nature's work were neither irritated by heat nor turned back by cold, he commonly recovered. But infinite persons died suddenly of it, before the manner of the cure and attendance was known. *It was conceived not to be an epidemic disease, but to proceed from a malignity in the constitution of the air, gathered by predispositions of seasons ; and the speedy cessation declared as much.'*

It certainly seems impossible to conclude certainly that the earth's inhabitants are safe from all extra-terrestrial influences. When we remember, too, that a connection has been traced between comets and meteors, we can believe that possibly the fear with which comets have been regarded may not be altogether so ill-founded as astronomers have been led to believe of late years. Certainly there is small risk from any effects of collision with comets, since we have learned that the mass even of the largest comet is inconsiderable. But the inter-mixture of cometic matter with the atmosphere of our earth might not always be a perfectly innocuous process. We do not as yet know what are the gases which are the chief constituents of the vaporous parts of comets, nor the proportion in which solid and liquid matter may be present in the heads and nuclear parts of comets. But there are few gases which, added in very large quantity to our air, would do no harm; and any considerable addition of solid matter, first vaporised and afterwards settling as a fine dust through the air, might severely injure at least those of delicate constitution.

There are some eventualities, indeed, which are very startling to contemplate, yet not altogether inconceivable. Suppose, for instance, that a comet composed in the main of hydrogen should mix with our air, until the oxygen of the air and the hydrogen of the comet were in the proportion in which these gases are present (chemically combined) in water. Then unless every fire and light in the whole earth were extinguished there would be a tremendous explosion, followed instantly by a deluge of water, and leaving the burnt and drenched earth no other atmosphere than the nitrogen now present in the air, together with relatively small quantities of deleterious vapours.

We need not greatly trouble ourselves, however, with the fear of such a calamity. If hydrogen comets were common, the earth would probably have encountered one long ago, in which case her condition would certainly not be such as it is at present. It is, however, not at all improbable that the earth is not merely exposed to mischief, but that her inhabitants have actually suffered, more or less seriously, at intervals, from the meteoric and cometic matter which falls upon her as she journeys onward through showers.[1]

[1] The medal commemorating the great plague of London, which was associated, it will be remembered, with the appearance of a comet, pictures the comet as scattering pestilence from its tail. According to this curious medal, pestilence was scattered in the form of small pothooks. Defoe's remarks about this comet, and the one which appeared a year after, are curious :—' A blazing star or comet appeared,' he says, ' for several months before the plague, as there did the year after, a little before the fire ; the old women and the phlegmatic hypochondriacal part of the other sex, whom I could almost call old women too, remarked, especially afterwards, though not till both those judgments were over, that these two comets passed directly over the city, and that so very near the houses (! !) that it was plain they imported something peculiar to the city alone; and the comet before the pestilence was of a faint dull languid colour, and its motion very heavy and slow ; but that the comet before the fire was bright and sparkling, or as others said, flaming, and its motion swift and furious : and that accordingly one foretold a heavy judgment, slow but severe, terrible and frightful as was the plague ; but the other foretold a stroke sudden, swift, and fiery, as was the conflagration ; nay, so particular some people were, that as they looked upon that comet preceding the fire, they fancied they not only saw it pass swiftly and fiercely, and could perceive the motion with their eye, but even they heard it, that it made a rushing mighty noise, fierce and terrible, though at a distance and but just perceivable. I saw both these stars, and I must confess, had had so much of the common notion of such things in my head, that I was apt to look upon them as the forerunners and warnings of God's judgments, and especially when the plague had followed the first, I

In my two next chapters I shall consider how the earth and other planets may be regarded as *growing* under the continual downfall of meteoric matter; and how, although this growth must be regarded as exceedingly slow in these our times, yet in past ages the members of the sclar system, and the sun himself, must have grown appreciably in volume and mass under the continual influx of meteoric matter.

yet saw another of the like kind, I could not but say, God had not yet sufficiently scourged the city.'

I.

IN considering the wonderful processes which are taking place within the limits of the solar system, and still more in endeavouring to trace back the course of events during former ages, we find ourselves surrounded by a hundred sources of perplexity. Nor is it to be expected, perhaps, that we should be able, either now or at any future time, to form clear ideas on a subject so involved in mystery. The powers of man—I am speaking of the race, not of individual men—are wonderful. The Almighty has enabled them to deal successfully with many problems which, even now that they have been solved, seem as though they had been placed beyond all reasonable hopes of mastery. But it has not been given to man to solve all the mysteries that surround him, and it may well be questioned whether it will ever be in his power to solve that great mystery, the origin of the wonderful scheme of worlds of which our earth is a member.

Yet there are steps which man can fairly hope to make on the path leading towards the great secret. There are processes still taking place which he can gauge and measure, thence inferring the probable nature of the corresponding processes in long past ages of the world's history. There are signs which are full of meaning, traces which can be followed for a great way—we do not yet know *how* far.

It is certainly a legitimate exercise of the powers given to man to follow out those paths, whether well marked or as yet little trodden, which seem likely to lead to new knowledge. We need not be troubled by doubts as to the way in which such paths may lead us, so that they really lead to the recognition of *facts*. We may learn many things inconsistent, perchance, with our present ideas as to the way in which it has pleased the Almighty to provide for His worlds. We may have to abandon some conceptions which had appeared very accordant with the might and wisdom of the Creator. But we may be sure of this, that whatever new ideas we may legitimately be led to, will prove not less worthy of Him. Increase of knowledge of His universe—whether of its various parts or of the various periods of its history—will enhance our conceptions of His power and wisdom, though still leaving those conceptions infinitely poor and feeble compared with the reality.

I make these preliminary remarks, because, strangely enough, many persons of religious mind seem afraid to enter upon the course here indicated, and follow with unwilling footsteps those who try to advance some short distance upon it. Of those who have such fears, the believing student of science (that is, of the knowledge of God's works) may justly ask the question, 'Why are ye so fearful, O ye of little faith?'

There are manifest signs in the present configuration and motions of the planetary system of a process of evolution by which in long past ages it *grew* to its present condition. There is, of course, nothing to prevent any man from believing that precisely as the solar system is now it was created so many thousands of years ago. The Almighty might have chosen that at a certain instant Neptune, Uranus, Saturn, and Jupiter—the zone of asteroids—and the family of minor planets, to which our earth belongs—should come into being, should be set revolving each on its proper orbit, and rotating each with its due period, should be clothed with atmospheric envelopes, diversified with oceans and continents, and in fine created just as they at present exist.

I say there is nothing to prevent anyone from adopting this view, because a Being of infinite power could have so arranged matters that all the evidence available on the subject should be precisely as it now is; and, as we have no record handed down by actual witnesses of the earlier history of the solar system, it is impossible to know certainly that this was not the actual order of things. *Now*, as in the days of Job, no man can answer when the questions are asked, 'Where wast thou when God laid the foundations of the earth? declare, if thou hast understanding. Who hath laid the measures thereof, if thou knowest? Or who hath stretched the line upon it?'

But it is reasonable to study the processes which are actually taking place around us, as well as the condition of those parts of the universe which we can examine, and to infer from such researches whatever is ascertainable as to the past history of created things. We may compare man's range of research to some region where races of shortlived insects have their being, and the processes which man can watch to those which take place within the cognisance of such creatures, supposing only that they had the power to investigate and to reason as man does. Let us imagine that such creatures noted the slow processes of change taking place in a tree near which they lived. To them these processes would seem infinitely slow compared with the rate at which *we* perceive these processes to take place. The growth of a leaf might, perhaps, occupy more time than the whole life of one of these creatures. Yet, if from one generation to another the knowledge gradually acquired were carefully handed down, it would be possible to recognise the nature of the growth and development of the tree. With further study, occupying perhaps the time and labour of several more generations, it would be possible to infer something of the fixture of the tree, and even perhaps to recognise the fact that at some (to them) very far distant epoch the tree would decay and perish.

But with such knowledge would come also the means

of inferring what had been the history of that tree during periods antecedent to the very existence of their race, and whose duration could not but appear to them as practically infinite. It might not be given to them to trace back the history of that tree to the time when the seed from which it sprang began first to germinate. Still less might they be able to recognise the law according to which tree succeeded tree—one form of the universe (in their eyes) succeeding to another form, according to the law of being of these tree universes. Their knowledge could be carried back to a certain distance, to a period infinitely remote to their ideas, but now beyond. It is not unlikely that they would regard the beginning of all things as lying just beyond the limits they were able to reach; and yet in reality, since the next step backwards would be but to the falling of a seed upon the earth, their conception of creation would be contemptible in the eyes of men.

I think we may very safely carry *our* investigations back as far as we possibly can. We cannot, I conceive, go very far; though we may imagine, if we please, that just beyond the period to which we carry back our thoughts lies the beginning of all things. Probably—nay, to my own mind, certainly—our ideas are as inadequate and feeble, compared with the reality, as those which I have pictured as the ideas of ephemeral insects. And certainly any conception of creation which placed its epoch just beyond the limits to which our powers enable us to reach in our retrospective researches, would appear contemptible to beings in existence when the foundations of the universe were laid, 'when the morning stars sang together, and all the sons of God shouted for joy.'

In my last article I mentioned that the earth is growing. Day by day and year by year meteors are falling upon the earth, not by hundreds and thousands, but by thousands of millions. This process of growth is, however, exceedingly slow. Estimated indeed by the actual quantity of matter falling year by year upon the earth it seems like a real appreciable growth. For let us suppose that on the average each meteor of more than 140,000 millions which fall per annum weighs but a single grain. Then the earth's weight is increased each year by 20 millions of pounds, or by more than 90,000 tons. Yet this is a mere nothing compared with the actual weight of the earth. Supposing the matter thus received to be spread uniformly over the whole surface of the earth, it would form a layer less than the 800,000,000th part of an inch in thickness. So that at this rate 400 millions of years must elapse before the earth's diameter would be increased a single inch. Thus it may fairly be said that though the earth is really acquiring new mass year by year, yet she is no longer growing appreciably in dimensions.

We see here a process which may be compared to what takes place in a tree when it has acquired its full dimensions. And as the mere life of a tree no longer growing yet teaches us by what processes the tree grew, so I conceive that the gathering in of meteoric matter which now takes place at so low a rate as to produce no appreciable *growth* yet indicates the nature of the processes by which in bygone ages the earth and her fellow-planets grew to their present dimensions. The meteors now being gathered in are but as a remnant. They are necessarily being reduced in number year after year, and we have only to look far enough back to recognise a time when they were so numerous that their downfall sufficed to produce a real and appreciable increase in the bulk of the planets.

I have mentioned certain indications in the solar system of past processes of evolution. These are in their way as sufficient as the indications afforded by the successive rings in the section of a tree's trunk. Let us briefly consider what the solar system thus teaches us about its past history.

All the planets travel the same way round. This is true not only of the eight primary planets but of the asteroids, now more than a hundred and thirty in number. Again, all the secondary planets or satellites travel the same way round (this direction of revolution being the same as that in which the planets revolve round the sun) —except the satellites of Uranus, which, however, can hardly be said to have any direction of motion with reference to the general level in which the planetary system circuits, for they travel in planes nearly square to that level. Lastly, as respects direction of motion, all the planets whose rotation has been observed, including our earth and the moon, and the sun also, rotate on their axes in the same direction. It must be understood that this direction is one and the same for all these motions—the revolutions of the planets around the sun, of the satellites round the planets, and of the planets on their axes.[1]

Now, there is no reason, in the nature of things, why this uniformity of direction should exist. If some planets went round one way, and some the other, it would still be as well with the solar system as at present. If our moon, or the moons of Jupiter or of Saturn, went round the other way no harm would follow. If the earth or any other planet turned on its axis the other way round, the inhabitants would be as well off as they are at present. It seems natural to infer that the uniformity is the result of some general condition affecting the whole scheme from the beginning. Of course we may argue that the uniformity exists because God so willed it, precisely as our illustrative insects, if they lighted on some old tree stump lately sawn, and perceived the circular rings in its section, might argue that the shape of these was in no way connected with the growth of the tree, but that the rings were circular and concentric because the Almighty had pleased to create them so. Such reasoning

---

[1] Looking down on the solar system from the northern side, these motions would all be the reverse of that in which the hands of a watch move.

on the part of ephemeral and feeble insects appears ridiculous in our eyes, who are so long-lived, so strong, and so wonderfully knowing. Let us not be too sure, however, that we are not falling into a mistake equally ridiculous in the eyes of the All-knowing, in regarding the coming into being of the solar system as synchronising with the beginning of all things.

If we reject this view as narrowing (preposterously, perhaps, if the truth were known) the range of time within which created things have existed, we have no choice but to regard the observed uniformity as the result of the action of some process of evolution, since the peculiarity is a most marked one. Setting the matter as a question of probabilities, the chances are many millions of millions to one against the observed state of things,[1] except as the result of express contrivance on the one hand or of a uniform process of evolution on the other.

Now, the French astronomer Laplace showed how all

[1] Taking the revolution of the planets in one common direction alone, and counting 140 planets (all at present known), the odds against the observed coincidence of direction are as 2 multiplied into itself 138 times to unity (or in technical terms, as 2 raised to the power 139 to unity). (The odds are as 2 raised to the power 140 to unity against the planets all going round in the actually observed direction, but only one-half this against their all going the same way round, that way being indifferent.) Now, 2 raised to the power 139 is a number of 42 digits, beginning 69,370, &c., and the antecedent odds against the observed relation are represented by the proportion of this enormous number to unity.

[Since this was written the 133rd asteroid has been discovered, raising the odds to 138,740, &c. (43 digits) to one.]

these motions would have resulted if the solar system had once been a great mass of intensely hot vapour turning round and round as upon an axis. This whirling mass of vapour would contract as it parted with its heat, and, as it contracted, would whirl more swiftly. This increase of its rotating movement would cause the outer parts to be separated, and a ring would be thus thrown off. This ring would eventually break up and form a minor vapour mass, circling around the remainder of the contracting mass. Moreover, Laplace showed that the mass thrown off would rotate in the same direction in which it revolved. Now, we have only to conceive this process repeated several times as the vapour mass continued to contract to understand the formation of the primary planets. We have only to suppose further that the larger vapour masses thrown off, as supposed, themselves contracted in the same way, and thus formed subordinate systems, to understand the existence of satellite systems like those circling around Saturn, Jupiter, Uranus, and Neptune. A ring such as the ring of asteroids or the Saturnian rings would, under exceptional circumstances, be formed instead of a single planet or satellite. And thus the main features of the solar system are accounted for.

But this ingenious theory does not account for some peculiarities which are scarcely less remarkable than those on which it has been based. In particular it does not account for the strange disposition of the masses of the solar system. Why should the inner family consist of minor bodies, in the main unattended, while the outer consists of giant orbs with extensive families of satellites? Why should the innermost members of the outer family of planets be the largest, while just within there lies the family of asteroids, not only individually minute, but collectively less (as Leverrier has proved) than Mars or even Mercury? Why should the two middle planets of the inner family be the largest members of that family? Laplace's theory gives no account of these peculiarities; nor perhaps could it be insisted that these peculiarities should be explained: yet, if any other theory should give an account of these features, explaining also the features which we have seen accounted for, then such theory would have a decided advantage over Laplace's. It is to be noticed also that Laplace's great nebulous contracting mass is a very unsatisfactory conception to begin with. No such mass *could* rotate as a whole. And lastly, Laplace's theory does not in any way correspond with processes still taking place within the solar system. It gives no account of the immense number of meteor flights and comets still existing within the solar domain.

In the next chapter I shall attempt to maintain a theory of the evolution of our solar system which has in these respects the advantage of Laplace's, and which I believe to accord much better, on the whole, with the real order of events in the past history of the solar system.

II.

It will be remembered that in my last chapter I mentioned the peculiarities of the distribution of the masses composing the planetary system as an objection to Laplace's theory of the formation of that system. These peculiarities have long been recognised as a stumbling-block in the way of any uniform theory of growth. Humboldt (of whom, however, it is necessary to remark that he is not of authority as an astronomer) noted long since the very peculiar arrangement of the planets as respects their dimensions, and specially as respects their mass. I propose, briefly, to indicate the evidence on this point.

First, let us see how the masses are arranged. The following table is useful for this purpose:—

	Mass (Earth's as 1000).	Distance from the Sun (Earth's as 100).
The Sun	315,000,000	—
Mercury	65	39
Venus	885	72
The Earth and Moon	1,012	100
Mars	118	152
(Here intervenes the family of the Asteroids.)		
Jupiter	300,860	520
Saturn	89,692	954
Uranus	12,650	1,920
Neptune	16,773	3,004

The mass of all the asteroids together amounts probably to 100 on the above scale, or about one-tenth part of the earth (Leverrier has shown that the asteroids cannot be equal to a fourth of the earth in mass); and we may set their mean distance of about 275 on the above scale.

Now, here we see that the system is divided into two families perfectly distinct from each other, and each consisting of four primary bodies. If we add up the masses of each family, we get for the inner family 2,068, and for the outer family 419,975—that is, the outer family exceeds the inner in mass more than 200 times. The sun, however, exceeds even the outer family about 750 times in mass; and the inner family exceeds the intermediate family of asteroids about twenty times, probably, and certainly more than eight times in mass.

Here is already a wide diversity of distribution. And taking the families in order from the sun—the great ruling mass—we find nearest to him neither the most massive nor the least massive family, but the family of medium mass. The family of least mass has the medium position in the system, and the family of greatest mass is outside.

Again, while the most massive family travels outside the two other families, the two most massive members of that family travel within the two of inferior mass. Yet of these two the outermost is the larger.

A like diversity of structure is found in the innermost family, to which our earth belongs. The least primary member of the family travels nearest to the sun, the second is much larger, and the third larger still. But there the progression stops, the third being the largest of all, and the fourth the smallest but one of the primary members of the inner family.

I do not know of any means of accounting for all these peculiarities of arrangement. It would perhaps be as difficult to account for all the peculiarities of shape and development in a tree. But as the general features of a tree are accounted for by what we *know* of the laws of tree growth, so I conceive that any true theory of the growth and evolution of the planetary system should be competent to account for the general features of that system. It appears to me that Laplace's theory of the evolution of the system through the gradual contraction of a vast rotating disc of vapour accounts for none of these general features, but, on the contrary, the processes he conceived would lead to a general uniformity of structure such as the planetary system does not possess. I do not mean that all the planets would be equal in mass if the system had been formed as Laplace supposed, but that they should be arranged in order of mass according to some recognisable law connected with their arrangement in order of distance.

In searching for another theory of the evolution of our system we may take into account the point to which I referred in my last chapter—viz. that Laplace's theory does not correspond with processes taking place at the present time. We may enquire whether any process of development is now taking place, actively or otherwise. And then, if we can recognise any such process, I think it will be worth while to consider whether this process in some former more active season of its action might not be found to give a better account of the evolution of the planetary system than that impossible process of nebulous rotation which Laplace conceived before it was as yet known that the process *is* impossible.

It seems to me that this is the proper way to search for an explanation of the growth of our system. If we were ephemera and were desirous of determining how a tree had arrived at its present condition, we might, if we pleased, imagine that some great mass of vegetable matter had shrunk into tree shape, or we might equally well at the beginning of our labours imagine that the tree had grown from some prior inferior form until it had assumed its present dimensions. But if, as ephemeral life proceeded, generation after generation gathering knowledge, we ascertained that the tree was still growing (though very slowly) by such and such processes, I conceive that the natural result would be to prefer the theory of growth to the theory of contraction. If further enquiry showed the theory of contraction to be inadmissible, because it was found that no vegetable masses, such as those which had been *conceived* to produce trees by a process of contraction, either did or could exist, we should find ourselves still further attracted to the theory that the tree had grown. And if, on careful examination of the evidence, it was found that the general features of

9

the tree could be explained by supposing that the present process of growth had once taken place much more actively, then I think a reasonable May-fly could form but one opinion.

He might not indeed conclude certainly that the tree had grown by those particular processes; but I think he would not be a rash ephemeron if he regarded that view of matters as altogether more probable than any theory of contraction.　Nor, I think, would he deserve to be blamed by other ephemera (not given perhaps to original investigation, and greatly submissive to the authority of eminent names) who would point out that the contraction theory had been advocated in former ephemeral periods by a highly distinguished ephemeron, whose opinion was not to be lightly opposed.　I conceive that our modern and innovating May-fly might reasonably reply to such censure, that while the memory of the eminent ephemeron of former hours was certainly to be held in all respect, yet his views could properly be opposed, for the simple reason that much new knowledge had been gained respecting the universe—that is, the tree—in the hours—nay, even whole days—which had passed since his hour.[1]

Viewing our universe in the same way, I think we can

---

[1] A student of astronomy, not wholly unknown to me, has used some such arguments in defending himself from the charge of audacity in maintaining new views respecting the stars against the authority of the deservedly eminent astronomer Sir W. Herschel, and in controverting the arguments of the great mathematician Laplace respecting the evolution of our solar system.　I think his reasoning is fair enough.

more hopefully discuss past processes resembling in nature, though not in degree, those at present taking place than the contraction of impossible nebulous masses.

Now, so soon as we turn our thoughts to meteoric indraughts as the source whence planets gathered their substance, we begin to see reasons for the general features of the solar system.

In the first place, we should expect planets near the sun to be small. For the sun's enormous might, exerted from the beginning of his existence as a central aggregation, would cause all meteors which passed within moderate distances from the sun (within such distances, let us say, as two hundred millions of miles) to have at those distances enormous velocities. We know what such velocities would be, supposing such meteoric masses to have travelled sunwards from very great distances. Quite close to the sun the velocity would be about 380 miles per second, and 200 millions of miles from him it would be about eighteen miles per second. It would be meteors rushing along with velocities ranging between these which would have to be captured to make planets within moderate distances of the sun. Velocities so great would give them power to escape for the most part. Only those actually impinging on the gathering minor aggregations would be captured.

It would be at some great distance—say, such a distance as Jupiter's—that the first really important secondary aggregation (the sun being regarded as the great primary aggregation) would be formed. Here there would be still abundance of material, but the great reduction of velocity at this distance (whether matter arriving at its journey sunwards were considered or matter voyaging away after close passage round the sun) would give a gathering mass the power to capture more matter, and so by growing rapidly to acquire fresh influence, and soon to become pre-eminent among all the subordinate aggregations.

Here, then, we should have the giant planet of the universe—not so far from the sun that the matter travelling hither and thither would be too greatly reduced, but so far away that such matter would not move too rapidly to be readily captured.

Outside this great secondary aggregation there would be aggregations smaller and smaller, owing to a reduction in the quantity of matter not compensated by the now slow reduction of the velocities. For while in the sun's neighbourhood a distance of 200 millions of miles reduces the velocity from 380 miles per second to eighteen miles per second, the velocity at Jupiter's distance is eleven miles per second, at Saturn's eight, at Uranus' six, and at Neptune's nearly five miles per second, a very much smaller proportionate reduction.

And I think that the general features of the system within the orbit of Jupiter are fairly accounted for by the theory of meteoric aggregation. For close to the sun the great velocities would enormously overbalance the great excess of material here. We should see then the least member of the inner family nearest to the sun. There would be a gradual increase of size and importance until a maximum was attained in the case of the earth, and then as gradual a falling off towards the zone of asteroids—the region, on this view, where the influence of Jupiter on the one hand and the sun on the other would each operate to prevent the formation of a subordinate aggregation, though not preventing a cloud or flight of relatively insignificant aggregations from forming.

I do not enter further here into the details of this theory, because I have already considered them fully in my 'Other Worlds.' I must, however, note one point. It may seem at a first view that this theory of the evolution of the solar system is inconsistent with the views I have enunciated as to the formation of the larger comets by eruption from suns, and of minor comets by eruption from the major planets. But it is not to be supposed that in the earlier stages of the history of our system matters were as they are now, and even now it may well be believed that enormous quantities of as yet ungathered materials are moving hither and thither throughout space. Growth and decay go on *pari passu.*

To revert to the tree which has already afforded so many illustrations of evolution theories—and illustrations so just in my opinion—we see that trees are continually throwing out matter, in leaves, buds, bloom, and fruit, which, falling eventually from the tree, is in a sense lost from its substance. This may be compared to the eruption or other emission of matter from the sun, and probably from the major planets of the system, as well in the present time as in long past ages. But this does not prevent us (and should not prevent a reasoning race of ephemera) from believing that the tree has grown continually even while such processes of throwing-off or loss have continued. Indeed, so constantly do we find the continuous gain of bulk which we call growth accompanied by as continuous a loss of matter, that it would be almost a fatal objection to any theory of the evolution of our system if it should fail in presenting *this* analogy to other known forms of growth.

But, indeed, it would be a mistake to suppose that we have gone back to the beginning of our system's history in showing how its present condition was probably evolved from a former condition. To quote words which I used two years ago in my book on the sun, ' In thus looking back at the past history of our system, we have passed after all but a step towards that primal state whence the conflict of meteoric matter arose. We are looking as into a vast abysm, and as we look we fancy we recognise strange movements, and signs as if the depths were shaping themselves into definite forms. But in truth these movements show only the vastness of the abysm, these depths speak to us of far mightier depths within which they are taking shape. ' Lo ! these are but a portion of His ways ; they utter but a whisper of His glory ! '

OUR DAILY LIGHT.

God said, Let there be light, and there was light.—Genesis i. 3.

We are in the habit of regarding the sun as a constant source of light and heat, to which we may always trust, day after day, year after year, and century after century. And yet if we follow the only evidence which we have upon the subject—apart, of course, from that continual supply of light and heat which the sun has afforded during past ages—we might well be disposed to feel doubt on the subject. When we consider the stars, and remember that they are suns like our own, we may look to them for information as to the general laws according to which the suns which people space exist—our own included. If we find among the stars the signs of change, some stars growing fainter, others growing brighter, some fading altogether from view, and others which had been invisible becoming conspicuous objects, we should be led to doubt whether the light of our sun may not one day wane or wax in lustre, whether he may not lose so much of his brightness as no longer to supply the wants of the creatures living upon the different planets of his system, or, on the other hand, blaze forth with so surpassing a splendour as to destroy those creatures by his excessive glory.

Now, although the stars do not teach us in this way to regard the sun's light and heat as *likely* to change very remarkably in the course of a moderate interval of time, yet changes sufficiently remarkable take place among them to show that we cannot place absolute reliance on the permanence of our sun's light and heat. I propose to consider a few instances of such changes.

Everyone knows the group of stars called Charles's Wain, consisting of seven conspicuous stars, three of which have been compared to the horses, while the remaining four indicate the outline of the wain or waggon. We have it on the authority of the most ancient records respecting the stars that these seven stars were once nearly equal in brightness. And in star lists made rather more than two hundred years ago we find that each of the seven was recorded as a star of the second magnitude.

We know further that Bayer, who assigning the Greek letters to the stars of a constellation followed as nearly as he could judge the order of brightness, gave to the middle star of the *seven* the *fourth* letter of the Greek alphabet, Delta. Now anyone who looks at that star group can see at once that this middle star of the set of seven is very inferior to the others in brightness. It is, in fact, now ranked as a star of the fourth magnitude, which implies, according to the best modern measurements of stellar brightness, that it gives out now about one-third part of the light that it gave out in former years. It is not known when the change took place; but it is certain that the star has thus sunk in brightness within the last two hundred years.

Now, this star is probably a larger orb than our own sun. There are reasons for believing that the five middle stars of the seven—that is to say, all but the farthest horse on one side, and the opposite angle of the wain on the other—are orbs forming a single family; and from a certain peculiarity which these stars exhibit in common, when examined by the spectroscope, it is inferred that they belong to a class of suns far larger than our own. But, whether this be so or not, it is certain that the four bright stars of the five are not inferior to our sun in the quantity of light they give out. The same was formerly true, of course, of the star which has lost, as we have seen, so large a proportion of its brightness.

Now let us try to picture what is meant by the change. Let us try to conceive what would have been the fate of creatures inhabiting our earth if the sun's light and heat had decreased in the same degree during the same short interval of time. Two hundred years may seem, indeed, a long period when compared with the duration of a single human life; but compared with even the history of a nation, it is little; while it sinks into insignificance by comparison with the intervals of time which history has to deal with.

Imagine what must have happened if, since the reign of Queen Elizabeth, our sun had lost his light and heat until he gave out less than a third of his usual supply. The loss of light and heat, so far as it affects merely the comfort of creatures living on the earth, would be of small importance. We bear without inconvenience the darkness of a cloudy day, or of many cloudy days in succession. We can endure protracted seasons of cold, so that, though we should be doubtless rendered uncomfortable by the change, it would not be absolutely unbearable so far as its direct effects would be concerned. But we must remember how wonderfully the various forms of life on our earth are adapted to the conditions which surround them. This is true of animal life, though some animals can bear change of climate and of place better than others: but it is especially noteworthy in the case of vegetable life. Every region of the earth has its own forms of plant life, unsuited to other regions, and incapable not merely of thriving but even of living anywhere save in their own *habitat*, or at least in some region very closely resembling their native place in all the chief circumstances which affect plant life. Now, a loss of even a third part of the sun's light and heat would correspond to a change in the conditions of the various forms of vegetable life which could not possibly be survived except by a few of the hardier sort. But if the sun, like the star Delta of the Great Bear, lost two-thirds of his lustre, it is certain that in a very short time scarcely any form of vegetable life would remain upon the earth. And it need hardly be said that animal life would inevitably perish if vegetation were destroyed from the face of our globe.

But the changes which have taken place in some stars have been far more remarkable.

In the constellation of the ship Argo there is a star which was recorded in Lacaille's Catalogues (in 1751) as of the second magnitude. Now, in 1677 our English astronomer Halley had described this star as of the fourth magnitude only; so that in the interval of eighty-four years (or less) this star had increased as greatly in brightness as the star Delta in the Bear has diminished. In 1811 and 1815 this star had again sunk to the fourth magnitude. But no long period elapsed before it had resumed its position as a star of the second magnitude. This was in 1826, and here it might be supposed were changes sufficiently remarkable. But a year later this star had risen to the first magnitude. Then, after returning for a while to the second magnitude, it increased again in brilliancy, until in 1838 it was one of the brightest of the first magnitude stars. It then diminished slightly, still, however, remaining in the first rank, until 1843, when it increased again until it very nearly equalled Sirius itself in brightness. From that time it diminished rapidly, until in 1863 it could only just be seen on the darkest and clearest night. It has remained thus faint during the last ten years.

Changes such as these—or even one of these changes

—if occurring in the case of our own sun, would destroy life very quickly from the face of the earth, and probably from all the inhabited planets of the solar system. The mere change from the second magnitude to a brightness approaching that of Sirius implies an increase of emission of light and heat more than tenfold. But from this amazing access of splendour how wonderful has been the falling off by which the star has been rendered almost invisible. It is absolutely certain that this star, once doubtless a sun, and probably like our own sun the centre of a scheme of circling worlds, gives out, day by day, far less than the hundredth part of the light and heat which it gave out daily only thirty years ago.

There are also cases where stars which had long been known to astronomers have disappeared altogether from view, so that their place knows them no more. It is possible that they may still give out some degree of light and heat, but the most powerful telescope fails to afford any sign of their existence, so that so far as our astronomers are concerned these stars must be regarded as extinguished suns. It is at least certain that they have lost so large a proportion of the light and heat they once possessed, that the change must seriously have affected the condition of beings living in the planets which doubtless circle around these once brilliant orbs.

But the sudden appearance of a new star is even more suggestive of the possibility of future change. Astronomers now know that those stars which have appeared for a short time, shining with great brilliancy, insomuch that they have sometimes surpassed even the leading stars of the heavens in brightness, are not in reality new stars. They are known stars, which after shining for a long time with but a faint lustre, have suddenly blazed out, owing to some mighty catastrophe which has taken place.

An instance of the kind occurred seven years ago, when a star suddenly appeared in the constellation of the Northern Crown, shining as a star of the second magnitude. It was found that it occupied the same place as a star of the tenth magnitude, and no doubt now exists that it was this known faint star which had thus suddenly acquired a new brilliancy; for though the star soon lost its great brightness, it can still be seen, as before, as a star of about the tenth magnitude. Now, when the star (appropriately called the Blaze Star) came to be examined with the spectroscope, it was found that a great portion of its light came from glowing hydrogen. Doubtless, by some circumstances the exact nature of which we shall never know, there had been a tremendous conflagration in that distant star. It was estimated that the brightness of the star increased fully eight hundred fold while this conflagration was in progress.

If a change such as this took place in our own time— and who shall say that such a change is impossible?—the prophecy of St. Peter would be fulfilled: ‘ The day of the Lord will come as a thief in the night; in the which the heavens shall pass away with a great noise; and the elements shall melt with fervent heat: the earth also, and the works that are therein shall be burned up.' For aught that is certainly known, the mere daily continuance of the sun's light and heat may be due to causes which need only be excited to unusual activity to produce such a catastrophe. We know now that the sun is undergoing processes which, although regular in their effects regarded as a whole, are locally irregular. Sometimes there are outbursts in the sun, which suggest very significantly the possibility of much more terrible, because more general catastrophes.

It seems, for instance, that a great local increase of solar action is produced when large meteoric masses fall upon the sun. Now, if it chanced that some large comet, arriving from outer space, should fall directly upon the sun, it is most probable that (as Newton once suggested) the effect would be a great, though temporary, increase in the sun's light and heat. Some comets have come near enough to remind us of the possibility of such a catastrophe. Newton's Comet (1680) passed at a distance of less than a third of the sun's diameter from his surface, and the comet of 1843 came even nearer. A very slight change in the direction of either comet, when still at a great distance from the sun, would have led to the catastrophe Newton feared. It may be that the catastrophe would do little harm, or would only affect the comet itself. But for my own part I cannot but think that the inhabitants of this earth have far more to fear from the fall of a comet upon the sun than from the once dreaded collision of a comet with our earth. It is no unreasonable inference that the great conflagration which caused the star in the Northern Crown to blaze out so remarkably, was produced by the downfall of a comet or flight of meteoric masses upon that orb. In this case it is quite within the bounds of possibility that our sun may one day experience a similar fate.

We are apt to forget these possibilities, 'for since the fathers fell asleep all things continue as they were from the beginning of the creation. For this we willingly are ignorant of, that by the word of God the heavens were of old, and the earth standing out of the water and in the water; whereby the world that then was, being overflowed with water, perished; but the heavens and the earth which are now, by the same Word, are kept in store, reserved unto fire against the day of judgment and perdition of ungodly men. But one day is with the Lord as a thousand years, and a thousand years as one day. . . . Seeing then that all these things shall be dissolved, what manner of persons ought we to be in all holy conversation —looking for the coming of the day of God, wherein the heavens, being on fire, shall be dissolved, and the elements shall melt with fervent heat.'

THE FLIGHT OF LIGHT.

Be not ignorant of this one thing, that one day is with the Lord as a thousand years, and a thousand years as one day.—2 PETER iii. 8.

ONE of the most startling thoughts suggested by the study of the heavens on a dark and clear night, is the recollection that what we look at is not what is actually in existence as seen. We turn our eyes to the blazing Sirius, and it seems incredible that in reality we are not looking at that noble sun as it is now, but as it was fifteen or twenty years ago. Yet nothing is more certain. The rate with which light travels has been measured in several ways, and no question can remain as to the accuracy of the result. It is certain light does not travel at a greater rate than 190,000 miles per second. Again, it is certain that Sirius lies at least a million times farther away from us than our sun.

Now, light takes more than eight minutes in reaching us from the sun, whose distance is more than 91,000,000 of miles; and it is easily calculated that the long journey from Sirius cannot be traversed in less than fifteen years. More probably it requires upwards of twenty years; and the greater number of the stars we see on a dark and clear night lie very much farther away than Sirius. Some of them certainly lie at distances which light can only traverse in hundreds of years. So soon as we turn, however, to telescopic stars, the range of time over which our vision extends is enormously increased, and it is certainly not too much to say that some of the fainter stars revealed by the great Rosse telescope lie at distances so enormous that their light has taken more than a hundred thousand years in reaching us. Then beyond these stars lie millions and millions of orbs yet farther away. There is no limit to the range of space occupied thus with the work of God's hands. All that has been taught us by astronomy suggests the lesson that every moment light reaches this earth from unseen orbs so far away that the journey over the vast abysses separating us from them has not been completed in less than millions of years.

And here a wonderful thought presents itself. We see the starlit heavens with the small organ called the eye, opening by a circle less than a quarter of an inch in diameter upon all these wonders. The telescope has enhanced the power of this organ, but the telescope does not, like the unaided eye, show the whole of the starlit sky at once. Yet again, even the telescope is but a minute instrument when compared with the very least of the celestial objects which it reveals. Now, if it be remembered that our estimates of the wonders of creation have been formed by these imperfect, these utterly feeble means, we begin to perceive that our conceptions of the universe are as nothing compared with the reality.

Imagine for a moment what would be seen if each one of us possessed a power of vision exceeding a million-fold that given by means of the Rosse telescopes. This conception, startling as it seems, does not alter the reality. The wonders we should then see exist, though they are unseen. They may be manifest to beings unlike ourselves, to the angels and ministers of the Creator. But whatever opinions we form on this point, we must not doubt that to the Creater Himself they are more than manifest. All our senses cannot suggest to us the absolute knowledge which He possesses of all His universe. We see, and touch, and smell, and taste, and hear, and thus come to know some little about the things nearest to us. But our knowledge even of such things is imperfect. And these senses are but five among myriads of possible senses, each one of which would add some new knowledge about every existent object.

The range of our senses, also, is exceedingly limited. We can understand this even from what we know of other creatures. The sense of smell in the dog, for example, is a sense utterly unlike our human sense in the information it conveys to the animal possessing it. A dog lives and moves among smells even as a man lives and moves among sights; it is probable even that some dogs can recognise the shape and something of the constitution of objects by the sense of smell, as perfectly as man by the sense of sight, and in some cases even more perfectly. The insect, again, possesses a range of vision and of hearing, possibly also of feeling, and smell, and taste, altogether unlike the corresponding range in the case of our senses. There are noises too shrill to be heard by our ears, which are clear to the audition of the insect. There are colours which to our eyes are as darkness, while to the insect they are beautiful, though with a beauty we are unable to conceive, since so feeble are our mental senses that we cannot even picture to ourselves colours, or imagine sounds, which our experience has not rendered familiar to us. And on the other side of the range of the senses, it is probable that the elephant, rhinoceros, hippopotamus, and bison, possibly also the whale and other large creatures, can recognise sounds too deep for human ears,[1] and perhaps colours beyond that red end of the spectrum where human vision ceases to distinguish colour. It may be added that even among men the range and the power of the senses vary considerably, thus reminding us of the fact that the senses are limited in their action, and indicating the possible existence of senses of the same kind, but of far greater range and power.

But so soon as we have taken these considerations fairly into account we begin to see that the aspect

---

[1] The deep mooing of the ox is probably the medium note of that animal's sound scale, and a similar conclusion may reasonably be formed in the case of other animals whose ordinary tones are exceptionally deep.

presented to us by the universe, either as actually seen or as revealed by the telescope, depends solely upon the powers and attributes given to man by his Creator. What we know of the universe is what our senses enable us to know, and is very far indeed from affording a true measure of the real universe, either in extent or in the complexity of its structure, or in the splendour of its various parts. In particular, and it is to this point that the considerations I have been dealing with have been directed, our senses are such that only one of them, sight, gives any evidence at all of the greater part of the universe, while this sense is so related to the peculiar form of motion we call light, that it can only tell us about any single part of the universe, as *that* part *was* at a particular instant so many years ago. It cannot bring into one picture the universe (or that portion of it which it reveals to us) as it all existed at any given time.

We learn by a view of the heavens that twenty years ago Sirius was shining with such and such brightness; that a hundred years ago some other star was shining with *its* degree of lustre, and so on; but the star depths are never revealed to us exactly as they are at the moment, or exactly as they were at any moment. Yet this is merely due to the imperfection of our senses. We judge by the light of these objects, and this light travels at such and such a rate. It is conceivable that creatures might have a sense enabling them to judge by some other form of action, exerted by the stars, as for instance by the action of gravity. If gravity were the action thus effective, the information conveyed respecting the universe would be far more nearly contemporaneous, since the action of gravity certainly travels many thousands of times faster than light,[1] even if it do not travel with infinite velocity as some philosophers suppose.

Thus we see that even only imagining the Creator to possess senses such as we have, but much more powerful, the aspect of the universe to Him would be very different from that which is presented to ourselves; and still more would this be the case if we conceived Him to possess senses by which other forms of force than our senses deal with would convey their information respecting the universe. Not only would a contemporaneous picture be presented through the action of some of these senses, but other senses would convey information such as our ordinary senses do not convey.

For the present, however, let us confine our attention to the teachings of the sense of sight, and reflect on some of the lessons which are suggested by the thought of what would follow from a great increase in the power and range of this sense. Let us dwell, in particular, on the startling thought that this sense, so enhanced, would

---

[1] This is not a matter of conjecture. It has been shown that if gravity travelled with a velocity equal only to that of light, the motions of the planets would be utterly different from those which have been observed since astronomy was a science; and a difference readily detectable would have resulted, even though gravity travelled a thousand times or a million times faster than light.

reveal to the creatures possessing it the history of long past events.[1] I use the word 'history' because, as a matter of fact, sight, like the other senses, conveys information about an event, and does not, as we are in the habit of supposing, reveal the event itself. The information is in all ordinary cases so direct and immediate, that it seems to us as though the event itself had been disclosed. But what has really happened has been that certain light-waves have communicated certain impressions to the optical nerve, and thence to the brain, and so the lesson has been conveyed that such and such events had transpired.

To return, then, to the creatures supposed to possess enhanced powers of sight :—They would be informed of the past. We are thus informed of the past history of the stars we see. But imagine only that we could see those stars (from our distant stand-point) so clearly that not only the shape and dimensions of their globes, and the nature of the processes taking place around and upon them were revealed, but that the worlds circling around them, and all that is—no, that *was*—taking place upon them, could be seen! Then we should be looking on while events which really happened many years ago were represented before our eyes. In ordinary speaking, we

---

[1] It is, perhaps, hardly necessary for me to remark that many of the considerations which follow have already been dealt with by the anonymous author of the ingenious and interesting little work called 'The Earth and the Stars.'

should see these events taking place, and yet in reality not only would these events have happened (in the case of most stars) long ago, but probably the creatures taking part in them would long since have passed out of existence.

It is when we imagine a converse process applied to our earth that the thoughts suggested become most instructive. Events have happened on our earth and have been forgotten, which, nevertheless, are at this very instant of my writing visible from some one or other of the orbs which people space, if only there are creatures on those orbs possessing such enhanced powers of vision as I have spoken of; and there is no event of such a nature as to be visible from standpoints without the earth, which has not been thus rendered visible over and over again as the light-messages conveying its history have passed beyond star after star (in all directions from the side of the earth on which such events took place); no such event which will not be thus rendered visible over and over again hereafter as the light-messages travel onwards into the star depths for years, for centuries, for millions on millions of ages, until time shall be no more.

Now, the conception of such powers of vision in creatures made by God's hands may be regarded as fanciful, though I apprehend that our ideas in such matters are very imperfect and feeble, and afford no measure of what is possible. But that the Almighty Himself is cognisant of all these light-messages who can question?

To Him who is everywhere, the light-record of all that
has taken place on earth is being continually conveyed,
the remembrance is ever present with Him; 'the eyes of
the Lord are in every place beholding the evil and the
good,' 'His eyes are upon the ways of man, and He seeth
all his goings.'

But, lastly, let us remember that even these thoughts,
startlingly though they impress upon us the fact that
nothing that is done shall be forgotten, are altogether
imperfect. It is well for us to form some idea of the
all-seeing vision of God, by speaking of the eyes of God,
and by comparing His knowledge with that direct knowledge of events which we obtain by means of the sense of
sight; but we must not forget that this mode of speaking
is really as far from the truth as are the poetical expressions by which the inspired writers speak of the might of
God's arm, or of His holding man as in the hollow of His
hand. There *is* that continual record of events by means
of light-waves travelling for ever and ever through space;
and beyond question, the Almighty is as cognisant of
those light-waves as of any event actually taking place
in this world or in others. But His knowledge is infinitely more perfect and complete than any we obtain
even of the simplest events by means of our senses.
'God looketh to the ends of the earth, and seeth under
the whole heaven. No *thought* can be withholden from
Him.'

A CLUSTER OF SUNS.

There shall be no night there.—Rev. xxi. 25.

In the previous chapter I spoke of the existence of senses
—that is, means of judging of external things—unlike any
that are possessed by mankind. It appears to me that
the study of astronomy is calculated to suggest ideas of
the kind, thoughts of what is unfamiliar to us, conceptions
of states of existence even unlike any that we know of.
For in studying astronomy we find ourselves brought into
the actual presence of systems where much must necessarily be quite different from what we experience here on
earth. It is of a system of this kind that I propose now
to speak.

When we search the heavens with powerful telescopes,
we perceive besides the stars certain cloudlike objects,
which have been called *nebulæ,* from a Latin word sig-
nifying a cloudlet. There are many hundreds of these
objects of various orders. But my present purpose is to
consider only one class of celestial cloudlets—the star
clusters. For many of these cloud-like objects, when
examined with suitable telescopic power, are found to
consist of myriads of stars. Within a minute space of

10

the heavens, since even in the telescope many of these cloudlets remain exceedingly small, thousands on thousands of suns are seen, and probably many thousands of suns are there also which are unseen, because smaller than the rest. Some of these objects are amazingly beautiful and splendid, insomuch that it has been said of one of them—a cluster called 13 Messier in Hercules—that probably no one who has beheld this cluster for the first time in a telescope of great power has been able to refrain from a shout of wonder.

Now, it was formerly held that these clusters of stars are in reality galaxies like our own Milky Way, sidereal systems whose stars are suns like our own separated from each other by distances like those which separate our sun from his neighbours among the stars. But certain very simple considerations oppose themselves to this view of the nature of the star-clusters, and show that they are really distinct in their nature from that part, at any rate, of the sidereal system to which our sun belongs. When we see one of these clusters of a rounded figure as a whole, and also gathering more and more richly towards its centre, always with a uniform roundness for each order of richness, we are certain that we have in view a globular system of suns. And when we look at any globe-shaped object of any apparent size, we know within what limits of relative distance the different parts of that object lie.

To explain my meaning—if there is a soap-bubble an inch in diameter, and a yard from the eye, we know that the farthest point of that bubble is farther than the nearest point by a thirty-sixth part of the bubble's distance; so much we could learn, let us say, by measurement: but if that bubble, so placed, looked just as large as a balloon very much farther away, then, although we could not tell by measurement how far off the balloon was, we should know without measurement that precisely the same relation held in the case of the balloon—namely, that *its* farthest point was farther away than its nearest point by a thirty-sixth part of the balloon's distance. And if the soap-bubble just concealed a star-cluster, or the sun, or moon, or in fact any globe-shaped object at any distance whatever, precisely the same relation would hold. Accordingly, though astronomers have no means of measuring the actual distance of any star-cluster—or, at any rate, have not yet succeeded in effecting such measurement—they can infer with great certainty within what limits of relative distance the parts of such clusters lie, because they can very accurately measure the apparent size of any star-cluster. Only, before passing from the soap-bubble illustration, let me warn the reader not to imagine that any star-cluster is so large as that illustration might suggest— a pin's head, at a yard's distance, would look larger than most of the chief star-clusters.

Now, when such a process has been applied, it is found that the farthest star in a star-cluster of the brighter and richer order cannot be at a relatively much greater distance than the nearest star of such a cluster;

and when due account is taken of the enormous number of stars in such clusters, it follows that, on a very moderate computation, the distance separating star from star in the heart of a rich cluster must be less than a millionth part of the distance separating the cluster from our sun.

But we can see the separate stars of these clusters, and sometimes with telescopes of no great power. We may, then, regard the stars thus seen as of at least the twentieth order of magnitude—that is, shining as brightly as stars of the first magnitude removed to but twenty times their present distance.[1] If, therefore, we could approach one of these clusters until we were within one-twentieth of its present distance, we should see its leading stars shining as stars of the first magnitude. But we should still be fifty thousand times farther from the cluster than its component stars are from each other, at least in the rich central region of such a cluster. What, then, would happen if we could continue our imagined journey until we were in the very heart of the cluster of suns?

It is very easy to answer. Suppose we were then midway between two leading suns of the group, then we should be at a distance from either equal to only the one hundred thousandth part of that which had

---

[1] These statements are all far within the truth, and are presented in their present form to avoid the necessity of a detailed account of the estimates of astronomers respecting star magnitudes.

separated us from the cluster when its leading brilliants shone as first magnitude stars. These two suns then would shine, not a hundred thousand times, but a hundred thousand times a hundred thousand times more brightly than our first magnitude stars. That is, they would shine ten thousand millions of times more brightly than Arcturus and Betelgeux, Capella, Vega, and Aldebaran. But this is equivalent to saying that they would each shine as a sun not quite so brilliant as our own sun, but still with much more than sufficient brightness to give broad daylight to any world placed where we have supposed our voyager to have arrived.

This, however, is far from being all. I have spoken thus far of but two stars out of the thousands on thousands composing the star-cluster. All these thousands would shine with a brightness enormously exceeding that of any of the stars we see, and many hundreds among them would appear as suns, smaller than the two nearest suns before considered, but bright enough with their sole lustre to banish night.

It follows, then, that to a globe placed as we have supposed, and travelling around one or other of the suns composing the cluster, night would be absolutely unknown. There would be different degrees of daylight, from the broadest day on the part of the globe turned fully towards the nearest sun, to a less brilliant day on the opposite part turned to other suns, but always day, often very much brighter than our summer noon, and seldom fainter, since the number of suns would make up for the comparative smallness of each.

Here, then, is a state of things utterly unlike any with which we are familiar. We can hardly suppose that those distant star-clusters are mere barren lights, when we remember that they are among the most stupendous creations in the universe. We know that the component stars are suns such as ours; we know that these suns are counted by thousands and tens of thousands: we cannot imagine that all this wealth of matter is glowing without any purpose. We conclude, then, that there are worlds within that cluster, and the condition of such worlds can be no other than that which has been described above. There is perpetual light, a perpetual supply of heat; there are no seasons, no days, and, so far as we can judge, it can be a matter of no moment to the inhabitants of such worlds whether the orbs they live on circulate in orderly paths around some particular sun of the system, or travel now for a while round one, then around another, wandering from sun to sun, even as astronomers suppose that the comets have wandered which come from out the inter-stellar spaces to visit our solar system.

Of course it would be idle to attempt to form any idea of the nature of beings inhabiting such worlds. It is quite out of our power to judge in what way the inconveniences which we should certainly experience in these regions may not only be altogether obviated, but replaced by advantages of which we can form no conception.

We can, however, form some idea of the wonderful scene presented to the inhabitants of such a world, because in reality it is no other than that which would be presented to ourselves if all the stars seen on the darkest and clearest night were to grow suddenly in lustre until the faintest shone with light enough alone to banish night. The wonderful scene thus presented must be carried round by a stately motion of rotation precisely as happens with our own star sphere. Suns must be always rising and always setting, only the magnificent colours which adorn our skies at sunrise and sunset must be wanting there, banished by the excess of splendour. It is manifest that, at least when the sky is clear, there can be no shadows in the landscapes on those distant worlds, since every quarter of the sky must have its suns. When the sky is partially clouded, there will be shadows, though not well defined shadows such as we recognise, but rather the lightest possible shade on those sides of objects which lie towards the clouded portion of the sky.

But there is one circumstance in the condition of the inhabitants of these worlds which is not only interesting but instructive. Doubtless there are among them reasoning beings who are led to enquire into the nature of the universe. In pursuing this enquiry they must in the first place encounter precisely the same difficulties which our terrestrial astronomers have met with. Each world must seem to the ordinary senses of its inhabitants the centre of the universe—the largest, finest, and most important of all created objects. But doubtless the careful study of the motions of the heavenly bodies has led many races of reasoning creatures in worlds placed amidst the star-clusters to the conclusion that the seemingly small orbs which shine in their skies are much larger than the worlds they inhabit; and we may readily believe that in some cases these beings have been able to form just ideas of the system or scheme of suns forming the star-cluster they belong to.

But *here* their researches into the extent of the universe must certainly cease. For the blaze of light from the thousand thousand stars of their firmament must blot out all light from beyond. Their whole sky—by which I here mean the illuminated air which in the case of our own daylight limits our range of view, and forms a veil beyond which we cannot penetrate—their whole sky must be far more resplendent than ours, because every part has its hundreds on hundreds of suns. In this great splendour exists a perpetual limit to all extension of their researches into the constitution of the universe. The light of their myriads of suns blinds them to lights which lie beyond: their system of suns is their universe; and though the universe thus revealed to them is magnificent and stupendous, yet we can see how minute it is compared with what is revealed to ourselves, when we remember that we can perceive many hundreds of such systems of suns.

Thus we learn how an excess of light may hide more than it reveals. We may picture the inhabitants of worlds in some glorious star-clusters rejoicing in their knowledge of the splendour and extent of their sun system, all unknowing of the far greater glories which the perpetual light of their skies conceals from them ; even as the man of science who trusts to science alone is too apt to glory in what is known, forgetful how the pride of material knowledge may blind him to far more important truths. Light is good, and science is good, but not *all* knowledge comes either with the light of day or with the light of man's unaided reason. Night has its revelations, more wonderful in reality though less splendid in seeming than the sun which rules the day. A true poet (though one that sang not often) has well said—

> Mysterious night! when our first parent knew
> Thee from report Divine, and heard thy name,
> Did he not tremble for this goodly frame,
> This glorious canopy of light and blue?
> Yet, 'neath a curtain of translucent dew,
> Bathed in the rays of the great setting flame,
> Hesperus with the host of evening came,
> And lo! creation widened in man's view!
> Who could have thought such darkness lay concealed
> Within thy beams, O sun! or who could find,
> Whilst fly and leaf and insect stood reveal'd,
> That to such countless hosts thou mad'st us blind!
> Why do we then shun death with anxious strife?
> If light can thus deceive, why may not life?

WORLDS RULED BY COLOURED SUNS.

IN the heavens there are stars of many colours; for one
star differeth from another in glory. But the colours we
see with the unaided eye are far less beautiful and less
striking than those which are brought into view by the
telescope. And among the coloured stars seen by the
telescope there are none more beautiful than the coloured
pairs of stars. Amongst these we find the most strongly
marked contrasts—such combinations as green and red,
orange and blue, yellow and purple; then, again, we
sometimes see both the companions of the same colour;
and yet again we find combinations where the contrast,
though not so striking as in the pairs first mentioned, is
nevertheless exceedingly beautiful, as when we have gold
and lilac, or white and blue, or white and green stars;
and, lastly, we find among the smaller companions of
double stars such hues as grey, fawn, ash-coloured, puce,
mauve, russet, and olive.

It was long thought that at least the more strongly
marked colours, in the case of small companion stars,
were due merely to contrast. Thus, if the larger of two

stars were orange, the smaller if really white would look blue, as anyone will perceive who will place on a sheet of dark paper a large orange-coloured wafer and close beside it a small white one. In like manner, if the larger star were red, the smaller would look green; if the larger were yellow, the smaller would look purple; and *vice versâ*: only I may as well remark here that while the larger star of a pair is often red, orange, or yellow, it is never blue, green, or purple—at least, such colours are never strongly marked in any leading star of a pair or in any single star.

But the supposition that the colours seen in double stars are due to contrast has been in several instances completely disposed of, by so arranging matters that one star only of a pair is seen at a time. This can readily be arranged where the stars are not very close, and in a great number of cases it has been found that the small star, seen alone, was really blue or green or purple, as the case might be. The experiment was in one case tried in the case of a very close pair, in a very interesting way. The star in question is the ruddy Antares, called also the Scorpion's Heart. This star has a minute green companion, far too close to the red primary star to be seen alone by any arrangement of the telescope. But advantage was taken by an eminent observer of the passage of the moon over this star. In a moment or two the moon hid the larger star, leaving the other shining alone, and then it was seen that the small star was unmistakably green.

The colours of the double stars, then, are real, so that if we could pay a visit to one of these pairs we should find coloured suns—red, orange, and yellow ruling suns, and green, purple, or blue minor suns, or, as the case might be, lilac, puce, mauve, russet, or olive suns of the smaller sort. Nor must we think of these smaller suns as really small in themselves. It is only by comparison with the leading orbs of unequal pairs that the lesser is called small. In reality it is probable that many of the lesser suns of these double systems are very much larger than all the planets of the solar system together.

But before proceeding to consider the state of affairs in worlds governed and illuminated by double suns, a point as to the colour of these suns has still to be considered. I have said that the colours are real; but it is to be noticed that there are two ways in which this may be explained. The light of a star may be actually coloured; or it may be white, but shine through some coloured transparent substance. We may take for illustration of a coloured light of the former kind the red fire, blue fire, and so on, of fireworks. Here the light is really coloured. As an illustration of coloured light of the second kind we may take red and green railway signals. Here we have lights which in one sense may be said to be really coloured, since their colours are not due to contrast or imagination or any like cause. Yet we know that the light is really white, and only appears red or green according as it shines through red or green glass. Now, it is manifestly a very interesting question to decide whether the colours of the double stars are to be explained in one way or the other. Of course we know that the coloured stars are not shining through any substance resembling glass. But since it has been ascertained that the light of every star in the heavens (at least every star yet tested) shines through vapours which must to some degree modify its colour, the question is naturally suggested that in the case of the very marked colours of certain double stars the real cause of the colour is to be sought in the nature of the vaporous envelope.

This has, in effect, been found to be the case in the few instances where it has been possible to try the experiment. It will not be difficult to convey an idea of the general principle on which the enquiry depends. When we examine the light of a star through a series of properly arranged prisms of glass, we get a rainbow-tinted streak of light, as in the case of the sun, only of course very much fainter. Also, precisely as in the case of the sun, the star's rainbow-tinted streak—or *spectrum*, as it is called—is crossed by a multitude of dark lines, which we know to be due to the presence of a number of vapours in the atmosphere of the star. Here I used the word atmosphere, but the reader must not fancy I mean anything resembling our own air.

Every one of these stars has an amazingly complex atmosphere of glowing vapours, so intensely hot that such substances as iron, copper, and zinc are not merely melted, but turned into vapour. Now, all stars are not alike as respects these vaporous envelopes. Some have substances in their atmosphere which others have not. And, again, some have apparently a much greater proportion of some substances than of others. Accordingly the dark lines across their spectra are differently arranged. Some have many dark lines in the red part of the rainbow-tinted streak, so as in fact to have a great part of the red light cut off, and to shine therefore with a superabundance of the yellow, green, and blue. Such stars have a greenish light. Others have most of their dark lines in the yellow, and so assume a purplish colour. And others have most of their lines in the blue part of the rainbow-tinted streak, and so shine with an orange light. And of course it happens in many instances that the dark lines are spread with tolerable uniformity over the whole length, or the greater part, of the rainbow-tinted streak.

The reader will see at once that the method of observation here indicated supplies the means of answering the question whether the colours of the double stars are inherent or caused by the absorbing action of the vaporous envelopes surrounding these stars. The process has been applied very successfully to a beautiful double star called Albireo, or Beta Cygni (that is, the second star of the Swan). This star is seen, even with a small telescope, to be double, and one of the stars, the brightest, is orange, while the other is of a beautiful blue colour. Now, when Dr. Huggins, the eminent spectroscopist, examined the spectra of these two stars, he found that whereas in the case of the orange star there are several strong dark lines in the blue part of the rainbow-tinted streak, in the case of the blue star there is quite a cloud of fine lines in the red and orange portions. Hence we learn that the two stars owe their colour to the nature of their vaporous envelopes. Each star glows in reality with a white light; but the white light has in one case to pass through vapours of a somewhat ruddy hue (because absorbing blue light), and therefore this star looks ruddy, while the light of the other star shines through bluish vapours, and therefore this star looks blue.

We do not yet know how it chances that the vaporous envelopes of these stars, and of other pairs of stars, differ in this way. Perhaps we shall never know. It is, however, an important gain to our knowledge to have ascertained that the colours of the double stars are not inherent, but that these stars are, as it were, celestial signal lamps, shining through coloured matter.

And now let us turn our thoughts for a brief space to the consideration of the state of the worlds circling around coloured pairs of suns. It is not quite clear what sort of arrangement would commonly prevail—whether such worlds would circle round the pair, travelling outside both, and having as the true centre of their motions the centre of gravity of their ruling pair of suns, or whether each sun of the pair would have its own family of dependent worlds. It may be that both arrangements would sometimes prevail in one and the same system. To show how this might be, we may conceive the following modification of the solar system.

Suppose Jupiter somewhat larger than he is, and attended upon by a larger and more important scheme of worlds. Also suppose Jupiter to be a subordinate sun—blue, green, or purple, as may best please the imagination. Then the other planets would be regarded as the sun's family, and of these, four—Mercury, Venus, the Earth, and Mars—would revolve as now around the sun, and within the path of Jupiter, his companion sun; the other three—Saturn, Uranus, and Neptune—would revolve outside both the pair of suns; and, lastly, there would be a scheme of worlds circling specially around the smaller of the two suns.

In some cases, however, very different arrangements would be requisite for the stability of the system. For in our illustrative case Jupiter travels nearly in a circle round the sun; but some of the double stars move on very eccentric paths. Now, when the smaller star of the pair, travelling along with a family of dependent worlds, came sweeping close round the leading star, it would not only be exceedingly probable that some of the family would be left behind owing to the superior attractive power of the chief sun, but it would certainly happen that all the creatures living on the worlds thus brought into unusual proximity to a sun much larger than their own would suffer seriously, *unless* the family of worlds belonging to the smaller sun were close to their own ruler. To use Sir John Herschel's expressive words, ' unless closely nestled under the protecting wing of their immediate superior, the swoop of their other sun in its perihelion passage round their own might carry them off, or whirl them off into orbits utterly incompatible with the conditions necessary for the existence of their inhabitants.' We may well agree with what Herschel proceeds to say, that ' we have here a strangely wide and novel field for speculative excursions, and one which it is not easy to avoid luxuriating in.'

In whatever way the systems depending on double suns are arranged, this at any rate is certain, that the beings inhabiting any world in any one of these systems have two suns. There may be, and in many cases there must be, a great inequality between the apparent size and brightness of the two luminaries, but we cannot question that even the lesser (in appearance, as viewed from any particular part of a double sun system) must be a veritable sun.

Taking the lesser suns of an unequal pair as seen from the earth, it must be remembered that that orb which looks so faint is in reality glowing with so great an intensity of heat and inherent lustre, that its light has passed to us after travelling over the tremendous abysses that separate us from the fixed stars. It is not an opaque orb shining by reflected light, but a mass of matter instinct with fire. We know this from its spectrum, which shows that in its atmosphere are the vapours of elements which our fiercest furnaces can only liquefy. If, then, we could approach that self-luminous orb, we should find long before we reached the confines of its system that it is a true sun. And within its system—as seen, in fact, from a distance which, though enormous, is reduced to absolute nothingness when viewed from *our* enormous distance— it is certain that the star is a sun in this sense, that it is capable of dispelling night, that when it is above the horizon of any world having airs like ours there must be a glowing sky like that which, during our own day, hides the stars from our view.

Thus every one of the worlds, in systems belonging to a double star, has a quadruple alternation, in place of that double alternation which we call day and night. There is, first, 'double day,' when both suns are above the horizon; next, single day with one sun; then, single day with the other sun; and, lastly, true night when both suns are below the horizon.

In my next I shall consider some of the results which must follow from these singular vicissitudes as well as the peculiarities of scenery, &c., which must prevail in worlds circling around coloured double stars.

I WILL consider, first, the case of a world circling as our earth does in her orbit, but around a sun of a rich orange colour, while a companion sun of a blue colour travels around the same sun [1] on a path resembling that of the planet Jupiter. The blue sun would be a large and brilliant orb, as seen from the world whose condition I propose to describe; but the orange sun would necessarily be far more brilliant and look far larger, being in reality the larger sun, and also the nearer. We will assume that the world we are considering has a moon somewhat like our own, and we may reasonably imagine that several other planets travel around the orange sun, others around both suns (that is, outside the path of the blue sun), and that, again, the blue sun has several planets travelling in immediate dependence upon it.

Now, in the first place, let us take the case where the world is between the orange sun and the blue one, and let us suppose that the season corresponds to our spring. Then it is manifest that since one sun illumines one side

---

[1] Speaking exactly, we should say that the two suns circle around their common centre of gravity; but here I deem it sufficient to use such expressions as accord best with ordinary modes of speaking.

of the globe, and the other illumines the other, there can be no night; it is orange day to one half of the world, and blue day to the other. Moreover, since the season corresponds to our spring time, it follows that orange day lasts exactly as long as blue day, and using for convenience the division of the day into twenty-four hours (which may or may not be nearly the same as our terrestrial hours), there are, all over the world, twelve hours of orange day and twelve hours of blue day. This, however, would not last very long, any more than on our own earth we have Jupiter visible all night for any length of time. The blue sun would gradually take up the position which Jupiter has when he is an evening star.[1]

Now, we can easily see what would follow from this. The blue sun would, in fact, rise before the orange sun had set. Thus there would be orange day as before, but towards orange sunset there would be two suns, the orange sun nearing the west, the blue sun passing over the eastern horizon. Then would come orange sunset and blue day; but the blue sun would set before the orange sun rose, and there would be therefore a short night, though no doubt not a dark night, since there would be blue twilight in the west and orange twilight in the east. Gradually the length of this night would increase, the length of the double day also increasing, but the orange and blue hours gradually shortening. At

---

[1] This would happen at least if the blue sun were going the same way round the orange sun that the planet was going.

length the blue sun would have drawn quite near to the place of the orange sun in the heavens, and there would be double day and night, but neither orange day nor blue day alone. The double day would probably be white, since the colours of the two suns are supposed to be complementary. After this the blue sun would pass to the other side (the west) of the orange sun, and would be placed like Jupiter when he is a morning sun. There would then be blue morning, white day, orange evening, and night, the night gradually growing shorter and shorter, until at length the blue sun would be opposite the orange sun, and there would be no night, but simple alternation of blue day and orange day, as at first.

I have not, in following these changes, taken any account of the varying seasons, because except when the two suns are together or opposite to each other, the considerations involved become rather more complicated than is desirable for these pages. But I will now, without following the blue sun round again, consider the effect of seasonable peculiarities when the two suns are on opposite sides of the earth. (When the two suns are together, the effects are of course the same as those recognised in our ordinary seasons.) Now, first, be it noticed that whatever be the pose of the earth, if the two suns are on opposite sides of her there cannot be any night, since one sun must illumine one half, the other sun illumining the other. *But,* whereas when the earth is posed as our earth is in spring, or autumn, there is everywhere equal orange day and equal blue day, this is not the case at other times.

Thus suppose the northern pole bowed towards the orange sun, as the northern pole of our earth is bowed towards our sun in summer, then in northern regions there is a long orange day, and a short blue day, and the reverse in southern regions. All round the northern pole—that is, within the regions corresponding to our Arctic regions—the orange sun does not set and the blue sun does not rise throughout the twenty-four hours; while in the corresponding southern regions the blue sun does not rise, and the orange sun does not set. At the equator, however, orange day and blue day are equal. Of course all is reversed when the southern pole is bowed towards the orange sun.

But now let us consider how curiously the moon of our imagined earth must vary in aspect. I will consider just a few cases to show how wonderfully complex and beautiful must be the variations of a moon belonging to a double sun system.

Suppose the two suns on opposite sides of the earth. Then it is clear that the moon's globe must (precisely like the earth's globe) have one half lit up by orange light, and the other half by blue light. Now the orange half will pass through all the phases that our own white moon exhibits. It will be in turn round, half-full, gibbous, full, gibbous again, half-full, round, and new. But the part of the moon which with us appears dark, or wanting, will be blue. Probably, as there will be no night, the moon thus coloured will not be at all conspicuous; yet it is not likely to be so faintly seen as our moon is in the daytime, simply because the peculiarities of colour must render it easily distinguishable from small clouds.

But next take the case where the blue moon is halfway round towards the place of the orange moon. Then the moon will have one half lit up by orange light and another half (not the opposite half) lit up by blue light; these hemispheres of her surface will overlap equally, so that half of each will be lit up both by blue and orange light. Thus in fact the moon's globe will be divided into four equal parts (like four quarters of an orange), one of which will be orange, the next black, the next blue, and the fourth white. How singular must be the aspect of a moon so illuminated, as it passes through the ordinary lunar phases with respect to either sun, on the skies of the earth whose condition we are endeavouring to picture!

Very singular also must be the aspect of the different planets which are variously illuminated by the orange and blue suns. Instead of shining as the planets of the solar system shine, with a nearly constant colour—their own inherent colour—the planets of a double sun system must vary in aspect according to their positions with respect to the two suns which illuminate them.

There is but one circumstance in which the celestial scenery presented to ourselves surpasses that which must be exhibited to the inhabitants of such a world as we have been considering. The glories of the star depths are seldom seen from such a world; night is the exception, and often for many weeks in succession there can be no real night, but an alternation of coloured days scarcely separated by brief periods of coloured twilight when the orange and blue suns are but slightly below opposite horizons. It may be that on this very account night, being rare, is more valued, and the magnificence of the night sky more imposing than with ourselves. But it is a strange thought that the astronomers of those distant worlds—for such worlds we must believe there are—may, in their zeal for science, undertake long journeys *to obtain more night* during which they may study the wonders of the starlit heavens.

Then, again, how wonderful must be those more special phenomena which correspond to our eclipses of the sun and moon, but are produced when one sun eclipses the other, or when one sun is eclipsed by a moon while the other sun is above the horizon, or when a moon is eclipsed as respects one sun while illuminated by the other! How strange the gradual change from white light to blue light as an eclipse of the former kind proceeds; or from orange to blue light, or from blue light to orange, as the moon conceals one or other luminary; while, when the moon is shining with white light produced by the combined lustre of the two suns, how strange must be the gradual appearance of a blue or orange shadow, according as the earth cuts off from the moon the light of the orange or blue sun !

And this leads us to consider the strange aspect which must be presented by ordinary objects—mountains, hills, buildings, plants, animals, and so on—when the two suns are both above the horizon. Where the light of both suns is falling there must be white light, or rather objects must appear, as they do in the white light of our own sun, with their natural colours. But parts which are in the light of but one of the two suns must show the colour of that sun, combined of course with their natural colour. There will only be true shadow where neither sun sheds its light. Or we may say that every object will throw a blue shadow opposite the orange sun, and an orange shadow opposite the blue sun, and that the part where the two shadows cross will alone be in true shadow. It will be manifest that natural scenery must present many beautiful varieties of effect altogether unfamiliar to us terrestrials, who know of no colours in scenery except those inherent in the objects themselves which form the landscape. Living creatures also must present a singular aspect, and to our conceptions an aspect not altogether beautiful, but too much like harlequinade to accord with terrestrial tastes.

The skies, however, must be often exceedingly beautiful. Our clouds have their silver lining, because it is the white light of the sun which illumines them. Our summer sky presents glowing white clouds to our view, and at

11

other times we see the various shades between perfect whiteness and an almost black hue, corresponding to the various degrees in which the illuminated side of a cloud is turned towards us. But imagine how beautiful the scene must be, when those parts of a cloud which would otherwise appear simply darker, shine with a fuller blue light or (as the case may be) with a fuller orange light. How gorgeous again must be the colouring of the clouds which fleck the sky when one or other sun is setting! At such times on our earth we see the most beautiful tints, owing to the various degrees in which the atmosphere affects the light of our single sun; but how wonderful must be the varieties of colour when, in addition to this cause of varying tints, there is a sun of complementary colour illuminating those parts of each cloud which would be simply dark were there no other sun but the orb which is actually setting!

I have, however, taken but the case of a single world in a particular double sun system, and I have considered but few of the various relations presented by the skies of such a world. The actual varieties of appearance even in one such world must be almost infinite. Then in each double sun system there are several orders of worlds, even as in our solar system there are major and minor planets, asteroids, satellites, and so on, to say nothing of comets and meteor systems. Doubtless the several members of each order are as wonderful in variety of structure and condition as the several members of our solar system.

Again, there are infinite varieties of arrangement depending on the relative dimensions of the suns of a double system, as well as on the shape of the paths they pursue: and in their colours again there are many varieties, as mentioned in my last paper—yellow and purple suns, red and green suns, equal suns of golden yellow, cream white, rose colour, and so on, companion suns of lilac, russet, citron, fawn, buff, and olive hue, in endless numbers.

Let it not be forgotten, in conclusion, that though there may be no world precisely like the one I have imagined, there must be many globes in double star systems where scenes very like those I have described are presented ; and that an almost infinite variety of arrangements must prevail among the thousands on thousands of such systems which astronomers have discovered. I conceive that few thoughts can be more striking and instructive than those suggested by this infinite wealth of beauty and variety. We see throughout the whole universe the same splendour on a large scale which is bestowed on a small scale upon the flowers of the field, which ' toil not, neither do they spin, yet Solomon in all his glory was not arrayed like one of these.'

THE KING OF SUNS.

WHEN we learn how enormously the sun surpasses all the members of the planetary family in bulk and mass, and how vast is the power represented by his light and heat, the idea is naturally suggested that the sun is either the leading orb in the universe or at least co-equal with those other suns the stars which exist in such countless numbers throughout space. It is sufficiently amazing to conceive that that glorious orb which astronomy pictures the sun to be, the scene of processes so stupendous, of outbursts so overwhelming, girt about by the wonderful corona and zodiacal light, attended on by a scheme of worlds among which our earth is but an insignificant body, and so mighty as respects attractive power that matter drawn to his surface from outer space reaches him with a velocity of nearly 400 miles in a second, should be repeated (as it were) hundreds and thousands and millions of times within the sidereal universe. But what is this thought even, amazing though it seems, to the consideration that our sun is not only inferior to a few suns, here and there, but actually belongs to an inferior order of suns; that the class to which he belongs bears to the chief known order of suns a relation as inferior as that of our earth and her fellow terrestrial planets to the giant orbs, Jupiter and Saturn, Uranus and Neptune, which circle outside the zone of asteroids?

Such, however, is the result to which scientific researches tend. I am not about to present the full evidence for the general statement I have just made, reserving the point for another article. What I now propose is to compare, so far as comparison is possible, a number of the leading order of suns—*the white stars*—with our sun, a member of the second order of suns—*the golden yellow stars*. I am about to describe what is known about the glorious star Sirius—the blazing Dog Star of the ancients. I speak of this star as the King of Suns, not as assuming that he is indeed the largest sun in the universe, but because he is the brightest star of his order visible to us, and the only sun in the universe of which it has been *demonstrated* that, taking light as the measure of magnitude, he surpasses our sun at the very least one thousand times in volume.

But how, it may be asked, can we estimate the magnitude of a star from its brightness, or, indeed, form any idea as to the dimensions of a body which even in the most powerful telescope appears as a mere point? For this is indeed the case with Sirius, notwithstanding the fact that in a powerful telescope we seem at a first view to see in this star a bright glare covering a considerable space. Attentive scrutiny soon reveals the fact that the glare is a merely optical phenomenon, and that the true

image of the star is a very bright point of light. It is
clear that if by any increase of optical power we could see
a star with a measurable disc, we should only need to know
the star's distance to infer the real dimensions of its
globe. But we can see no disc, and except in the case of
about a dozen stars, we cannot measure star-distances, and
only know that the stars lie beyond that distance which
our instruments are capable of measuring. How, then, can
we form an opinion as to real star magnitudes?

I proceed to explain what has been done towards the
solution of this difficult problem, noting that if the reader
should be dissatisfied with the nature of the evidence, he
must bear in mind that the astronomer has no choice but
to deal with the evidence supplied to him. It would be
very convenient if he would invent evidence, and he might
in this way give a much more striking and satisfactory
account of the mysteries of the star depths. But what we
want is the truth ; and the truthful astronomer must often
be content to give that answer which was the favourite
reply, we are told, of the eminent French mathematician
Lagrange, ' I don't know.' [1]

---

[1] This answer is not so favourably received, in general, as it should be. I
remember how on one occasion I was asked at the close of a lecture on the star
depths why I had not told my audience the true shape of the sidereal universe—that is, its relative length, breadth, and depth. I replied in effect
that before I could give this information I must first possess it myself, and
that as yet no man possessed it. I could perceive that the audience were
very far from satisfied with this reply. But I might have occasioned even
more dissatisfaction if I had said, what is in all probability the real truth,
that not only is man now ignorant of the configuration of the sidereal universe, but he can never hope to attain exact knowledge on the subject.

To determine the distance of an inaccessible object we must compare the direction in which it lies as seen from two stations sufficiently far apart. This, which is a principle of ordinary land-surveying, is equally true of the celestial objects. The astronomer determines the moon's distance by observing her from the northern and southern hemispheres, as from the Greenwich Observatory and the observatory at Cape Town; or else he takes advantage of the fact that the earth rotates on her axis, and so carries any given station from one side to another in a given time. The distance of the sun can be measured in no other (direct) way, and although we hear of the transits of Venus as means of which the astronomer avails himself to determine the sun's distance, yet the very same principle is involved—the value of a transit of Venus depending solely on the fact that the observers at two distant stations can in point of fact regard her as a celestial index, traversing the sun's face as an index plate, so that they possess, as it were, an instrument of survey more powerful than any terrestrial instrument.

To measure star distances the earth's dimensions are altogether too small. No instrument which man will ever make would show the slightest difference in the direction of any star as seen from opposite sides of the earth. But precisely as the measurer of the moon's distance need not leave his observatory, or have a companion observer working at a distant station, if he prefers to trust to the earth's rotation to sway his station from one side to the other—so the astronomer, unable to leave the earth to seek, as he would wish, a station millions of miles away, can nevertheless avail himself of the earth's motion of revolution around the sun, which in the course of six months will carry the earth from one side of her path to the opposite side, *one hundred and eighty-three millions of miles away.*   One place and the other (any two opposite points of the earth's orbit) may be regarded as two observing stations at the ends of a base line of this enormous length, laid down, as it were, to extend astronomical survey from the solar system to the stars.

It might be thought that this base line could not but be amply sufficient for the purpose in view.   But so much vaster are the distances of the stars, that until quite recent years this base line proved altogether too short for effective measurements, and even now only one star has had its distance fairly measured, while some nine or ten have had their distances roughly estimated.   All the rest which have been tried lie so far beyond our means of measurement as to show no signs whatever of change of place as the earth circuits around that orbit which to our conceptions seems so enormous in extent.

Now, the one star whose distance has been measured—Alpha Centauri—is found to lie more than 200,000 times farther away than the sun.   Moreover, the light of this star has been compared by means which need not here be described with the light that we receive from the sun, and has been found to be equivalent to about the 17,000 millionth part of the sun's light. But we can tell how much light we should receive from our sun if he were removed to 200,000 times his present distance. His light would be reduced not to the 200,000th part of its present amount, but to the 200,000th part of *that* reduced amount —or, in fact, to the 40,000 millionth part of his present lustre. So that he would shine *much less brightly* than the star Alpha Centauri if he were removed to the same distance. According to the best estimates of the star's distance, it must emit about three times as much light as the sun.

. But Sirius is much farther away than Alpha Centauri, and, moreover, shines much more brightly. Sirius is one of the nine or ten stars mentioned above as lying at distances not absolutely immeasurable. We cannot place much reliance on the results obtained in the case of Sirius, because his actual change of place as the earth circuits round the sun is so exceedingly minute. The best estimates assign to Sirius a distance exceeding that of Alpha Centauri five-fold—or rather that is the mean between the two best estimates. Taking this value, it follows that if Sirius shone no more brightly than Alpha Centauri in appearance, he must nevertheless give out twenty-five times as much light. But a careful comparison of his brightness with that of Alpha Centauri shows that he is about four times brighter. Therefore in reality he must give out about *one hundred times* as much light.

We have seen, however, that Alpha Centauri gives out .

about three times as much light as our sun. It follows that Sirius shines in reality *three hundred times* more brightly than the sun. Now, this implies that if the surface of Sirius is of the same intrinsic brightness as the sun's—that is, if on the average each square mile of the surface of Sirius gives out the same quantity of light as each square mile of the sun's surface—then the surface of Sirius must be 300 times as large as the sun's. It would follow that the diameter of Sirius is between 17 and 18 times as large as the sun's. (For 17 times 17 are less than 300, and 18 times 18 are greater than 300.) Hence the volume of Sirius would be about 2,200 times as great as the sun's (this number 2,200 being obtained by multiplying 300 by $17\frac{1}{3}$, which is nearly equivalent to multiplying $17\frac{1}{2}$ twice into itself). This is on the supposition of equal surface-lustre; and it cannot be regarded as certain that Sirius is not considerably brighter than our sun as respects his actual surface. Of course if this is the case, we cannot assume that Sirius is larger in so great a proportion as when we suppose his intrinsic lustre the same as the sun's.

But it is worthy of notice that the eminent French physicist St. Claire Deville considers it impossible that under any circumstances a surface can be much hotter or more luminous than the solar surface. We shall probably be within the limits of fact if we regard the surface of Sirius as not more than twice as bright as the sun's. This would leave his surface 150 times larger than the sun's, or, for convenience of reckoning, say 144 times; his diameter would thus be twelve times the sun's, and his volume 1,728 times the sun's.

Have I not rightly called Sirius a 'king of suns'? From that glorious orb, nearly 2,000 such orbs as the sun, that great and mighty globe, instinct with fire and life, might be formed, each fit to be the centre of a scheme of circling worlds as important as that over which our sun bears sway! And then conceive how vast must be the scale of the planetary scheme which Sirius doubtless rules over. Indeed, it *must* be vast for the mere security of its inhabitants. An orb placed as far from Sirius as Mercury or Venus, or the earth or Mars from the sun, would be scorched with a heat so intense that no life would be possible upon it. The distance of Jupiter would be better, but even there the supply of heat would be six times as great as that which we receive from the sun. At Saturn's distance a world would be illuminated and warmed half as much again as our earth. Only at a distance about one-fifth greater than that of Saturn, so long regarded as the most distant member of the solar family, would an attendant on Sirius receive the same supply of light and heat as we receive from the sun. In short, a scheme of planets bearing the same relation to Sirius as respects the supply of light and heat, which the planetary system bears to the sun, would have to be constructed on a scale twelve times vaster.[1]

---

[1] It would not even then resemble the planetary system in other respects; for the light and heat and attractive energy of Sirius are reduced at

After all, however, the most wonderful circumstance is that of which alone we are certain. We know nothing of the family over which Sirius bears sway; but we are well assured as to his own splendour and surpassing volume, and these are the features which afford the most surprising evidence of the wonders of the star depths.

In the next chapter, however, I shall have to consider yet greater wonders; I shall have to deal not with a king among suns, but with an order of kingly suns.

the square of the distance; and to make them equivalent to those in the solar system we have supposed all the distances enlarged in the same degree as his surface exceeds the sun's. But his might is more probably proportional to his volume, in which case the attraction he exerts remains still twelve times greater in the corresponding planets of the imagined system than our sun's attraction on the respective members of his family. Therefore, unless we further modify our supposition, we must set all the Sirian planets circling much more rapidly than the corresponding members of the solar family. They must, in fact, move $3\frac{1}{2}$ times as fast, and therefore have years correspondingly shortened. Thus the one corresponding to our earth would have a year of about $104\frac{1}{4}$ days, and the others in proportion.

In my last chapter I described a sun—the star Sirius—
so superior to our own in splendour, and doubtless in
magnitude, that it must be regarded as belonging to a
superior order. We might, indeed, if there were no
evidence to the contrary, regard Sirius as the king of
suns, not as a member of a higher order. We might
suppose that he is perhaps the central sun of the star
system, in which case his superiority over our own sun
would not be surprising, since it would correspond precisely with the superiority of the sun over the members
of his planet family. Indeed, this view was adopted
before it was known how enormously Sirius exceeds the
sun in magnitude. The great German philosopher Kant
regarded Sirius as the central sun of the universe, because
it appeared to him from other considerations that the
central sun should lie towards the region occupied by
the constellations Orion, the Hare, and the Two Dogs;
and Sirius being the leading star of that region (as indeed
of the whole stellar heavens) appeared to Kant very well
suited to be the ruling orb of the universe.

But, apart from all other considerations, the enormous
distance of Sirius shows conclusively that be cannot be

the orb which our sun obeys, far less the ruling orb over the stars lying far away beyond our sun towards the constellations Hercules, the Eagle, and so on, which occupy the region opposite to that in which Sirius is the leading orb. It requires no elaborate calculation to prove this. Roughly speaking, Sirius is a million times farther away than the sun; and since attraction varies as the square of the distance, his attractive influence is a million million times less than it would be if he were only at the sun's distance from us. Supposing his mass the 2,000th part of the sun's, it follows that his influence on the sun is but the 500 millionth part of the sun's influence on the earth.[1] This would be altogether in-

---

[1] It may, perhaps, interest the reader to learn precisely what the influence of the sun on the earth is, and so to infer the influence of Sirius on the sun. We must of course consider equal quantities of matter, and for convenience we will take that quantity of matter which we call a ton—that is, the quantity of matter which, placed on the earth's surface, weighs a ton, or produces that amount of downward pressure. Now, a ton of the earth's matter tends sunwards with a force only equal to that which would be produced on the earth by the downward pressure of 1 lb. 3 oz. 200 gr., or roughly 8,500 grains (New Avoirdupois, which is the same as Troy measure) Accordingly, on our assumption as to the mass of Sirius, which is probably above his real mass, a ton of the sun's mass tends towards Sirius with a force corresponding to the 500 millionth part of 8,500 grains, or roughly the 59,000th part of a single grain. This is probably the greatest attraction which any individual star exerts on our sun, and indicates the exceeding feebleness of the forces exerted on each other by the stars, regarding these forces as *moving* forces. The total quantity of attraction between Sirius and the sun is of course enormous, because the sun's mass is so enormous. But this total quantity is not what we have to consider in enquiring into that star's fitness to rule our sun. For its magnitude, we see, depends on the sun's magnitude, and of course his magnitude gives him independent power. In all such cases we have only to compare the attrac-

sufficient to sway the sun appreciably from his course. If, indeed, there were no other bodies in the universe than the sun and Sirius, our sun would circuit around Sirius, though the period of revolution would be enormously long. But as it is the attraction of Sirius is only one among thousands of attractions, exerted by the leading neighbouring stars; and the sun obeys the combined influence of these attractions, not the power of any particular star. Every other star also, including Sirius, is similarly influenced by the combined influence of all the rest.

Still Sirius, for aught that has yet been shown, might be distinguished above all other suns, and his influence, though far inferior to the combined influences of other suns, might still be paramount in the sense of being far superior to that exerted within the universe by any other sun whatever.

But we have now to consider evidence which points to Sirius as one only of a class or order of suns, and an order including a great number of stars.

I have spoken in former chapters of the teachings of the spectroscope respecting the stars; and in so doing I have mentioned specially what has been learned in this way about the colours of the stars. It has been shown

---

tions exerted on equal quantities of matter. Thus we may speak of Sirius's moving power on the sun as less than the moving power which our earth has on bodies near her surface (that by which she causes them to fall if unsupported), in the same proportion that the 59,000th part of a grain is less than a ton, or roughly as 925,000,000,000 to 1.

that the light of every sun is that arising from the in-candescence (or whiteness) of matter intensely hot; and that the colours of the stars originate in the gaseous envelopes surrounding the glowing core or heart of each. These envelopes are themselves intensely hot, glowing indeed with heat; yet compared with the fierce heat of the matter they surround they may be regarded as re-latively cool. They possess, according to their constitution, the power of cutting off various parts of the light issued by the suns to which they severally belong. For the spectroscope spreads out that light for us into a long rainbow-tinted streak, and across that streak we can see the dark lines showing where light of this or that particu-lar colour is wanting, absorbed by some special vapour in the star's atmosphere.

Now, I think it will appear very clear to the reader that if the stars really are of various orders, the spectroscope may probably possess the power of distinguishing one order from the other. A star very much larger and more massive than our sun should have, one would suppose, a different spectrum; for it is difficult to imagine that under the very different attractive power which such a globe would exert on its atmosphere the various vapours of that atmosphere would not be differently related to the glowing centre.

For example, if hydrogen were present in the same relative proportion in the atmosphere of so massive a sun, we might imagine that this gas, being the lightest of all known gases, would be extended above all other vapours in the star's envelope, as we see in the case of our sun; but also we should expect to find a much greater quantity of hydrogen outside the other envelopes of the larger star. And then the region where enormous pressure liquefied or solidified the core or crust of such a sun would lie relatively nearer the region where the hydrogen began to be mixed with other vapours. For light though hydrogen is, it would produce an enormous pressure in the atmosphere of so monstrous a sun as Sirius; and at the bottom of the hydrogen envelope (pure or nearly so) there would be a much greater pressure than at the corresponding part of the atmosphere of our own sun.

So that I think we should expect to find the hydrogen dark lines much stronger relatively in the spectrum of Sirius than in that of our own sun. And if this turned out to be the case, we should regard the peculiarity as characteristic of a very large sun; and if other stars gave the same kind of spectrum, we should be led to believe that they were also very large suns. We should not be prevented from adopting this belief by the faintness of such stars, unless we knew their distance; for they might be very much farther away than Sirius, and so rendered apparently faint, while really emitting as much light as he does. But our opinion would be very much strengthened if we found that the stars giving this particular spectrum included some of the brightest orbs in the heavens, orbs also known to lie either at enormous estimated distances, or so far away that all attempts to estimate their distance had failed. Our opinion would be still further strengthened—nay, I think it would grow into conviction —if we found that the stars giving this spectrum also showed a general resemblance to each other in tint.

Now, this is precisely the evidence which we have on this matter.

The star Sirius gives a spectrum ' crossed by four very strongly marked dark lines, which are those corresponding to the gas hydrogen.' Of six hundred stars examined by the Italian astronomer Secchi, about three hundred were found to give a spectrum of this kind. Most of these stars are distinguished by their great brightness and by their somewhat bluish tint. The class includes Rigel, the bright star on the advanced foot of Orion; Altair, the leading brilliant of the Eagle; Wega, the splendid gem adorning the Lyre; six of the stars of Charles's Wain; and other bright luminaries.

May we not infer with some confidence that these stars belong to a higher order than our sun—an order whose real importance is indicated by the demonstrated superiority of Sirius? It is true that Sirius is the only member of the order whose real lustre relatively to our sun's has been estimated. But this is only because the other stars of the order lie too far away to give any measurable indications of their true distance, or therefore any means of estimating their real lustre. And even as it is we can indicate in the case of most of them a great superiority to the sun, our only difficulty being in determining *how* great that superiority is. Take Rigel, for example. This star shows no signs of displacement as the earth circuits on her wide orbit round the sun. We may safely assume, then, that this star is *at least* twice as far away as Sirius, which *does* show a measurable displacement. So that if Rigel were put where Sirius is, he would shine *at least* four times as brightly as at present. But this would make his lustre equal to two-thirds of that of Sirius, or his real brightness 200 times that of our sun. Taking his intrinsic lustre, mile per mile of surface, as twice our sun's, we find his surface 100 times our sun's, his diameter 10 times, his volume and presumably his mass 1,000 times the sun's—*at least*, be it remembered. Precisely the same reasoning applies to Wega, whose distance has indeed been estimated to be twice that assigned to Sirius.[1]

We must not assume that because half the stars observed by Secchi gave this particular spectrum, therefore half the suns of our universe are of the larger order; for it must be remembered that the largeness and bright-

[1] By myself in my last chapter. There are in reality two estimates of the distance of Sirius, one by Henderson, the other by Cleveland Abbe. I take the mean of the two. It serves to show how extremely difficult all measures of such very distant bodies must necessarily be, to mention that Abbe's measurement exceeds Henderson's as 5 to 3. This, however, does not affect the inference of enormous distance.

ness of these bodies render them more amenable to spectroscopic investigation.

It remains to be shown, however, that other stars present different appearances under spectroscopic analysis. The evidence on this point is very clear. About one-half of the three hundred remaining stars examined by Secchi were found to give a spectrum similar in character to that given by our sun, only of course very much fainter. Among the stars belonging to this class are Capella, Pollux, Dubhe in the Great Bear, Procyon, and others.

But it is, perhaps, when we turn to Secchi's third order of stars that the most singular revelation awaits us. For he tells us that the stars of this order have a spectrum resembling that of a sun-spot; and he infers that the stars of this order are covered with many spots. An interesting confirmation of this view presents itself. We know that the spots on the sun are variable. Sometimes there are many, sometimes few or none. Now, a sun much more spotted than ours ever is would be exposed to yet greater variations, insomuch that we should expect its light even to vary as a whole, and perhaps to a considerable extent. Now, Secchi's third order includes the most remarkable variable stars in the heavens: Mira, the Wonderful Star in the Whale; Betelgeux, the singularly variable orange star, which is ordinarily the leading brilliant of Orion, but sometimes surpassed by unchanging Rigel; and other variable orbs.

A fourth order remains, respecting which I shall say

little, because in point of fact little is known. It includes about thirty of the stars observed by Secchi, chiefly inconspicuous orbs, but remarkable for their deep red colour.

Such is the evidence thus far obtained by the newest instrument of science.

THE DEPTHS OF SPACE.

WHEN we look around us into the regions which surround the solar system, and see the myriads of myriads of stars which are spread through space, it is impossible not to feel strongly the desire to penetrate the mystery of the star-strewn depths. We have learned much respecting the earth on which we live, and not a little of the system to which the earth belongs. We have at least so far solved the problems presented to us by the planetary scheme as to recognise the subordinate position which our earth holds within it, and that the sun is the mighty ruler whose sway guides all the planets in their courses. But the enquiring spirit of man is not satisfied with these discoveries. No sooner has he learned to regard the earth as but one of a system of worlds circling round the sun, and that that system has such and such proportions, and presents such and such forms of motion, than he desires to regard our sun as but one of a system of suns, and to ascertain what may be the nature and the scale of this higher system, what the movements taking place within it. This was the noble problem which the elder Herschel set as the great end and aim of all his labours: 'A knowledge of the construction of the heavens,' he said, towards the end of his wonderful career as an observer, ' has always been the ultimate object of my observations.'

It is in contemplating this problem that man is most forcibly taught the insignificance of the earth on which he lives—in point of size at least, though we must remember that ' great and bright infers not excellence.' So long as the study of external nature is limited within the bounds of the solar system, we are able to measure not merely the proportions, but the dimensions of the objects we study, but so soon as we pass beyond our solar system, the power of measuring is wanting—or at least is so limited as to serve us but for a short distance. We have learned the distances of about half a dozen stars, and even those distances have been only roughly ascertained; all distances beyond are immeasurable, and for the most part must remain so, it would seem, unless some new method of estimating star distances should unexpectedly be discovered.

We have to judge of the star depths around us, then, in some other way than by actual measurement. We must scrutinise them attentively and be on the watch for indications of various nature by which to form some idea of the laws of stellar grouping.

To this problem few astronomers indeed have devoted their energies, probably because it presents difficulties so enormous. The elder and younger Herschel, William Struve, Mädler, and one or two more, are all who can be named as having actually taken these questions in hand as astronomers, though Kepler, Kant, Lambert of Alsatia, Wright of Durham, and a few others have speculated more or less ingeniously respecting the sidereal system.

It is to the original mind of Sir W. Herschel that science owes the bold idea of *gauging* the star depths, of actually attempting to apply a measuring-line from our tiny earth by which to determine how far the stellar system extends in this direction and in that, until its whole figure should have been determined. The process, he suggested, might be compared to that by which the nautical surveyor charts the sea bottom, marking its depths and shallows, its hills and depressions, its peaks and mountains, its valleys and ravines. Precisely as the lead line of the seaman passes through more water where the depth is greater, and through less where the shallows lie, so Herschel conceived that the telescopic line of sight would pass through more stars where the stellar system has its greatest extension from us, and through fewer where the boundaries of that system are nearest to us.

He threw out the visual plumbline again and again, now sounding, *as he conceived*, the profundities of the star system, and now finding that the limits of the system were relatively close to us. He found that when the line of sight was directed towards the zone of the heavens where we see the Milky-Way, the telescopic field of view was nearly always rich with stars; but when he turned his telescope away from that zone, and especially when it was turned nearly square to the general level of the Milky Way zone, few stars could be perceived.

Accordingly, he concluded that the system of stars is flattened in shape, extending farthest where we see the Milky Way, and having boundaries which lie relatively close in, towards the parts of the heavens which lie farthest from the galactic zone. It was on this evidence that he based what has been called the ' cloven flat disc ' theory of the sidereal system. For the Milky Way has two branches through a considerable portion of its circuit, so that the greatest extension of the star system lies towards two planes, where the Milky Way is cloven. A good general idea of the shape of the stellar universe according to these results may be obtained by taking two wafers, and after wetting one-half of one of them—that is, a semicircle of its surface—applying the other thereto, so that we have a double wafer; but one-half of the double wafer has its two leaves disjoined. Now, if these two semicircular portions be slightly separated from each other with the point of a knife, so that they slope away from each other, we have a figure something like the cloven flat disc of Herschel's theory. Only it will be understood, of course, that he did not suppose there was anything like regularity in the shape which at this time he ascribed to the stellar system.

But as he went on with his observations, Herschel gave up the principle of star-gauging and its results. It is well to notice this carefully; because the text-books of astronomy say little on the subject, and what they say is for the most part inexact. Herschel began to perceive that there are laws of physical association, binding the stars together in schemes subordinate to the stellar system regarded as a whole. And he came to regard the Milky Way itself as a subordinate system, or as at least distinct in character from the parts of the star system lying around us. He wrote thus in 1802, seventeen years after he had enunciated the cloven-disc theory. 'Although our sun and all the stars we see may truly be said to be in the plane of the Milky Way, yet I am now convinced by a long inspection and continued examination of it, that the Milky Way itself consists of stars very differently scattered from those which are immediately about us.' And again in 1811 he said, 'When the novelty of the subject is considered, we cannot be surprised that many things formerly taken for granted should, on examination, prove to be different from what they were generally,[1] but incautiously, supposed to be. For instance, an equal scattering of the stars may be admitted in certain calculations; but when we examine the Milky Way, or the closely compressed clusters of stars, this supposed equality of scattering must be given up.' Now, it will be clear to all that the cloven-disc theory, and the principle

---

[1] It may be necessary to explain that the word 'generally' here does not refer to the number of those who have adopted the view referred to, but to the general sense in which the view had been adopted. No one can doubt this who has read Herschel's series of papers.

itself of star-gauging, were necessarily based on a belief in the generally equable scattering of the stars. In giving up this belief as a general rule for guidance, Herschel was in effect giving up the hopes he had formed when he thought of the method of star-gauging, as well as all the general results to which he had been led by the application of that method.

When Herschel was a very old man, close on the four-score years which so few attain without some signs of failing mental powers, he invented another method, commonly confounded in our text-books of astronomy with the method of star-gauging, but in reality quite distinct from it. In star-gauging he had estimated the distance of the boundary of the star system by the number of stars he could count in the telescopic field; in the new method he estimated the distance of star groups by the telescopic power required to resolve them into separate stars. A group like the Pleiades, or like the Beehive in Cancer, which can be resolved into stars with a very small telescope, lies relatively near to us, according to this theory; a group which can only be resolved with one of the mightiest of the telescopes which Herschel used lies very far away; and some groups which none of his telescopes could resolve lie at distances incalculable until some larger telescope can accomplish the resolution of the group.

I shall not say much of this principle. I believe Herschel himself would have abandoned it had he lived to test it thoroughly. A little consideration will show that it implies a uniformity of structure throughout the stellar system which is very little accordant with what Herschel had himself discovered while making those observations which led to the abandonment of the star-gauging method. It will presently appear that other and more decisive evidence of variety of structure has been obtained since Sir W. Herschel's time.

The reader will begin to see the nature of the methods by which alone the astronomer can hope to penetrate the mystery of the star depths. Each of the methods just described must be regarded as a kind of survey of the heavens—not of the heavens presented to ordinary vision, but of the heavens brought into view by the penetrating eye of the telescope. For if the human eye could suddenly obtain the power of telescopic vision, those wealths of star-strewing which it is the province of star-gauging to measure would be revealed to our view, not piecemeal, as under telescopic scrutiny, but at once as in a grand celestial panorama. Those varieties of distribution to which Herschel applied his resolution test would be clearly recognised. Here the stars would be seen spread richly over a region of the heavens, but clearly separated from each other; elsewhere would be regions where the stars would more closely cluster, though still separately discernible; but in parts of the heavens veritable star-clouds would be seen, regions where the stars gather so closely together that even the enhanced powers of vision I have imagined—nay, though the power of the Rosse telescope had been acquired by man—would fail to show discrete stars, the sky in those parts being aglow with condensed star-light, on which, as on a splendid background, brighter stars would be seen spread with inconceivable richness.

Such a scene might not be intelligible at a first view; it might even baffle all attempts at interpretation, all efforts to estimate the relative distances and proportions of its several parts. But our only path to the solution of the noblest problem in science is by presenting to the mind's eye such a picture of the great star-strewn sphere which surrounds us on all sides; when that has been done, we shall begin to know whether the great problem is altogether beyond our mastery.

Herschel's two methods having practically proved insufficient, it remains to be seen by what other methods we may render more distinct our mental picture of the star depths.

It occurred to me very early in my enquiry into the great problem, and before I had fully investigated the long and noble series of researches by which Sir W. Herschel had attempted to master it, that this was a case where the mental vision must be assisted by the bodily vision. It is singular that hitherto, so far as I know (and I think little that has been done on the subject has escaped my reading), the idea of *picturing* the results obtained by telescopic scrutiny had been altogether overlooked. I do not here refer to pictures illustrating theories of the universe. Every student of astronomy knows that Sir W. Herschel was careful to give diagrams illustrating his successive conceptions of the structure of the universe. But such illustrations as these, though necessary and useful, cannot throw any light on the structure of the universe, since they illustrate theories already formed, not facts on which theories are to be based. What seemed to me most desirable was that charts should be constructed on which the results of telescopic observation should be carefully mapped down without reference to any preconceived opinions, and solely with the intention of interpreting as satisfactorily as possible whatever laws of stellar distribution may really exist. It appeared to me that mere lists of numbers could afford but unsatisfactory evidence on such points.

Even the mind of a Newton might well shudder before the stupendous problem of attempting to educe a true theory of the stellar universe from a few laws of statistical distribution; while, on the other hand, pictures of the star sphere, or of parts of it, if suitably devised, might at once suggest true views. It is easy to illustrate the difference between the two methods. Suppose we wished to form true ideas respecting the actual distribution of clouds in the air, on some day when the whole sky was flecked with clouds of various form, colour, and shape; but that we had no way of examining the sky except through a movable tube which showed only a small part of the sky at a view. Now, if the two following methods were available for the enquiry (by combining the observations made by a great number of persons), is it not manifest which would be the most instructive? By one let the sky be assumed divided by a series of circles parallel to the horizon, and by a series of half-circles square to the horizon, and therefore all crossing at the point overhead; and let the enquirer be supplied with lists informing him of the number of clouds in these various sections of the sky. By the other let a picture be painted, in which all the features of the sky as ascertained by the different observers are combined artistically into a single view.

I think no one can doubt that while clear ideas would be formed from the study of the picture, not all the statisticians in the world could derive just views from the analysis of the lists of numbers.

I propose in my next chapter to tell the reader some of the facts which come into view, when pictures of the star depths are constructed on a certain plan devised to make them as instructive as possible, and then to indicate a scheme which I have devised for continuing and extending the enquiry. I think I shall be able to show not only that there are reasons for hoping that a true general theory of the stellar system may one day be formed, but that the facts which are already known, or may be inferred, are full of interest, and exhibit the universe of stars as far more wonderful in extent, in variety of structure, and in complexity of detail than had hitherto been supposed.

.

CHARTING THE STAR DEPTHS.

In my last chapter I pointed to the necessity of charting the heavens, even as they would be seen by means of a very powerful telescope, if we really hope to ascertain the laws of the sidereal universe.

But it is manifest that we must not begin by thus combining in a single picture all that such a telescope would reveal. For let it be considered how incomprehensible the scene so presented would appear to us. The dome of heaven, even as we see it with the naked eye, presents a perplexing display. Those suns seem as the sands on the sea-shore for multitude; the glorious streams of stars called the Milky Way lie in complex clouds before us. The problem even thus presented appears to lie beyond our powers. What, then, would be the scene when for every star we see thousands and tens of thousands would be revealed? How should we be perplexed when the clouds of the Milky Way, as now seen, appeared only as the brightest masses in a perfect sky of star clouds, in which every variety of form, of aggregation, and of constitution should be presented to our view!

Even more incomprehensible would be the streams of cloudlets which astronomers call *nebulæ*. Yet even there the wonders of the scene would not be at an end. For by our assumption the powers of the human observer would be so enhanced that he would perceive the motions of all the millions of stars, one group tending hither, another thither, one region instinct with diverse and seemingly random motions, another bearing onwards its wealth of stars in one compact body, if a system could be called compact whose several orbs were seen to be separated from each other by thousands of millions of miles. Even our solar system, if viewed under such conditions, would present a most perplexing scheme to one not already acquainted with the laws pervading it; but the orbs of the stellar universe are a million times more numerous, are arranged according to laws infinitely more complex, travel with motions infinitely more varied: and though we need not doubt that, if we could but perceive the real dependence of the various parts upon each other, a perfect harmony would be found to pervade every portion, yet that harmony can only be manifest to Him in whose eyes a thousand years are as one day.

We must approach the solution of the great problem, then—that is, such solution as we are likely to attain to —by gradual steps. We must not attempt to survey the whole domain of sidereal astronomy at once, but gradually open our eyes to its full extent. This expression is not simply figurative. The conception of a gradually increasing telescopic power corresponds to the idea of a gradual opening of the eyes. Half closed at first, the eyes of our imaginary enquirer are veiled from the overpowering glories of the great star-multitude, they reach not very far beyond the range of ordinary human vision; but gradually they become better able to endure these wonderful glories, and to understand the full significance of the scene; then they are opened to fresh wonders: until at length all that the powers of the telescope can reveal to man is disclosed to their view.

In working, then, by the method of charting I began (for I may as well note that I have been practically alone in this work) by charting the stars that we can see, according to a plan by which the laws of distribution should be clearly recognised; for the charts I drew were so contrived that equal spaces on the celestial sphere should be represented by equal spaces in the chart. It quickly became clear that the stars are not scattered at all uniformly over the heavens. There are rich and poor regions; and these are so arranged that while the whole of the galactic region is exceedingly rich in naked-eye stars, two opposite rich regions, one in the northern and the other in the southern heavens, are separated from each other (except where the Milky Way on opposite sides passes from one to the other) by singularly barren regions. It appears a noteworthy circumstance that near the centre of the great southern rich region are found those two wonderful objects called the Magellanic Clouds, vast globe-shaped conglomerations (scarcely any other word seems so suitable) in which are contained not only myriads of stars of all orders of magnitude after the seventh, but also every kind of star cloudlet.

This was only a first step; though I may remark that to this particular part of my work alone I was able to apply a somewhat novel but very effective method of research. It seemed desirable to ascertain how far the apparent aggregation of stars in the rich regions I have mentioned, and their segregation from other regions, was a real phenomenon—in other words, to test the eye's power of forming an opinion on this point. I therefore made separate copies of the northern and southern charts on the smoothest and most uniform paper I could obtain, and then cut out the poor and rich parts of the chart and weighed them in a very delicate balance. This process told me their relative extent better than any way of measurement applicable to such strangely shaped regions. I found that, as might have been expected, the eye had judged quite correctly, and that when comparison was made between the poorer and richer regions, the wealth of the star distribution was in some of the latter regions fully five times as great as in some of the former.

But already a remarkable and important feature of star distribution had come to light. It was manifest that the Milky Way is a region much more richly strewn with naked-eye stars than are other parts of the heavens. Now, if the glow of light in the star clouds forming the Milky Way were simply due to the great extension of the star-system towards these directions, it is very plain that the milky light would be produced by stars not separately discernible to the naked eye, and that whatever bright stars were spread on the Milky Way background would be quite unconnected with the great star-strewn regions producing the milky light. Thus there ought, on this supposition, to be no difference in the richness of bright stars over the Milky Way and over the rest of the heavens. The fact that there is such a difference, and to a very marked degree, as we have seen shows beyond all possibility of question that at least the extra number of bright stars on the Milky Way, if not all the bright stars on that region, are actually associated with those other stars, separately undiscernible, which produce the milky light of the galaxy. But this being the case, it follows that those bright and seemingly large stars are *really* very much larger than the other stars of the galaxy, that they owe their superior brightness not to relative near-ness, but to inherent superiority over the stars surround-ing them.

This result is well worth noticing, for this chief reason, that it exhibits to us a new order in the universe. Pre-cisely as we have learned to recognise during the present century the existence of a class of bodies in our solar system—the asteroids—which are quite distinct as an order from the planets, forming a zone or band of small planets, a kind of scheme before not thought of by astronomers, so here in the star clouds of the Milky Way, with interspersed superior orbs, we recognise an arrangement which hitherto had not been met with in the universe.

But when this result had been discovered, it seemed to me that it would be interesting to follow up the discovery, by searching for evidence as to the distribution of the intermediate order of stars—stars not so bright as to be visible to the naked eye, but yet considerably brighter than the great multitude of stars which Herschel had found strewn through the Milky Way when he examined it with his most powerful telescopes. Now, it chanced that a few years ago the German astronomer Argelander had completed the cataloguing and charting of the stars seen in the northern heavens with a telescope $2\frac{1}{2}$ inches in opening—just such a telescope, so far as size is concerned, as we commonly see in opticians' windows. But even such a telescope as this brings into view thousands on thousands of stars which the naked eye cannot perceive.

Although Argelander and his assistants swept rapidly over the northern heavens (dividing it into zones), not going more than twice over each part, and doubtless on hazy or moonlight nights passing over many stars which would have been perceived on a dark and clear sky, they yet charted no less than 324,198 stars, of which 310,000, or thereabouts, belonged to the northern half of the star sphere surrounding us.[1] Now, on very dark and clear nights we can perceive on the half of the heavens which at any moment may be in view about three thousand stars. So that Argelander's telescope showed at least one hundred times as many stars as we can perceive with the unaided eye. Conceive the glorious scene which would be disclosed if, for every star we see on the darkest and clearest winter nights, a hundred stars should suddenly leap into view, the stars of our familiar constellations growing at the same time correspondingly brighter, insomuch that we should recognise the glories of Orion and Auriga, the Bears, the Herdsman, and the Lions—in fine, all the constellations known to us, but revealed only by their superiority over a hundred times as many stars shining as brightly as those few thousands which we now perceive.

Argelander's work was presented in a series of forty large folio charts; and it was necessary to combine these in a single chart on the same equal-surface method which I had used when mapping the six thousand stars seen with the naked eye. I made the circle enclosing the proposed chart twenty inches in diameter, and then divided it into ninety-two concentric zones by suitably drawn circles, and drew from the centre 360 radiating lines, so that the whole surface was divided into more than twenty

----

[1] They carried their charts two degrees beyond the celestial equator for comparison with a corresponding series of southern maps one of these days (or some of those southern nights) to be completed.

thousand pencilled spaces, corresponding to the spaces in Argelander's charts. Then into these spaces the stars were marked in, being copied by eye-draughts from the charts. It will be seen, therefore, that the various degrees of richness in stellar distribution were accurately represented in the resulting chart; and it needed but an examination of the chart to show whether the stars included within the range of Argelander's telescope were gathered more richly along the Milky Way or not. But in reality no examination was required, since so richly were these stars strewn on the Milky Way, that its figure was as it were shaded in by the mere aggregation of the dots representing stars.

Here, then, is fresh evidence of the wonderful constitution of the Milky Way. We see that this complicated aggregation of star streams, for such is the true description of the galaxy, consists in the main of a multitude of relatively minute stars, amidst which many stars, so large as to be visible to the naked eye, are scattered, while also stars of intermediate orders are gathered with great richness in the same region of space.

It follows that when Sir W. Herschel was endeavouring by means of his powerful telescopes to resolve the cloudy light of the Milky Way into separate stars, he was not really penetrating, as he supposed, to the remotest limits of our stellar system, and bringing into view stars which were at a relatively enormous distance, but in many cases at least was simply scrutinising more and more closely certain definite aggregations of stars, of many orders of real magnitude, all intermixed together in the same region of space. So that we no longer have any evidence, certainly not such convincing evidence as Sir W. Herschel supposed, that the limits of our star system can be reached. We have nothing to show that far away beyond the star groups which he so resolved there may not lie other groups which his telescope would not even bring into view, far less separate into stars, and all forming parts of the same system. Our stellar universe, in fact, no longer presents the uniform aspect which it had assumed as interpreted by Sir W. Herschel, but shows varieties of structure and of aggregation corresponding with, but far surpassing in degree, those which we recognise in the solar system.

Here for the present I pause, though I might readily dwell on processes of research by which the star-charting I have commenced may be extended to far greater depths, and the whole heavens surveyed with telescopic powers gradually increasing from the small telescope used by Argelander to the largest telescopes yet made by man. When that has been done, and the results have been duly studied, we shall begin to form clearer and worthier ideas than hitherto of that amazing scheme of bodies of which our sun is a member. We shall find in that system an infinite variety of structure. As I have written elsewhere, ' besides the single suns, the universe contains groups and systems and streams of primary suns ; there are galaxies of minor orbs; there are clustering stellar aggregations showing every variety of richness, of figure, and of distribution; there are all the various forms of star cloudlets, resolvable and irresolvable, circular, elliptical, and spiral; and, lastly, there are irregular masses of luminous gas, clinging in fantastic convolutions around stars and star systems.   Nor is it unsafe to assert that other forms and varieties of structure will yet be discovered, or that hundreds more exist which we may never hope to recognise.'

THE STAR DEPTHS ASTIR WITH LIFE.

I DO not know which thought is more stupendous, that
the millions of suns which people space should all be
fixed or should all be in exceedingly swift motion. It
is an impressive conception that multitudes of suns, each
competent to rule over a scheme of circling worlds, should
remain steadfast each in its own domain, that the infinite
universe should be divided, as it were, into separate
kingdoms, ruled over in the main by single orbs, but
some governed by multiple suns, and each, undisturbed
in its integrity by rival empires, constant and stable for
all time. But it is a no less impressive thought that
each of these great ruling orbs should be urging its way
through space with a velocity compared with which the
swiftest motions known to us are as absolute rest—that
the mighty star kingdoms of the universe should have
constantly changing boundaries, or rather, since every
subordinate orb in every star kingdom must partake in
the motion of its ruler, that these kingdoms are carried
bodily onwards, in every second of time passing over
many miles of their wonderful flight through space.

But more impressive than either thought is the consideration that to our apprehensions *both* these conceptions are true. Each sun of our universe of suns is indeed in swift motion, as is our own. Each bears its family of dependent worlds along with it at an amazing velocity. Each star domain is continually changing not in boundary alone, but altogether. And yet so enormous is the scale on which the universe of stars is constructed that while momentarily changing it may be regarded as more unchanging than any object within its own infinite extent. If there could be constructed on any scale which would not be too large to prevent the whole being seen at once a perfect model of the stellar system, or rather of the part of the stellar system which lies within man's cognisance, and if within that model motions took place corresponding to those which are actually taking place in the stellar universe, then ages must elapse before the appearance of the system would be appreciably altered.

The most seemingly unchanging objects—a block of granite, a mass of steel, a diamond—are in reality undergoing moment by moment changes of structure, shape, and condition which surpass infinitely in extent those which would represent the changes in the stellar universe, even though the imagined model of that universe were as large as some great metropolis. If, passing beyond such puny and inadequate conceptions, the distance separating our sun from his nearest neighbour among the stars were represented by a mile—in which case the model would probably have to be as large as our earth—

and supposing that nearest star moving with respect to our sun (regarded as at rest) at the rate of 100 miles per second, then the motion of the star in the enormous model would be so slow that in an hour it would amount but to the 850th part of an inch, and it would require thirty-five days to traverse a single inch relatively to our sun as represented in the same model. It will be conceived, therefore, how absolutely unchanging a model on any ordinary scale would appear. For probably no star moves with respect to any other at the rate of 100 miles per second; and a model of the star universe, so far as our telescopes reveal it, would require to be several miles across, in order that the distance separating our sun from the nearest star should be represented by a single yard.

In the star universe, then, we have a strange combination of the changing and the unchanging. It is astir with energy, instinct with the most amazing vitality, and yet it is to our feeble senses constant. Only in the eyes of Him to whom a thousand years are as one day, and one day as a thousand years, is the life of the universe a reality. He alone recognises harmony and perfection in the system of star motions. *We* cannot see the harmonious relations of the universe regarded as a whole, simply because we do not recognise the laws of stellar motions. We see stars gathered together in one place and sparsely strewn elsewhere, apparently without law or order—precisely as an observer of our solar system from some distant stand-point would see no signs of regularity in the momentary distribution of the planets.

But precisely as the astronomer knows that, regarded not alone in all its parts, but with due reference to all its motions, the solar system is a regular and orderly scheme, so to the All-knowing Creator the stellar universe, inharmonious in all its parts if regarded without reference to the motions actuating its various members, is a scene of regularity and system, because not only are the actual places of the stars known to Him (which is not the case with astronomers), but the complete series of motions which are taking place within the system is recognised and understood.

Let us, however, consider how astronomers first ascertained that the stars are not absolutely fixed, and what has since been ascertained respecting the stellar motions.

The actual recognition of the displacement of a star by its own motion is a work which can only be accomplished by means of a powerful telescope, well mounted, and so arranged as to afford the means of determining any star's place with extreme nicety. In fact, this amounts to saying that the motion of the star must be very much magnified before it can be perceived.

But although this is true of any given astronomer, no star moving fast enough to be appreciably displaced to ordinary vision in any man's lifetime, yet in the course of centuries a star may shift so much in position as no longer to occupy the same relative position with respect to other stars. And the first recognition of star motion was, in point of fact, effected without telescopic assistance. In this way: The ancient astronomers noted the passage of the moon over certain stars, recording the date and hour of the occurrence, and the part of the moon at which the star disappeared and re-appeared. Now, the moon's motions have been very accurately determined, insomuch that astronomers can trace back her steps and learn certainly that she was at such and such a distant past epoch at such and such a part of the heavens.

Supposing any star whose concealment by the moon has been recorded by ancient astronomers to have remained in the same place during the interval which has since elapsed, the moon's motion traced back to the date of the event would carry her over the present place of that star. But if at that epoch the star had a different position, it is to that ancient position of the star, not to its present position, that the calculation would carry back the moon; and if one judged from the present position of the star, one would infer that there had either been no concealment of the star, or that the circumstances of the concealment were different from those actually recorded.

It was thus that astronomers first discovered that some at least among the stars are slowly changing their place in the heavens. We owe the discovery to Halley, the friend and contemporary of Sir Isaac Newton. So soon, however, as the fact was recognised in this comparatively rough though effective manner, astronomers perceived that by carefully determining the places of the stars with the telescope they could detect star motions much more satisfactorily. This would not be the place to describe the methods in use among astronomers to determine with great exactness the place of any star. It must suffice to note that in these methods the astronomer takes advantage of all the refinements of mechanical ingenuity, and that the magnifying power of the telescope in reality acts to magnify any effects of star motion. So that if a magnifying power of 100 is used, the astronomer could detect in one year any motion which, to the naked eye, would only be discernible in one hundred years.

Very few motions are discernible to ordinary vision (aided, of course, by an instrumental index devised to determine a star's place) in so short a time as one hundred years. But notice that in twenty or thirty years a telescopist, using the very moderate power named, would be able to detect a motion which ordinary vision would be able to recognise after the lapse of two thousand or three thousand years. And our astronomers are not limited to twenty or thirty years. They can compare their observations with those made by such observers as Bradley and his contemporaries nearly a century and a half ago. This amounts, with moderate telescopic power, to the observation of effects equivalent to those which would be presented to the naked eye in the course of more than ten thousand years. It will not be wondered at, then, that effects of change should be recognised by astronomers, possessed as they are of this power of in effect extending time by magnifying its operation.

It may be mentioned that so far as observation has extended very few stars in the heavens have unchanging apparent positions. It is highly probable that in reality every star is in motion. But of course the motions of some stars among the thousands dealt with in astronomical observations are directed almost exactly towards or from the earth, and therefore cannot be recognised by any displacement of the star.

The determination of the actual rate of any star's thwart motion is impossible unless the star's distance be in the first instance determined ; and, as I have said in a former chapter, we know very little about star distances. If we take the case of Sirius, whose distance has been set at about a million times the distance of the sun, we find that the annual thwart motion of this star is such as to indicate a real rate of thwart motion of about twelve miles per second.

But it might seem that we are after all in a very unfavourable position to form anything like complete or satisfactory ideas respecting stellar motions, since we can only recognise the thwart motions, and cannot estimate even these as actual rates of motion at so many miles per second. It has lately chanced, however, that a method of spectroscopic observation has enabled astronomers to recognise, and even to measure in miles per second, the motions of stars directly from or towards us. The principle of the new method may be thus briefly indicated : The spectrum of a star is a rainbow-tinted streak, crossed by certain dark lines. If a dark line can be recognised as due to any particular vapour, as hydrogen, magnesium, or so on, then we know that its place corresponds exactly to some particular part of the spectrum's length—some particular tint of the red, or orange, or yellow, or green, or blue, or indigo, or violet. But tint in light corresponds to tone in sound. In one case the number of light waves reaching the eye, in the other the number of sound waves reaching the ear, in a given time occasions the peculiar quality which we call colour in one case, or tone in the other.

Now, the longer light waves make the red, orange, and yellow colours, while the shorter make the green, blue, indigo, and violet. Again, the longer sound waves make the grave tones, and the shorter make the acute tones. And we know that motion affects the tone of any sound. If the whistle of a railway engine is sounding while the engine is passing, it will be noticed that as the engine approaches the observer, the tone is acuter than as the engine is receding from him, there being a sudden lowering of the tone as the engine passes.

The reason is readily perceived. For when the train is approaching more sound waves reach the observer in a given time, since the approach of the train is continually bringing nearer to him the point whence the sound waves

18

come, and so shortening their journey towards him and of course the time in which they reach him, the reverse taking place when the train is receding. So that the ear, which knows nothing of the train's motions, simply conveys to the brain at one time the intelligence of waves arriving at a certain greater rate, leading to the sensation of an acuter tone, and afterwards the intelligence of waves arriving at a lesser rate, leading to the sensation of a graver tone.

Applying this to an approaching or receding star, we see that if only the rate of approach or recession bears an appreciable proportion to the velocity with which light travels (182,000 miles per second), any given colour of the star's light will be changed to a colour nearer the violet end of the spectrum, while the change will be towards the red end of the spectrum if the star is receding. This would not affect the colour of the star as a whole, but any dark line in the star's spectrum being shifted in this way would no longer agree in position with the corresponding line of the same element—hydrogen, magnesium, or the like—in the spectrum obtained by the chemist from that element in his laboratory. If the two spectra—that of the element at rest, and that of the star carrying that element along with it at an enormous rate —can only be compared, we can recognise and even measure the star's motion of recession or of approach.

In this way Dr. Huggins discovered two or three years ago that the star Sirius is travelling from us at the rate of more than twenty miles per second. Since he made this discovery a telescope better suited for the work has been placed in his hands by the Royal Society, and with this he has recognised motions of recession or approach in the other bright stars, some of these motions taking place at the rate of more than fifty miles per second.

In another chapter I shall describe certain peculiarities which characterise the stellar motions, and in particular (1) the evidence which the star motions afford as to the motion of our own ' bright particular star,' the sun, with his scheme of dependent worlds, and (2) the evidence of certain drifting motions among particular star groups.

THE DRIFTING STARS.

In former chapters I have compared man to the May-fly, and his conceptions of the universe, or what he calls the universe, to the ideas which a reasoning May-fly might form of the objects amidst which his brief career is passed. And surely there is no subject of research which suggests such a comparison more forcibly than the study of star movements. A child is born into the world, grows to manhood, becomes, perchance, what we call great, lives to the threescore years and ten, or even to those four-score years which bring with them weariness of life; and during all those years the great universe of stars which encompasses us on every hand remains to ordinary percep-tions unchanged. Let the heavens be studied on the first night after that man was born, and let them again be studied on the first night after his death, and no change in the distribution of the stars shall be perceived.

And yet during all the years which have elapsed every one of those orbs which seem so steadfast has been rushing onwards at a rate compared with which the swiftest forms of motion with which we are acquainted—

the speed of the express train, the flight of the bird, even the rush of the missiles which we poor ephemera employ to destroy our fellow-creatures—are as absolute rest. In every second yon busy star which seems so still has urged its way thirty or forty miles upon its wide and as yet undetermined career. Not for a moment does it rest, even when unseen by human eyes; and yet the career of the most long-lived of our race passes while that star remains to all ordinary perceptions in an unchanging position.

Yet our short-lived race, puny and feeble though it appears compared with the wondrous orbs amidst which the earth on which we live exists, has deliberately undertaken and not unsuccessfully carried out, the daring scheme of determining according to what laws the stars move, and in particular (for in reality this scheme is the most daring of all) of ascertaining from the seeming motions of the stars how the sun, that vast orb of which our earth is a minute dependent upon whose surface man is a most minute moving creature, is moving through star-bestrewn space.

We owe to Sir W. Herschel the first conception of the method by which the star motions were to be analysed for the detection of the motion of our own sun. It is clear that if all the stars were at rest, and our sun were moving in their midst, then the other stars would appear to be affected by motions corresponding to the real motions of the sun. If the sun were travelling on a great level plain, upon which lay all the other stars, we might say that the stars to right and left of him would appear to be moving backwards, precisely as the trees, houses, and other objects at rest on either side of the track of a moving carriage seem to be travelling backwards. But as the stars do not lie on a plane surface, but are scattered throughout the length and breadth and depth of space, we cannot so describe their apparent motions. Nevertheless it is clear that stars on *all sides* of the sun must appear to travel *backwards* if he is travelling in any direction *forwards.*

It is common to find it stated that the stars of the region towards which the sun is travelling would appear to *open out,* just as the trees of a forest seem to open out from each other as the traveller advances towards them; and that the stars of the region which the sun is leaving would seem to draw closer together. But no such effect could be expected to be recognisable, because the distances of the stars are so great. Precisely as when we are travelling in a carriage the objects on either side are those chiefly affected by apparent motion, so with the stars: those on every *side* of the course of the advancing sun would be more affected than those lying in regions towards which, or from which, he is moving.

But a difficulty is introduced in the case of the sun which does not appear in the case of some traveller moving onwards amidst a number of objects at rest. We only infer that the sun is moving because we have seen

that the stars are moving. And we cannot for a moment
suppose that all the star motions are merely apparent,
and due in reality to the sun's motion. For why should
the sun, which is only one among many hundreds of thousands of suns, be the only one which is moving? Apart
from this, the motions of the stars are altogether too
diverse in character to be ascribed to any such simple
cause as the motion of the sun alone, even if that were
in itself a reasonable or likely supposition. So that the
astronomer who wishes to learn in what direction the sun
is moving has not the same sort of evidence to guide him
which is afforded to one travelling amidst a number of
objects at rest. The sun is surrounded by a multitude of
moving objects, and, to make the determination of his
motion infinitely more difficult, those objects lie at unknown distances, are moving in unknown directions, and
have unknown velocities.

Very wonderful is it, therefore, that Sir W. Herschel
first, and afterwards several other astronomers have, by
the careful study of the stars' movements, ascertained,
with what amounts practically to absolute certainty, that
our sun, with his whole family of planets, is moving
towards the part of the heavens occupied by the constellation Hercules. Every investigation of the evidence has
led to the same general result in this respect. But as to
the rate of the sun's motion, which is not uncommonly
presented as though it rested on the same footing, the
evidence is very much less convincing. It has been said

that the sun is travelling at the rate of three or four miles in every second of time. But when one examines the evidence one finds that this conclusion depends on assumptions as to the average real magnitude of the stars of various orders of apparent brightness. I was long since led to conclude that such assumptions were unsafe, and also to infer from certain evidence which I had collected that our sun moves much more swiftly than had been supposed. In fact, speaking generally, I may say that I had been led to the opinion that our sun is by no means so important a member of the star system as the majority of the leading brilliants of the heavens, and that consequently the real distances of those brilliants are greater than would be inferred from the supposition that they are the sun's equals only. Hence it follows, of course, that the signs of motion among these stars indicate much greater real motions with respect to the sun. This amounts to saying that not only the motions which those stars have within the star system, but those also which are only relative, and produced by the sun's real motion, are much greater than had been inferred. So that the sun's real motion to which these relative motions are solely due must (if my view were correct) be much greater than was supposed.

I think this view of mine has been confirmed by the evidence obtained to show that the sun belongs to an order of stars inferior to that including Sirius, Vega, and some three hundred stars studied spectroscopically by the Italian astronomer Secchi. Then the results of Huggins's labours, indicating motions of recession and approach by thirty, forty, and even fifty miles per second, render it extremely unlikely that our sun's whole motion amounts but to three or four miles per second.

I have said that as to the sun's motion towards Hercules little doubt can be entertained, because every investigation of the subject has led to the same result. But it is worthy of notice that the last and in some respects the most complete investigation of the matter, by my friend Mr. Dunkin, working under the general directions of the Astronomer Royal, while pointing to the same general result, showed also the effects of that difficulty to which I have referred above—the multiplicity of real motions among the stars. For after the calculation was finished which showed that the sun's motion towards Hercules accounts for a greater proportion of the observed movements than any other assumption, Mr. Dunkin proceeded to enquire what proportion of the observed movements was actually accounted for in this way. The result was to show that only about *one-thirtieth* part of the observed motions could be regarded (on the assumptions adopted) as due to the sun's motion.

Sir J. Herschel remarked on this, ' No one need be surprised. If the sun move in space, why not also the stars? And if so, it would be manifestly absurd to expect that any movement could be assigned to the sun, by any system of calculation, which would account for more than a very small portion of the observed displacements.[1] But what is indeed astonishing in the whole affair is, that among all this chaotic heap of miscellaneous movement, among all this drift of cosmical atoms, of the laws of whose motions we know absolutely nothing, it should be possible to place the finger upon one small portion of the sum total, to all appearance undistinguishably mixed up with the rest, and to declare with full assurance that this particular portion of the whole is due to the motion of our own solar system.'

When we add to this thought the consideration to which I have already adverted—viz. that the movements themselves are such that their effects in the course of the longest life are utterly undiscernible—the wonder is enhanced that men should venture to attack a problem so recondite, and that their daring should have been rewarded with success.

The thought has even been conceived that possibly something might be learned, not only as to the direction and velocity with which the sun is moving, but as to the shape of the path which he will describe in some enormous period compared with which the thousands of years which are included in what we call history, the millions whose

---

[1] In an Appendix to my 'Essays on Astronomy' I have indicated reasons for expecting, however, that one-half of the observed displacements would be accounted for by the sun's motions. This is mathematically demonstrable, and is in fact so demonstrated in the work mentioned. It follows that the smallness of the actual correction results from errors in the assumptions on which the calculation has been effected, a result according well with my inferences from other considerations.

passage is indicated by the condition of the earth's crust—
nay, even the thousands of millions inferred from the
condition of the solar system—are but as a single moment.

It was once thought that the German astronomer
Mädler had found the true centre around which all the
stars of the galaxy, including our own sun, are revolving in the star Alcyone, the leading brilliant of the
Pleiades. But it is now generally acknowledged that the
evidence on which Mädler based this view was quite insufficient.

Probably science will have to wait hundreds of years
before any just ideas can be formed as to the general laws
according to which the stars of the galaxy are moving.

In the meantime, however, it appears desirable and
useful to search for subordinate laws of motion. The
idea occurred to me three or four years ago that if the
motions of the stars could be *mapped*, instead of being
merely tabulated as hitherto, signs would be traced of
such subordinate laws. In particular it seemed to me
not unlikely that a community of motion would be
recognised among stars really forming subordinate star
families.

The method I used for charting star motions was as
follows :—I drew charts, including all the stars whose
thwart motions have been recognised, and to each star I
attached a small arrow showing the direction in which
the star is moving. Moreover, I made the length of the
arrow proportionate to the rate of the star's thwart motion

on the heavens. Each arrow was made just so long that
while one end indicated the present place of the star the
other end or point indicated the place which the star will
have *thirty-six thousand years hence.* It will give an
·idea of the extreme slowness of the apparent motions to
mention that notwithstanding the enormous number of
years to which each arrow-length corresponded the greater
number of arrows were very short.

I have said that my object was to determine whether
any set stars show a tendency to drift together. I recognised several instances where, as it seemed to me, this
tendency to star-drift was strongly marked. One of these
I selected as the subject for a scientific prediction. The
stars affected by star-drift were five of the seven forming
the familiar Plough (or Charles's Wain), and the peculiarity of the case was this, that all five were drifting
nearly in the same direction as regarded their apparent
thwart motions, and nearly at the same rate, this motion
taking place in a direction nearly opposite to that due to
the sun's motion in space.

I knew that Dr. Huggins would soon be able to apply
to the leading stars of our northern heavens that spectroscopic method of determining motions of recession and
approach which I sketched in the last chapter. Now, if
the five stars in the Plough are really drifting in space,
it would follow that they have a common motion of recession or approach, whereas if the drift were apparent
only, there would be no such community of motion in

the line of sight. To indicate, therefore, the confidence which I had in the reasoning which had led me to the opinion that those five stars really are drifting together through space, as a single system, I predicted that whenever Dr. Huggins should apply to them the new spectroscopic method he would find that they were either all approaching or all receding, and at a common rate.

This prediction was exactly confirmed by the event two years later. It happened that Dr. Huggins had forgotten which of the seven stars form the drifting set of five, supposing the 'two pointers' or *hind* wheels of the Plough, the other two or *front* wheel-stars, and the first horse to be the five, whereas the five are the farthest pointer from the pole, the front wheel-stars, and the stars representing the two horses next to the wain. The observation of the pointer nearest to the pole showed that that star is approaching, and the observation of the pointer farthest from the pole showed that that star is receding at the rate of nearly twenty miles per hour. So Dr. Huggins judged that I was mistaken, at any rate as respected those two stars, which were seen to be travelling in different directions. He proceeded, however, with his observations. He found both the remaining wheel-stars receding at the rate of about twenty miles per second. The star representing the first horse was found to be receding at the same rate, and lastly the star representing the second horse. Here, then, were five stars receding at the rate of about twenty miles per second; but Dr.

Huggins supposed at the moment that these were not the five stars respecting which I had made my little prediction. On turning, however, to my 'Other Worlds' (published two years before his observations were made), he found that it was the set of five stars which he had found to be thus receding at a common rate which I had described as, in my belief, forming a drifting set.

I think the inference is fair that my general theory respecting local star-drifts is correct, and that among those stars which form our familiar systems there are groups travelling as systems through space. A strange thought truly, when we remember its consequences. It shows that, notwithstanding the enormous distances which separate these stars from each other, yet vaster distances, or rather distances of a higher order of vastness, separate that system of stars from the surrounding parts of the galaxy. It presents to us, also, the wonderful thought that cycles of revolution must exist within that system, compared with which the longest periods of motion recognised within our solar system must be regarded as absolutely insignificant. We are shown in such star systems an order of created things unlike any that before we had known. One other form of evidence has been given to show the infinite variety which pervades every part of the universe.

THE MILKY WAY.

Lo! these are but a portion of His ways; they utter but a whisper of His glory.—Job xxvi. 14.

If on a calm, clear night, when there is no moon, we regard the star-lit sky, we see spanning the vast concave of the heavens a zone of cloudy light. In our country, where the air is seldom free from haze and vapour, even when it appears clearest, this wonderful zone is faint and indistinct. Only in certain portions can we recognise its lustre so distinctly as to feel assured (unless acquainted with its figure and position) that we are not looking at clouds high up in the air. But in southern latitudes the Milky Way is aglow with light. There it is seen as a brilliant band athwart the heavens—

> A broad and ample road, whose dust is gold, ·
> And pavement stars, as stars to us appear.

We cannot wonder that the ancient astronomers should have looked with wonder on this amazing pheuomenon. Steadfast as the stars amidst which its course is laid, the galaxy shone night after night before their eyes, and offered a noble problem for their thoughts. Nor did they fail to perceive the meaning of that steadfastness which, to the unthinking, would have had no significance. ·They saw that the wondrous cloud must lie at an enormous distance; and that in all probability its light must be produced by the combined lustre of countless stars, removed to so great a distance as to be separately indistinguishable.

Manilius, their astronomical poet, puts forward this stupendous conception, and we find Ovid describing the Milky Way in terms not unlike (setting aside their Paganism) those in which one acquainted with modern astronomical results might poetically present them :—

> A way there is in heaven's extended plain,
> Which when the skies are clear is seen below,
> And mortals by the name of *Milky* know ;
> The groundwork is of stars, through which the road
> Lies open to the Thunderer's abode.

But it is when the Milky Way is studied with the telescope that the true glories of this wonderful zone are seen. A large instrument is not needed. Galileo saw the wonders of the galaxy with his small and imperfect ' optic tube '—a telescope which, in our day, though invaluable as a relic of the great astronomer, would be worth but a few shillings, so far as its optical performance is concerned. Wright of Durham analysed the depths of the Milky Way, and formed a sound opinion as to the true nature of the zone by means of a telescope only ten inches in length. The smallest telescope which opticians sell for star-gazing, when turned upon certain parts of the galaxy, will reveal a scene of wonder which is calculated to fill the least thoughtful mind with a sense of the infinite power and wisdom of the Almighty. Countless stars pass into view as the telescope is swayed by the earth's rotation athwart the rich regions of the galaxy.

There are stars of all orders of brightness, from those which (seen with the telescope) resemble in lustre the leading glories of the firmament down to tiny points of light only caught by momentary twinklings. Every variety of arrangement is seen. Here the stars are scattered as over the skies at night ; there they cluster in groups, as though drawn together by some irresistible power; in one region they seem to form sprays of stars like diamonds sprinkled over fern leaves ; elsewhere they lie in streams and rows, in coronets and loops and festoons resembling the star festoon which, in the constellation Perseus, garlands the black robe of night. Nor are varieties of colour wanting to render the display more wonderful and more beautiful. Many of the stars which crowd upon the view are red, orange, and yellow. Among them are groups of two and three and four (multiple stars, as they are called) amongst which blue, and green, and lilac, and purple stars appear, forming the most charming contrast to the ruddy and yellow orbs near which they are commonly seen.

But it is when we consider what it is that we are really contemplating that the true meaning of the scene is discerned, that the true lesson taught by the star depths is understood.   Then we may say with the poet, but in another sense—

> The floor of heaven
> Is thick inlaid with patines of bright gold;
> There's not the smallest orb which thou behold'st,
> But in his motion like an angel sings,
> Still quiring to the young-eyed cherubim.

The least of the stars seen in the galactic depths—even though the telescope which reveals it be the mightiest yet made by man, so that with all other telescopes that star would be unseen—is a sun like our own. It is a mighty mass, capable of swaying by its attraction the motions of worlds, like our earth and her fellow-planets, circling in their stately courses around it. It is an orb instinct with life (if one may so speak), aglow with fiery energy, pouring out each moment supplies of life and power to the worlds which circle around it. It is a mighty engine, working out the purpose of its Great Creator; it is a giant heart, whose pulsations are the source whence a myriad forms of life derive support: and until the fuel which maintains its fires shall be consumed, that mighty engine will fulfil its work; until its life-blood shall be exhausted, that giant heart will throb unceasingly. And more wonderful yet perhaps is the thought that where all seems peace and repose, there is in reality a clangour and a tumult compared with which all the forms of uproar known upon earth sink into utter insignificance.

We know something of the processes at work upon our

own sun. We know of storms raging there, in which fiery vapour masses, tens of thousands of miles in breadth, sweep onward at a rate exceeding a hundred-fold in velocity the swiftest rush of our express trains. We see matter flung forth from the depths beneath the sun's blazing surface to a height exceeding ten and twenty-fold the diameter of the globe on which we live. And we know that these tremendous motions, though they seem to take place silently, must in reality be accompanied with a tumult and uproar altogether inconceivable. We know that precisely as distance so reduces the seeming dimensions of these vapour masses, and their seeming rate of motion, that even in the most powerful telescopes they appear like the tiniest of the clouds which fleck the bosom of the summer sky, and change as slowly in their seeming shape ; so distance partly, and partly the absence of a medium to convey the sound, reduces to utter silence a noise and clangour compared with which the roar of the hurricane, the crash of the thunderbolt, the bellowing of the volcano, and the hideous groaning of the earthquake are as absolute silence.

What, then, must be our thoughts when we see thousands and thousands of stars, all suns like our own, and many probably far surpassing him in splendour, passing in stately progress across the telescopic field of view ? The mind sinks appalled before the amazing meaning of the display. As we gaze at the wondrous scene an infinite significance is found in the words of the inspired Psalmist : ' When I consider the heavens, the work of Thy hands, the sun and stars which Thou hast ordained, what is man that Thou art mindful of him ? or the son of man that Thou regardest him ? '

It has been said that with the telescopes with which the Herschels have surveyed the depths of heaven twenty millions of stars are visible. But these telescopes do not penetrate to the limits of the star system. In certain parts of the Milky Way, Sir W. Herschel not only failed to penetrate the star-depths with his gauging telescope (here spoken of), though the mirror was eighteen inches in width ; but even when he brought into action his great forty-feet telescope, with its mirror four feet across, he still saw that cloudy light which speaks of star depths as yet unfathomed. Nay, the giant telescope of Lord Rosse has utterly failed to penetrate the ocean of space which surrounds us on all sides.

And even this is not all. These efforts to resolve the galaxy into its component stars have been applied to portions of the Milky Way which (there is now reason to believe) are relatively near to us. But in the survey of the heavens with powerful telescopes streams of cloudy light have been seen, so faint as to convey the idea of infinite distance, and no telescope yet made by man has shown the separate stars which doubtless constitute these almost evanescent star-regions. We are thus brought into the presence of star clouds as mysterious to ourselves as the star clouds of the galaxy were to the astronomers of old times. After penetrating, by means of the telescope, to depths exceeding millions of times the distance of the sun (inconceivable though that distance is), we find ourselves still surrounded by the same mysteries as when we first started. Around us and before us there are still the infinite star depths, and the only certain lesson we can be said to have learned is, that those depths are and must ever remain unfathomable. Truly, the German poet Richter has spoken well in those wonderful words which our own prose poet De Quincey has so nobly translated; his splendid vision aptly expresses the feebleness of man's conceptions in the presence of the infinite wonders of creation :—

' God called up from dreams a man into the vestibule of heaven, saying, " Come thou thither, and see the glory of My house." And to the angels which stood around His throne He said, " Take him, strip from him his robes of flesh ; cleanse his vision, and put a new breath into his nostrils, only touch not with any change his human heart, the heart that weeps and trembles." It was done ; and with a mighty angel for his guide the man stood ready for his infinite voyage ; and from the terraces of heaven, without sound or farewell, at once they wheeled away into endless space. Sometimes with the solemn flight of angel wings they passed through Zaharas of darkness, through wildernesses of death, that divided the worlds of life ; sometimes they swept over frontiers that were quickening under prophetic motions from God. Then from a distance which is counted only in heaven, light dawned for a time through a shapeless film; by unutterable pace the light swept to them, they by unutterable pace to the light. In a moment the rushing of planets was upon them; in a moment the blazing of suns was around them.

'Then came eternities of twilight, that revealed but were not revealed. On the right hand and on the left towered mighty constellations, that by self-repetitions and answers from afar, that by counter-positions, built up triumphal gates, whose architraves, whose archways, horizontal, upright, rested, rose, at altitude, by spans that seemed ghostly from infinitude. Without measure were the architraves, past number were the archways, beyond memory the gates. Within were stairs that scaled the eternities around; above was below and below was above, to the man stripped of gravitating body; depth was swallowed up in height insurmountable, height was swallowed up in depth unfathomable. Suddenly, as thus they rode from infinite to infinite, suddenly, as thus they tilted over abysmal worlds, a mighty cry arose that systems more mysterious, that worlds more billowy, other heights and other depths, were coming, were nearing, were at hand.

'Then the man sighed and stopped, shuddered and wept. His overladen heart uttered itself in tears, and he said, "Angel, I will go no farther; for the spirit of man acheth with this infinity. Insufferable is the glory of God. Let me lie down in the grave, and hide me from the persecution of the Infinite, for end I see there is none." And from all the listening stars that shone around issued a choral voice, "The man speaketh truly: end there is none that ever yet we heard of!" "End is there none?" the angel solemnly demanded; "is there indeed no end? And is this the sorrow that fills you?" But no voice answered, that he might answer himself. Then the angel threw up his glorious hands to the heaven of heavens, saying, "End is there none to the universe of God. Lo! also, there is no beginning."'

www.ingramcontent.com/pod-product-compliance
Lightning Source LLC
Chambersburg PA
CBHW031044120726
47905CB00007B/2296